The Closet

Joseph MacNabb

Publisher's Note:

This is a work of fiction. All names, characters, places, and
events are the work of the author's imagination.

Any resemblance to real persons, places, or events is
coincidental.

Solstice Publishing - http://www.solsticeempire.com/

BK. gnd - '56 church school
bld. built & church formed 1828 -
Joe's gt. gt grandfather retired here after
being N Ga circuit rider - built house
at 15 Wesley which became family home -
Joe's g'mother on cornerstone committee when
current sanctuary built. Juvenile judge
(part time) over 30 years.

Original book 140,000 wds. - much
too long for murder/suspense genra - ended
up about 93,000 wds.

MacNabb house on wesley St is
house in book - Joe was never put
in closet -

To Patty

Themes: 1- Can/should a minister
kill a man? Should he be held to
a higher standard? 2- Obsession.
3- Small town life (still the way it
was in 1950 to certain extent)
4- Forgiveness - self and others

Prologue

Ten Years Earlier

Their little celebration begged for champagne, but it wasn't missed at all. Will and Leah Rowan swilled joy instead. They'd chosen their favorite French restaurant in the Highland-Poncey neighborhood of Atlanta to mark the occasion, and they were dining so early that no other patrons were even there yet. Doubtless for him, and surely for her, too, this was the most exciting of times. They smiled and laughed so much through their meal that they hardly found time to eat.

Leah was rightfully on center stage. Almost three years into her academic program, she'd completed her dissertation prospectus, and she was on the verge of becoming a doctoral candidate in philosophy at Emory University. "This afternoon, I went over my prospectus with Dr. Pylant, and he seemed to like it. I invited him to join us for this celebratory dinner, but he had some kind of faculty thing to go to. I told him you had a church meeting, so we would have to eat early, but he still begged off."

Will was sorry her assistant professor couldn't make their dinner. Dr. Pylant had served as a mentor as well as a teacher while she pursued her PhD in philosophy. "If he liked it, it must be okay."

She nodded, downing a mouthful of lamb from her cassoulet.

"So what's next?"

"This is so very good." She looked down at her plate. "All right then. I've just completed the hardest part. You can't imagine how tough it is to prepare a dissertation prospectus even though it's just fifteen pages, not counting the bibliography. Without going into all the details, it has to include a statement of my idea, how I'll develop it in a dissertation of up to four hundred pages, how long I think it'll take, and what research materials I have to support it."

"I guess it sounds like a major milestone then, but now what?"

"This afternoon, I made a few adjustments, and tomorrow I'll give the final copy to Dr. Pylant. He'll guide it through the committee process and then on to the graduate faculty. If I defend it to their liking, I will be a doctoral candidate!"

"After that, you can finally start writing your dissertation."

"Oddly enough, that will be the easiest part for me, and I have four years to do it if I want to take that long. But before any of that stuff happens, Will, I have something much more important to attend to." She patted her stomach and smiled.

Will laughed. "Thank you for recognizing that giving birth to our child is more important than your school work."

By then, she was laughing, too, but all at once she stiffened and sat upright.

"Is something wrong, Leah?" He tried not to sound alarmed, but he was.

"Just a twinge. It may be starting, but I don't think so. Let's just finish dinner. Okay?"

He nodded, but he didn't really think it was okay. She was two weeks short of being nine months pregnant, and at this point, every little 'twinge' made him nervous. And when they got home, he voiced his concern. "I don't have to go to my meeting tonight. Why don't I call and tell them I can't make it?"

She shook her head. "No, don't you dare do that. You go on to your meeting. You have a cell phone, and you'll only be twenty minutes away. I told you at the start that I didn't want the baby to affect your job, and I still don't. I'll be fine."

He sighed, saying nothing, and after leaving her at home, he headed for his church meeting. On the way, he thought of his own career path. It hadn't been easy either, but not nearly as arduous as hers. After graduating Yale Divinity, he'd served for two years as a provisional member of the Church's divisional conference in order to qualify for ordination as an elder. Once that was done, he'd received an appointment to Stokes Memorial Methodist Church on Peachtree Road in Atlanta, a plum assignment for someone of his age.

Of all of his duties at Stokes, the night-time sessions were the most wearisome. He preferred doing anything other than listening to the prattle of committee members. On this evening, he and two other associate pastors, both women, attended the meeting along with several church members. The senior pastor was absent, vacationing at Little Dix Bay, and he couldn't imagine what the senior must look like in swimming trunks.

The church had a large membership and a considerable staff, and talk about money often topped the agenda. Tonight was no exception. He'd once been idealistic enough to think that finances were a small piece of the typical church's pie, but it wasn't so.

Mercifully, the meeting ended much sooner than expected. Leah dominated his thinking as he walked across the parking lot to his vehicle. *Alone at home, a typical weeknight for her.* Before they married, he'd spent hours talking with her about the way it would be, what with his phone ringing at all hours and with most weekends and weeknights not being his own. She convinced him that she could put up with all of the trappings, but her parents, the Cuttinos, didn't share her conviction. They'd raised their only child to join the highest and best of Atlanta society, perhaps with an Emory surgeon or a rising star at a

Buckhead bank, and to their collective way of thinking, a mere minister could never take her there. At least that was his perception.

As he left Peachtree Road and headed down Piedmont Avenue, he called her. Her phone rang ten times before sending his call to voice mail. He tried their landline, but the result was the same. He left no messages and put his phone on the passenger seat. *She's gone to the Emory village for something and forgotten her phone. No, that's not like her. She has her phone, but she didn't hear my call. No, that's not it. Has she driven to the hospital on her own? Would she do that? Without calling me?*

He and Leah were house-sitters for an Emory theology professor who'd taken a position at the Pontifical North American College in Rome. Otherwise, such a house would have been well beyond their means. He'd always appreciated its relative close proximity to his church, but at present, it had never seemed so far away.

He couldn't recall locking the door on his way out, and on top of that, she rarely set the alarm, a situation that sometimes led to arguments. Now, the very idea gave birth to panic. As far as he was concerned, their elegant, Lullwater Road residence was a magnet for burglars, but she felt safe and secure in their neighborhood because she'd been raised in a very similar setting.

After he left Piedmont and turned onto Rock Springs Road, he doubled his speed. *Please don't let the baby come before I get there!*

Less than ten minutes later, he pulled off Lullwater into their driveway, parked behind her car, and took the quickest route into the house, the front door, relieved to find that it was locked. He stepped into the foyer, dropping his keys on a chest nearby and calling her name. Silence, so uncommon in their house, stopped him dead still. All at once, a bundle of loud and disturbing noises from the kitchen cracked the quiet, first shuffling and running footsteps and then the back door ripping open and slamming against the laundry room wall.

"Leah!" He dashed through the dining room and into the kitchen where he found a scene too grotesque to imagine. "My dear God in heaven!" he whispered, grabbing the nearest counter for support.

She lay on her back on the floor, next to the kitchen island. Her glazed-over, frozen eyes stared unseeing at the coffered ceiling. Her pale, unmoving, right arm stretched out toward an overturned chair as if she was reaching for something. *But what?* Her pink nightgown bunched near the top of her thighs, exposing her splayed, bare legs. Blood, a lot of it, oozed from a deep gash behind her right ear, forming a glistening, red pool under her blonde hair. Her labored, rasping breathing offered the only hint that she was still alive.

He fell to his knees beside her and reached for his phone. As he punched in 911, tears of despair and guilt rolled down his cheeks, leaving dark stains on his tie and shirt. While the call rang through, he lowered his head and whispered, "Oh, Leah…Leah…Leah…how can you ever forgive me?"

***

Leah died at Emory University Hospital a little more than twenty-two hours after Will found her. Dark days and endless nights followed.

Although the doctors couldn't save her, they did save their daughter. That the child would never know her mother or feel her loving touch robbed her birth of the joy it deserved. He named her Leah Anne Rowan and from the first, called her Annie just as they'd planned.

While she was in surgery, he'd called her parents, Phillip and Eileen Cuttino, at their mountain home in Cashiers, North Carolina. When they arrived at the hospital five hours later, the first words out of Eileen's mouth were unkind and combative. "And, Will, just where were you when Leah needed you? Let me take a guess. You were at another one of your revivals or committee meetings."

Things went straight downhill from there. The Cuttinos even tried to remove Annie from the hospital on false pretenses. A concerned nurse warned him, and he put a stop to it. From then on, he exercised the utmost care in all of his dealings with his late wife's parents, especially when it came to his daughter.

Atlanta detectives took three days to eliminate him as a suspect, including conference after conference at the police station. On day one, they pointed out that marital discord almost always led to violence such as that done to his wife. Of course, none had ever existed. On the next day, they revealed that Leah was hit on the head with a heavy, blunt object with a small, round face. After he confirmed his ownership of a hammer, they came and got it. On the third day, they apologized for considering him a suspect in the first place and related what they surmised. It all sounded like guesswork.

Evidence at the scene indicated that Leah's assailant knocked out a pane in the French-half back door to gain entry. "It's likely that he busted the window out with the same hammer he used to hit her. She was already in the kitchen, or the noise brought her there. Reverend Rowan, you told us that your wife sometimes didn't bother to set your alarm, and this must have been one of those times. We think the man had been watching your house for a while and knew which car you drove. With your car gone, he probably assumed that your wife was alone or out with you. Of course, a druggy—one who needed a fix—might not have cared who was in the house.

"There's no way to know exactly how long he was in the house either, but we think you got home just minutes after he attacked her. When you interrupted him, he grabbed everything within easy reach and took off."

Will nodded. The only items that the intruder took were right there in the kitchen. She usually left her purse on the built-in desk; her laptop was sitting on the island when he left for the church; she was wearing the rings he'd given her.

The last thing the detectives told him made him feel even emptier. They said there was little hope that her assailant would ever be identified unless he used one of her credit cards or tried to pawn her laptop or her jewelry.

"Maybe that's a good thing. If you don't find him, I won't have to worry about killing him," he said.

Both of the detectives gave him a questioning look, and one of them asked, "Are you serious about that, preacher, or just joking around?"

He shrugged. In truth, he didn't know, but it probably didn't matter anyway. Soon, the mantra of the police became, "I wish we did, but we don't." He imagined where the paltry product of their investigation went: into a file; then, into a stack on a detective's desk; then, into a filing cabinet in a detective's cubicle; and finally, into a graveyard of shelves housing hundreds of cold cases.

Leah's body went from the hospital directly to the State crime lab for an autopsy. Upon its return, a funeral service was planned at his church with burial in her family's plot at Westview Cemetery in Atlanta. In the meantime, he brought Annie home, and his mother, Amelia, came up from Savannah to help out. His baby's cries made him mindful of how miraculous it was that she was alive and how distressing that her mother wasn't. Thoughts of the autopsy routinely cropped up when he was holding the baby, and if she could have talked, she surely would have asked, "Why are you holding me so tightly, Daddy?"

Her funeral filled the church, but that was the extent of his memory of it. At the end of the day, his mother told him of meeting numerous friends, professors, ministers, and others at the funeral who reflected on Leah's life. "She was loved by so many people, Will. They couldn't stop talking about her tenderhearted ways and accomplishments."

He remained silent, avoiding her eyes. He had no recollection of seeing a single friend or colleague there other than family, nor did he remember a word of the eulogy.

"It's time you got yourself right, Will. You have a daughter to raise now."

He gave her a fleeting smile but said nothing.

***

When his doorbell rang three months later, Will was packing with Annie nearby making baby noises. He looked her way, deemed her safe, and answered the door. It was Julie Fowler, another philosophy student who'd been a good friend to Leah, and Henry Pylant, the assistant professor who was working with her when she died. After giving Julie a hug, he invited them in, apologizing for the mess.

"I hope it's not a bad time, Will," Julie said. "I wanted to see how Annie was doing and drop off this casserole for you. You may want to stick it in the freezer."

"And I brought this for your daughter," Dr. Pylant said, handing him a wrapped package.

"Thank you both. So thoughtful. Let me take this food to the kitchen and then open your package."

He asked them to have a seat, and when he returned, he unwrapped Dr. Pylant's gift, a large, pink, stuffed rabbit. "This is great. I think she has a version of every animal on Noah's Ark but this one." He put it in the crib beside Annie. They watched her touch it, making more unintelligible sounds.

"Dr. Pylant, I'm embarrassed that I've never thanked you for all of the help and support you gave to

Leah along the way. And Julie, I don't have tell you how much your friendship meant to her."

Julie glanced at Annie. She was cooing softly, 'talking' to her new rabbit. "She looks just like her, Will."

He nodded, suddenly heartsick.

"I've heard you're planning to move from Atlanta, but I hope that's not the case. Is the rumor true?" she added.

He sighed. "Honestly, after we lost Leah, I considered leaving the ministry altogether. The bishop and some of my friends convinced me not to. Annie had a lot to do with my decision to stick with it, too. I want to make a good life for her, and I know that a life in the church will provide that."

"Where will you be going?" Dr. Pylant asked.

"There's an opening at a small church in Harris County, and I've been assigned there. The bishop thought it might be good idea for me to get away from here, and I agreed." He sighed and looked around the room. "With Emory being right next door and with all the memories associated with this house, it's been tough. I haven't been in a good place mentally since it happened."

"I understand, and I feel for you. Maybe what I'm going to suggest will help out in some small way."

"At this point, I would appreciate anything like that. What do you have in mind?"

"It's about Leah's dissertation prospectus. As you know, she spent almost three years of her life seeking doctoral candidacy, and from what I saw of her prospectus, it spoke of an academic career that would've been outstanding."

Annie began crying, interrupting him. Will walked over and lifted her into his arms. When he carried her back to his chair, his eyes were teary, too. "It consumed her day and night until she got pregnant. After that, it took a back seat to the baby, but it was still so very important to her.

Believe it or not, she never even let me see her prospectus. She said she wanted it to be perfect in every way before anyone except you saw it."

Julie chuckled. "She wouldn't even tell me what was in it."

The professor cleared his throat and leaned forward. "Let me explain then what I have in mind. For years, the department has maintained a limited number of samples of what the faculty considers the best of all of the dissertation prospectuses submitted by university students. With your permission, I would like to add Leah's prospectus to that collection. It would not only be a way of memorializing her but also a wonderful guide for potential doctoral candidates. I'm confident the department head will want to include it."

Will smiled. "That would be very nice indeed, Dr. Pylant. It's a terrific idea. Thank you so much."

"There's just one problem, Will. She didn't leave a copy with me. On that last day, we met and went over it, but she wanted to make a couple of changes, so she took it with her. I know she completed it that afternoon because she called me and told me that she had. She was so overjoyed, so ready to celebrate…" His voice trailed off, and he looked away.

Will nodded slowly, reliving the terrible day in a rush.

"If you'll just make a copy for me…" Dr. Pylant started.

"Give me a second." Annie was sleeping on his shoulder now, and with great care he returned her to her crib and placed the rabbit beside her. In his chair again, he spoke in words both measured and soft in tone. "I have no copy of the prospectus to give you. It's gone."

"What are you saying?" Julie asked.

"The only copy of her work was on her laptop, and the man who attacked her took it. I know she saved it on a jump drive, but I haven't been able to find that either. I remember seeing her put the drive in her handbag once, but the intruder took that, too. Her laptop and handbag haven't been recovered, and I doubt they ever will be. I've looked high and low for printed pages, drafts, whatever, but no other copies exist."

Both of his visitors were silent, avoiding his eyes.

He lowered his head. "I was hoping to save it for Annie, but it's gone."

Dr. Pylant frowned. "All of that work, her research—lost forever. I really thought a lot of Leah, and I'm going to go back and try to come up with some other way to honor her memory; maybe some sort of scholarship would be suitable."

After they left, Will didn't return to his packing effort. Until Annie begged his attention again, he sat numb of mind and body, unmoving and whispering over and over, "I'm so sorry, Leah. I'm so very sorry. Please, please forgive me."

Chapter One

Present Day—Monday, Night

"Preacher, am I going to Hell?"

The voice rose above the roar of the midway at the Tanotchee County Fair and caught Will Rowan off guard. He and his ten-year-old daughter, Annie, had just left the Ferris wheel, the last of many rides they'd shared on a rare night of fun. He turned to see who'd spoken to him and in the process stifled a groan.

"What about it, Reverend Rowan? Will I go to Hell or not?"

Will studied the face of the old man looking up at him from a motorized wheelchair. Despite his age, the man gazed at him with bright and challenging eyes. A decal-laden baseball cap announced his status as a 'Vietnam Vet' in large, yellow letters. He was John 'Tolley' Tollerson, a member of his church.

No one ever asked Will about the prospect of ending up in Hell anymore. In the Methodist church, the issue harked back to a time of tent revivals, prayer meetings, and Cokesbury hymnals. "Mr. Tolley, why don't you drop by the church tomorrow morning, so we can talk about it? Right now, Annie and I are hoping to enjoy the fair, and I see that you're doing the same with your grandson."

Mr. Tollerson eyed his grandson, who tugged at his sleeve and pointed toward the bumper cars. He gave the boy a firm direction to 'hold still.'

At the same time, Annie motioned for Will to lean down. After he did, she removed two dollars from her shoulder bag and handed the bag to him. Then she whispered, "Daddy, don't worry about me. Go ahead and talk to Mr. Tolley. I'll be at that game booth right over there."

Not waiting for his response, she moved into the crowd and headed toward the booth. After he watched her go, he turned back to Mr. Tollerson. "I need to take care of Annie, Mr. Tolley. Will you excuse me?"

"I shot at a few gooks in my day, Reverend Rowan, but I only know of one that I killed for sure. It was near Loc Ninh, a V.C. with a machete in his hand. I blew his head off, a real mess. I need to know if I'm going to Hell for it."

The old man was talking about something that haunted his dreams, something that he'd told Will many times over. "He was a young man, just a boy, but it was him or me. I had to kill him. So, will the Lord forgive me for it? Please tell me. It's real important."

He put his right hand on the old man's shoulder. "Mr. Tolley, I really do have to go now."

"What if you had been in my shoes, Reverend Rowan? Would a preacher ever kill a man? Would a preacher go to Hell for something like that?"

***

Down the midway from Will and Mr. Tollerson, wooden clowns smiled at Annie from the back wall of the game booth. They all wore the same stupid grin. She'd thrown two rope rings at them already, missing both times. She looked at her only remaining ring, wondering what kind of tricky toss would catch a clown. *Dumb, little, white-faced, slanting clowns*, she thought.

The disgusting, heavy-set man behind the game booth counter snorted and spit onto the sawdust floor. "Hurry it up, kid. Others want a try."

She turned to see if her father was watching her, but he was still talking to Mr. Tollerson. She'd seen the old man in church almost every Sunday. He always sat down front in a special place set aside for wheelchairs. She'd seen his grandson, too, running up and down the halls, always into something.

It was Monday, her father's day off. "Why couldn't they leave him alone for just one night?" she whispered to herself.

For her, the fair had been wonderful so far. She loved the teeming crowds, the meaty cooking smells, the roaring, grinding sounds of the rides, and the garish, blinking lights filling the night sky. She liked stuffed animals, too, and this might be her last chance to take one home tonight.

She sighed at the laughing clowns. As she braced herself for one final throw, she noticed a man over to her right, standing at the edge of the outer wall of the game booth. He was sort of average, not tall like her father. He held a tiny, calico kitten that squirmed in his hands as if it wanted to get away, like his hold on it might be too tight.

She wondered what he wanted, this unknown man with the broad smile and dark hair under a baseball cap. He said something to her, but what he said was lost in the midway noise. For some reason, maybe just the sound of his voice alone, he seemed familiar.

He put the kitten down onto the matted hay at his feet. Then, he turned and disappeared behind the booth. The kitten curled up in the grassy hay, not moving and looking forlorn.

"Wait, Mister," she yelled, but the man didn't return.

She hesitated for a moment and then walked over to the kitten. It looked up at her and mewed. She picked it up and held it against her chest, feeling the soft, rapid thumping of its little heart. She'd always wanted a kitten, but she doubted her father would agree. She looked his way, thinking she might ask him now, but he and Mr. Tollerson were still at it.

She turned back toward the shadowy area behind the booth and said, "Mister? You can't just leave this little kitten here."

"I'm right over here, Annie."

She squinted into the darkness, and after a few seconds, her eyes adjusted to the gloomy setting. She saw the man again, standing several yards away near a chain link fence.

"I have all these kittens, a whole box of them in my car. My mama cat had a big litter a few weeks ago. I've got to find homes for them, or they'll end up at the pound. They'll be put to sleep. That's too terrible for me to even think about. I came to the fair hoping to give them all away. Won't you take the kitten you're holding? It seems to like you, but maybe you'd prefer one of the others I have right over here. Little girls and kittens just go together."

"I don't know. I'd have to ask my daddy first."

"You've seen me at the church, haven't you? From what I know of your dad, I'm sure he wouldn't care."

She looked at the cute kitten. It *did* seem to like her. Her eyes turned toward the man again. He knew her name, so he must be somebody from her father's church. She had no reason to believe he wasn't.

She agonized over what to do.

The man spoke again, soft and caring. "Come on, honey. Why don't you come on over here and see the other kittens? You may like one of them better."

She was almost sure she'd heard this man's voice before, but she couldn't remember when or where. *Was it at the church or somewhere else?*

She glanced toward her father. Mr. Tollerson still gestured with one hand while his grandson jumped up and down, tethered by his other hand.

Seeing her father standing there, listening to somebody from the church, she knew what she needed to do. She turned back in the direction of the man in the baseball cap. "Here," she said, holding out the kitten. "Please take it back. I can't keep it without permission."

When the man didn't move, Annie began walking toward him into the shadows.

Chapter Two

Monday, Night

Mr. Tollerson had moved on at last, guiding his wheelchair in the direction of the bumper cars with his grandson in tow. As Will watched them go, he felt for the old man with his mild case of post-traumatic stress. His heart seemed in the right place, and Will felt sure that there was a place for him in Heaven.

With a nod of his head, he turned to scan the midway for Annie. Seconds earlier, she'd been standing right there in front of the ring-toss booth, but now she was gone. *Where is she?*

He had a flash of nausea, and for a moment he thought it might even bring up the greasy hot dog he'd eaten earlier. He shook off the feeling and hurried over to the game booth. Inside, a man in denim overalls and a wrinkled, white shirt leaned against the wall, twirling three rope rings on his left index finger. The man looked at him and nodded. "Wanna play?"

Will leaned across the counter, explaining that he was looking for his daughter, a blonde-headed girl in blue jeans and a green T-shirt. He stood back and held his right hand up to a point just below his chest to demonstrate Annie's height.

"Over that way," the attendant said, pointing to his left. "She was talking to some man about something and walked off."

"What man?"

"Who knows, fellow? I heard him, but I couldn't see him."

"What were they talking about?"

"You got me."

Thanking the attendant, he turned to leave. At the same time, the man reached over the counter and grabbed his arm, giving it a hard squeeze. "Your kid has one of my rope rings, and I want it back."

Will frowned and pulled his arm away. The man's foul odor lingered in his nostrils. "Don't worry. You'll get your ring back."

He turned his back on the attendant and headed down the midway flanked on both sides by seedy game booths like the one he'd just left. Every half minute or so, he took out his cell phone and punched in Annie's number but got no answer. Leah Anne Rowan had a mind of her own, and she might be anywhere on the fairgrounds which all at once seemed as vast as the Grand Canyon.

***

Far from the fair, the man who claimed to have a whole box of kittens drove an understated, rental car down one of the darker streets of Catalpa. Soon he left the city and traveled into the countryside. He moved neither too fast, nor too slow, along a route both well thought-out and circuitous of his destination. As he drove, he tapped the steering wheel with the fingers of his right hand, humming a perfect, wordless rendition of 'Bella siccome un angelo' from *Don Pasquale*.

He had no litter of kittens. The calico one in his vehicle paced back and forth in a cardboard box on the floor in front of the passenger seat. Its mewing sounds grated on his otherwise pleasant mood, so he reached over and swatted it. He despised cats.

Because of the tiny feline, his car was rank, prompting a concern that it might need fumigating. The kitten had been in the box since early afternoon, whining and defecating. After following Will and Annie to the fairgrounds, he'd parked on the dark, service road behind the game booths, leaving it in the box while he stood in the shadows, waiting, hoping that Annie would come by. Nothing had guaranteed either her isolation or her seduction by the little cat, but in the end, it all worked.

On a dark, deserted stretch of Rickety Back Road, some ten miles or so from the fairgrounds, the man pulled his vehicle onto the grassy shoulder. He cut the engine and turned off the lights. Then he rolled down the window and sat for a moment, looking and listening for approaching vehicles.

Satisfied that no one else was nearby, he got out of his car and opened the passenger side door. He removed the box with the revolting kitten inside and placed it beside the road. Then he reached down for the animal, intending to place the rope-ring from the fair over its head and throwing them both into the woods. But once he had the little feline in hand, it began squirming, scratching, and biting. He dropped it and tried to kick it, but it eluded him and ran down the grassy slope next to the road and into the dark forest. "Good riddance," he muttered, hurling the rope ring from the fair into the trees after it.

He returned to his vehicle where Annie slept on the rear seat. Her cell phone was still in her pocket, and its ringing had been incessant. He took it out of her pocket, noting that all of the calls had come from her father. He removed the sim card and placed it and her phone on the asphalt road, smashing both into several pieces with a hammer he'd brought along for that purpose. He threw the pieces into the woods, too.

In his vehicle again, he turned to look at her. Her mouth was open, and her slender left arm draped down to the floor. The man smiled and drove away, picking up exactly where he'd left off on the aria from *Don Pasquale*. Meticulous preparation had at last borne fruit. This time, not one thing went awry.

***

After searching every ride, game booth, tent, barn, parking space, car, motor home, and open area at the fairgrounds, Will and three policemen found no trace of Annie. Near midnight, one of the policemen called and woke up his superior, Lieutenant Jack Carter, to ask for direction. He reported back that the lieutenant, upset at not being called earlier, was on his way.

Will waited in the fair operator's motor home which, according to a wall plaque, served as the 'international headquarters' of the carnival company. Beside himself with concern for his missing daughter, he sat with his head in his hands, praying, while the operator, Snipes, a bespectacled, short man, paced back and forth, mumbling things like, "Don't know how in the world the company could be held liable for this one," and, "Little girls run away all the time."

Soon, this self-serving harangue brought Will to the brink of losing his composure, and he fought an urge to jump up and pound the diminutive man into silence.

Annie's shoulder bag hung from his right hand. Made of light green suede with matching tassels, it featured a side-pocket zipper with a little, gold slider. She'd brought the bag to the fair because she wanted to use her own money until it ran out. He'd been holding it ever since she headed for the ring-toss booth. Looking down at it, he almost teared up.

Meanwhile, Snipes rattled on and on about the lowlifes drawn to the carnival whenever it arrived in a town. "Of course, this company has no control over who comes to a fair. It's the locals who sell the tickets, not us."

Without looking up, Will shook his head and said, "You disgust me, Mr. Snipes. My daughter's missing, and all you're worried about is a lawsuit."

The metal door creaked open, and Lieutenant Carter stepped inside. Before he could even offer a greeting, the operator started in again with his defense of the carnival. He stared at Snipes, saying nothing until he stopped talking. Then he turned to Will. "Come on, let's go outside."

As they left, the lieutenant looked back at Snipes. "You'd better just stay right there."

Jack was one of the first people Will met when he moved to Catalpa in June of the year before. At the time, they were waiting in the same line for a teller at a local bank. Their conversation led to a cup of coffee and a close friendship, and just having him here gave him some degree of hope.

The crowds were gone, and the carnival was closing down for the night. He followed Jack over to a merry-go-round, now abandoned and silent, and they sat on the edge of it. After a hot day, the mid-September night had turned cooler. Even so, the lieutenant took out a white handkerchief and wiped the freckled, light brown skin of his brow. "We're friends, Will. Why didn't you call me?"

"I wanted to, but the officers wouldn't let me. They said that Annie hadn't been gone long enough to bother you."

"At times, I wonder about some of our folks."

"She's been missing for over four hours, Jack. You know her. She wouldn't just run off. Somebody took her. They have her, and we've got to find her. What are we going to do?"

"You won't be doing anything. I want you to go home now and wait until you hear from me. Somebody may try to reach you on your landline." He stood and put his hand on Will's shoulder. "Come on with me."

"Wait! I can't leave. Something happened last summer, and I need to tell you about it."

"Will, time is really important right now. We can talk later, but tonight I've got to focus on finding her. Let's get you to your car."

He stood and grabbed his friend's arm. "No, Jack. I've got to tell you now."

"Tell me what?"

"A man tried to take Annie at the beach. It may be the same man!"

Chapter Three

Monday, Night

Jack frowned. "Are you kidding me, Will? Some man tried to take Annie last summer at the beach?"

"Yes."

Jack sat beside him. "Go ahead then. I'm listening."

Will took a moment, remembering, letting it all come back. It was in July. He and Annie and his friend, Mae Shaw, had gone down to Savannah to visit his mother, and after that, they headed over to Tybee Island. He hadn't thought about it much since then, perhaps just putting it out of his mind.

"Well?" Jack said.

"All right. I was trying to get it straight in my head. I took Mae and Annie down to Tybee Island last July. We stayed in my mother's beach house. One night, we went to the Crab Shack for an early dinner, but it was crowded. A girl was outside waiting for a seat, too. She was a marine biology student from the University of Miami, and she was involved in the Island Sea Turtle Project that summer. It was the nesting season, and she was hosting a night-time beach walk for a new group of volunteers later that evening."

Will paused, reliving the night. "The student told us all about sea turtles, how tourists don't realize the damage they do with noise and flashlights. She told us it causes them to abandon their nests without laying eggs, or it distracts hatchlings from finding the ocean. She invited us to join the group on the beach that night, and Annie wanted to do it."

On the fairgrounds, more lights went off on the other side of the midway. Jack was getting impatient. "When does something happen, Will?"

"I'm getting there. The girl cautioned us to bring red flashlights that were turtle safe, and we had some at the beach house. Annie was excited, and when it got dark, we hurried down the wooden walkway onto the beach.

"Without a moon, the only light streamed from the houses beyond the dunes. We could hear pounding waves, but we could see the ocean only when glimmers of light caught the waves as they rose and fell.

"Annie found the student and her group of volunteers first, and we headed down the beach to join them. The girl asked everyone to gather around, and we formed a circle with her in the middle. She educated us about the turtles, including the proper protocol for watching them at night. When she finished, she promised to lead us to a nest and asked us for silence.

"I was holding Annie's hand, but she pulled away. I let her go, thinking she wanted a better vantage point near the front of the group, but I was wrong. She left the group. Later, she told us everything that happened after that.

"It seemed that when we began to follow the girl to the nest, Annie noticed something moving near her feet. She looked down and saw a baby turtle go by, heading toward the ocean. She couldn't believe it. She wanted to yell to everybody to come and look, but the girl had told us to be quiet. Without telling us, Annie put her light on the turtle and followed it, just to see what would happen when it got to the water. But before it got close to the foamy water, it stumbled into a hole in the sand. She looked down at the little turtle and then at the ocean. The glistening water was dark, and she was afraid that it would get lost out there.

"She looked back toward the group and saw the leader's light at the top edge of the beach, near the dunes.

We were too far away for her to ask for help, and the little turtle was still struggling. Thinking it wouldn't hurt to pick it up, she reached down and lifted it out of the hole."

Jack put his hand on Will's shoulder. "Is this just about turtles, or is something else going on here? I've got to start looking for Annie."

Will lowered his head. "This is so hard. If I had just run after the man that night and brought him down…"

"Go on and finish the thing, would you? Time is precious."

Will took a deep breath and continued. "All right, Annie heard a man's voice from behind her. At first, the voice sounded like mine, but as he kept talking, she knew it wasn't. He told her to turn off her light. He said something like, 'Annie, if you don't, you'll hurt the baby turtle.' She thought he was part of the group, and he *did* know her name. So she did what he told her to do.

"Meanwhile, I assumed she was still with us. But after following the leader to the nest, I realized she was gone. I looked around, calling her name. When I got no response, I stepped away from the group and studied the dark beach. Seventy-five yards or so away, near the water, I saw a red light and knew it was hers. I ran through the sand toward the light, but Mae stayed with the group, unaware that I'd left.

"All of a sudden, the light went out, and I couldn't tell exactly where it'd been. I slowed, stopped, and screamed as loudly as I could for Annie to cut on her light, but the wind and waves swallowed my words. Darkness and sparkling water lay ahead, nothing else. So, I took off, running in what I thought was the right direction. I stumbled through the sand, yelling for her over and over again.

"Then, on my left, close by, the red light came on again. In its glow, I saw a man walking away down the dark beach. I yelled for him to stop, but he never turned around. He didn't run; he just didn't stop. I thought maybe he couldn't hear me. Ten yards later, Annie was safe in my arms.

"I should have run after the man. I should have knocked him down and beat the dickens out of him. Instead, I let him get away."

Jack shook his head. "What was he wearing?"

"Annie said that he had on a baseball cap, some kind of dark sweater, and dark pants. She called his shoes, 'sneakers.'"

"Weren't you concerned that he knew Annie's first name?"

"She didn't mention that until we were back at the house. If I'd known that on the beach, I would have gone after him."

Jack huffed. "And leave Annie all alone? Even if you *had* caught up to him, he might have killed you for the privilege."

Will was quiet.

"What else did the man do or say?"

"On the way up to the house, Annie told me more. After she turned off her flashlight, the man told her he'd seen a lot of other baby sea turtles just a few steps down the beach. He said they needed to return them to their mothers, or they might die. This worried Annie a great deal, so she let him take her hand to lead her over to the other baby turtles. But then, she heard me calling, telling her to turn on her light. She couldn't do it with only one hand, so she asked the man to let go. He wouldn't release her hand at first, but when she began to pull away, he did."

Jack leaned forward. "Was Annie upset? Did she seem okay?"

"Mae talked to her—girl to girl—back at the house to make sure that the man hadn't done anything. She was fine. She told Mae that the man didn't touch her at all except to take her hand. She wasn't upset. All she really seemed to care about was whether or not the little turtle had made it down to the ocean. She said that the ball cap obscured the man's face, and she never got a good look at him because she cut off her flashlight when he told her to."

Jack nodded. "You called the Tybee police, right, Will?"

He shook his head and lowered it. "No. We put Annie to bed and forgot about it. What could the police have done anyway? The man would have been long gone before they responded."

"So two months ago and five hours away from here, some man tried to take her, but you have no idea who he was or what he looked like."

"Do you think it was same man, Jack?"

"Could be." He stood again.

Will had to ask, "You think I should've called the police, don't you?"

Jack stared at him for a second, ignoring his question, and said, "Come on. Let's go." He turned toward the exit and began walking that way.

Will got in his path, trying to slow him down. "I want to help. You're crazy if you think I'll just sit at home while you're out there looking for her."

The lieutenant turned to face him, saying nothing. His silence brought on panic in Will.

"Annie's gone, isn't she? She's gone, and I'll never see her again."

"We'll get her back, but you've got to stay out of the way. You're a good friend, but I'm a cop. It's best that you just go on home and let us do our job."

"Isn't there something I can do?"

He was still holding Annie's shoulder bag. Jack looked down at it.

"Look, Will, I've been around you and Annie enough during the last year to know everything I need to know about her. The officers here at the fairgrounds have already talked to you, and I'm aware of everything you've told them about what's happened tonight. I don't need anything else from you right now. I want you to go on home and let me find her for you. Is that her pocket book? I'll want it for the dogs."

"Dogs? What…?"

Jack took the shoulder bag from him.

"If they can pick up her scent at the game booth and follow it, we'll have a much better idea of where to look for her. It's just one of the things we'll be doing tonight."

"I want to stay and see what they come up with."

"No. You will *not* be staying here. I want you at home to answer any calls until we can get something set up to monitor them. Can't you see how important that is?"

Will turned away and looked down the midway. It was deserted now, save a few carnival workers and the uniformed officers waiting for Jack. One by one, the lights for the rides and other attractions went out, engulfing the midway in deep shadows. To him, the growing darkness mimicked the shoveling of dirt into Annie's deep, dark grave.

"Will, I can't stay around here one minute longer. There's nothing else you can do. Get home and get some rest. Are you coming?"

He lowered his head and nodded. Bent and anguished, he followed the lieutenant to his car. Behind the wheel, he took one more look at the fairgrounds and then started his car and headed home.

Chapter Four

Monday, Night

Annie woke up with a bad headache. She felt like throwing up, the same way she'd felt sick when she had a stomach virus one time. And her arms and her legs—her whole body—seemed different somehow—slow and weak. Nothing was right with her. Her eyes came into focus but only after she blinked a lot.

She was in a room with an odd, slanted ceiling, a little bit larger than a closet. It was lit by a single, naked bulb set in a yellowed socket. She was fixed to a straight, wooden chair with a cane bottom, clamped somehow to the bare, wooden floor. Her arms and legs were free, but her torso was strapped to the chair from behind making it impossible to get up. She still wore the same clothes she'd had on at the fair, but she had no idea of where she was. She remembered going behind the fair booth to return the calico kitten to the man who'd left it with her but not one thing after that.

She thought of herself as brave, but all of this strangeness scared her to death. Then she noticed him for the first time. The man with the calico kitten sat on the floor near her feet, staring at her. He was older than her father. His legs were drawn up with his arms circling them, and he was smiling.

Beyond the man, she faced a closed door painted reddish black. The walls of the room were paneled in wood, and to her left and right, large, framed collages of pictures blanketed the walls. Her strap kept her from seeing what was behind her.

Her gaze returned to the man. "Why do you have pictures of me on your wall?"

Not responding, he continued to stare.

Annie put her head down and crossed her hands in her lap, unable to tolerate his staring eyes any longer. "Please. I want to go home."

"Not now, Annie. You and I have something we must do first. We each have a role to play."

His voice sounded kind. It gave her some courage, and she looked at him again. "You told me my father wouldn't care if I had a kitten."

"Yes."

"You don't know if he would care, do you?"

"No."

"It was a lie, wasn't it?"

"I'm sorry, but yes. It was."

"Do you even know him?"

"I know all about him."

"Who are you?"

"My name isn't important, Annie."

"But tell me your name anyway. I need to know it."

"Why don't you call me 'Iblis?' It isn't my given name or the name I have now, but I'll let you use it until I'm ready to tell you my name."

Tears filled her eyes. Even his name was strange. "What are you going to do to me?"

"Nothing."

"Is that really the truth, Mr. Iblis?"

"Yes."

"Please tell me what happened to the little kitten? Is it all right?"

He smiled and shrugged. "Kittens come and go."

His answer made her stomach feel even worse, and she looked away. "Are you sure you won't try to hurt me?"

"I'm positive. Before I leave, would you like to go to the bathroom again?"

"Again?"

"You probably don't remember that I took you before. You could hardly walk, and you were so groggy. Do you need to go now?"

She shook her head and placed her hand on her neck, reaching for a delicate chain hidden under her T-shirt, needing assurance that it was still there. When her hand touched it, she pulled it out and glanced down at it.

"I see you have a locket on your chain. May I look at it?"

Annie glanced down at her chest. "I don't want to take it off."

"You can keep it on. Just open it for me so I can look inside."

She opened the locket, and he leaned down to look at the picture inside it. He studied it for several seconds and then straightened up again. "Is that your mother?"

"How do you know she's my mother, Mr. Iblis?"

The question seemed to puzzle him for a moment. "Because you look a lot like her, of course."

A tear formed in her right eye and trailed down her cheek. "She died."

He nodded. "Yes."

"Did you know her?"

"The article about you and your father in the Catalpa paper last year informed me that she was gone."

She closed her locket, and he got up to leave. When he opened the door, she saw a dark hallway beyond. Watching him walk away reminded her of something from her past, something uncomfortable. *But what?* And then it came to her. "I know your voice, Mr. Iblis. You were the man on the beach that night."

He stopped but didn't turn around. "Yes."

"You wanted to take me away that night didn't you?"

He turned and looked at her, said nothing, and left, closing and locking the door behind him. Then the light went out.

She couldn't see a thing now, not even her hands in front of her face, and she had to touch her face to make sure it was still there. She heard a sound. *Was it a door closing?*

And then, everything was quiet. In the total darkness, she began to whimper, and not knowing what else to do, she whispered a prayer. "Oh, Jesus, please help me. Please, please, please help me."

Chapter Five

Tuesday, Wee Hours

Will sat at the kitchen table in the small, craftsman home he shared with Annie on Atwater Street in Catalpa. *I'm supposed to monitor my landline, but why be anchored to it?* It was no secret that he had a cell phone, too, and the number was there for the world to see on the church website and in numerous other places. He could be out looking for Annie right now and still be available to whoever had her. He thought of calling Jack to remind him of that but hesitated. He'd seen enough television shows to know that the police always told the parents of missing children to stay at home, to wait, to do nothing, to feel helpless, to agonize, and to expect the worst.

A bottle of Scotch whiskey and an empty glass sat on the table in front of him. He'd taken it down from a high shelf in his bedroom closet. Not long after his father died, his mother gave him three bottles of single-malt, Scotch whiskey from his father's stock. She told him that he might be glad that he had them someday. "Preachers need a drink every now and then, too," she said.

His mother's 'now and then' had come, but the bottle remained unopened. He couldn't go there yet because he still had hope. Later though, it might be just the place to visit.

He called Annie's cell phone over and over again. At first, his calls went to voicemail, but as the night wore on, a robotic voice answered them. "The person you're trying to reach is not available." He sent her text messages, too, and they were 'delivered' for a time, but later, not so. His darkest thoughts led him to conclude that Annie couldn't respond.

His cell phone was on the table, and his landline phone was a few feet away on the wall over a counter. He kept looking at one and then the other, but neither rang. Jack had promised to call the minute he knew anything. He'd also directed Will to get some sleep, but he hadn't even gotten undressed yet.

Annie's dog, a black Lab named Pete, lay at his feet. As soon as Will got home, the dog scratched at the back door to come in from the yard. After he let him in, he ran from room to room looking for Annie. When he didn't find her, he barked. His barking didn't stop until Will put food in his bowl.

He wished his father, Holland, was still alive. Better than anyone else, he would have known what to do. He wanted him here, too, so he could apologize for not taking his advice. If he'd just listened to him, he wouldn't be sitting in this little kitchen in Catalpa, Georgia, forsaken by God. He could hear his father now, belittling the ministry, begging him not to get into it. Will was still in college at the University of Georgia at the time, and he'd already been accepted at Yale Divinity School. Although his academics were sound, his partying record at Georgia belied any notion of his fitness for the ministry, and his fraternity brothers were in a state of disbelief over his future plans.

For years, Holland had expressed his hope that he would go to law school and then join the Savannah firm he'd founded. Will listened, but in the end, his heart wouldn't let him go in that direction. For months, he put off telling his father, but when Yale accepted him, it was time.

The circumstances were far from right. Holland, a respected and successful lawyer, lay in a hospital bed set up in the library at his home in Savannah, still clear-headed and strong enough to speak but soon to die from lung cancer. Over two days, as they talked, his father was less and less subtle about his feelings. "A lot of ministers are men who can't make a living any other way," Holland said, as emphatically as he could in his condition. "Some of them are con artists, who look and act like used car salesmen. You're smarter and better than that. Don't do it."

He looked away, saying nothing. Only the soft hum of an oxygen tank broke the silence between them until his father spoke again. "Really and truly, Will, what makes you think it's a good idea?"

His eyes met his father's. "Why did you become a lawyer?"

He nodded but remained quiet for at least two minutes while Will pretended to look at the books behind him. Then Holland took a deep, long breath and let it out slowly. "Okay then. Okay. I wanted some peace of mind, that's all. I needed to know that you were absolutely sure about it."

"I am, Dad. I feel called to do it."

He smiled and took Will's hand. "You'll make a damn good preacher. I don't doubt that at all. It's the right thing for you."

He died two weeks later.

Now at his kitchen table, Will would've given most anything for some of his father's sage advice, especially about how to handle the waiting and the not-knowing. He'd felt exactly the same way ten years earlier when his beloved Leah lay dying in a dark hospital room in Atlanta. He could do nothing then and nothing now, nothing but sit and wait, dreading an outcome that seemed inevitable.

He had a sinking feeling that Annie's disappearance and what had happened last summer were connected, and just the thought of it fueled his regret, magnifying his guilt for losing Annie at the fair.

He got up and paced back and forth with Pete matching his every step, the tapping of his nails on the wooden floor offering the only relief from the dreadful silence. As he walked, he thought of needing to call his mother, Annie's other grandparents, and his friend, Mae. When he got home from the fair, he'd rationalized that it was too late. But the truth was that notifying them would give the whole thing a sense of reality that he wasn't ready to face. If Annie wasn't found soon though, her story would leak to the media, and he wasn't about to let the people who loved her find out *that* way.

He picked up his cell phone and looked at the time. Almost three hours had gone by since he left the fairgrounds, and he'd waited long enough. Jack answered soon after he punched in the number. "I told you I'd call *you*, Will. Why aren't you in bed?"

"Just tell me."

"No, I won't. This is a police matter. I can't be telling you stuff."

"What are you keeping from me?"

Jack sighed. "The search dogs stopped at the alley behind the ring-toss booth. Tire tracks in the dirt suggest that she got into a vehicle."

"That's crazy. You know Annie wouldn't do that. What about her cell phone? Can't the police track it somehow?"

"We could if it was still in existence. From what we can tell, it's not."

"That's it? There's nothing more?"

A long silence followed and then, "We will find her. I promise you that, but right now, I've got to go. We'll talk in the morning."

"Wait, Jack…"

But much like Annie, Jack was gone, too.

***

At first light, Pete huffed and nudged him, begging to go out. Will wasn't sure how long he'd slept with his head on the kitchen table, but it couldn't have been for very long.

He put the dog out and returned the unopened bottle of Scotch to his bedroom closet.

After he showered and dressed, he called his mother. Amelia Rowan, an artist, would be up already. She liked to do most of her work in the gentle, diffused light of early morning. She responded to the awful news by offering to come up from Savannah, but he urged her not to.

"Oh, Will. I don't know how long I can stay away."

"After we've found her, that's when you should come."

She agreed to wait, but only if he kept her up to date on any new developments. "I'll call Harry for you," she said. "He'll be very upset." Harry was his younger brother, the only lawyer in the family now, the heir to their father's firm.

He dreaded the call to Annie's other grandparents, the Cuttinos. He guessed that they had already migrated back to their home in Atlanta after spending the summer in their mountain retreat. He gritted his teeth and punched in the number.

Eileen answered, firing one question after another, most raising issues of neglect on his part, some even hitting home. Soon Phillip got on the line, too, saying very little and nothing at all in Will's defense. The Cuttinos' reaction was a carbon copy of their response to Leah's death. Then, as now, they implied that he was responsible, and their questions served to throw gasoline on the fire of his guilty feelings.

Loud knocks on the front door brought his conversation with the Cuttinos to a merciful end. Eileen was still railing when he hung up, but he had to go. Two Catalpa detectives had arrived to search Annie's room for clues. They surveyed the house briefly before sending him back to the kitchen while they concentrated on her room.

Every question he asked them was directed to Jack. They were there for all of thirty minutes.

After the policemen left, Will called Mae Shaw, the woman he'd been seeing for several months. He guessed that she was still in bed, and he pictured her brushing back her short red hair as she answered the call. Even though it was the third time he'd related his bad news, it seemed much more difficult this time.

"Will? I was asleep."

"Annie is…missing, Mae. She disappeared…last night at the fair. We can't find her."

"What do you mean by 'disappeared?'"

"I'm not sure…they think she got into a car…I don't know what…" His voice trailed off.

"I'm coming over there right now."

"No, don't. They may want me to help them look for her."

"The police are involved?"

"Of course they are."

"I'm so sorry. Please don't try to keep me away. Will you be at the church later?"

"Yes."

As he put down his cell phone, his tears came. It was the first time he'd cried since Annie went missing. Hours had gone by, and it was so hard to have any hope at all.

Chapter Six

Tuesday, Early Morning

Twenty minutes later, Will's eyes were dry and squinting against the bright, morning sun as he pulled his twelve-year-old Land Rover into the parking lot of the First Methodist Church. The lot was empty.

The new church janitor, Rankin Turner, should've arrived before now, but his old, white, pickup truck was not there. He was glad because he didn't want to have to deal with him or any of the other staff members yet. He had deferred letting them know about Annie until this morning, and he wasn't looking forward to it.

He left the parking lot and headed for a side door leading into the administrative area of the church. On the way, he passed the church's older, massive, brick sanctuary with its buttressed, Gothic design and its elaborate sandstone trim. It bulked against the sky, dwarfing him, making him feel even smaller and more ineffective than he already did on this day. Entering the building, he walked across the hall, through the outer office of his assistant, Callie Rainwater, and into his own, larger office.

Behind his desk, he sat doing nothing, unfit for any task and consumed with thoughts of the fate of his lost daughter and where in the world she might be.

His despondency was in full flower when the security bell sounded at the side door. He walked over to Callie's desk, buzzed the caller in, and stepped into the hall. When no one came in, he walked over to the door. Through the glass inset, he saw an unsmiling Jack Carter holding up two steaming cups of coffee and motioning for him to open the door. He let him in, and they returned to his office, both holding a coffee cup.

Jack's tired faced competed with his wired demeanor. "Wimberley at the *Catalpa Times* called me. He'd already heard that Annie disappeared. I confirmed the bare bones but gave out few details. Newspaper and television reporters from Atlanta are calling the station, too, and they'll invade the city in short order. We directed all of them to refrain from contacting you or the church. Of course, that's a useless restraint."

"I don't care about the media. I want to know what's going on."

In response, he gave a report of sorts. He related that he'd already sent detectives to the fairgrounds to interview all of the carnival employees before they vacated the premises. "Unless we can justify keeping them around, the fair people will be gone by mid-morning, two days earlier than expected. My guess is they want to get out of town before a lawsuit is served on them."

"I have no interest in suing anybody. I just want Annie back."

"I know that you won't sue them, but they don't," Jack said, taking a long sip of coffee.

Will picked up his phone and looked at the time. The staff would be arriving soon, and he was getting antsy. "What else?"

"With all of the people at the fair, I don't know how the dogs picked up Annie's scent at the game booth, but they did. As I told you before, they followed her scent around the booth to the access road behind it. After that, it was obvious that she was put in a vehicle. Tire marks on the dirt road—one set of them—support the vehicle scenario."

"How could that have happened? She wouldn't have gotten into some man's car voluntarily."

"He probably chloroformed her at that point."

Will lowered his head and shook it.

"A forensic team has been at the fairgrounds since dawn. Because Annie was taken right after you last saw her at the booth, I doubt that they will find anything. They'll finish their work in a couple of hours, and if they do find something, I'll let you know.

"Our uniformed officers and sheriff's deputies are looking for Annie on roads throughout the county. We've rounded up registered sex offenders, and they're still being interviewed. State troopers had temporary roadblocks in place until dawn. An Amber Alert was issued."

"Is that it?"

"I wish I had more, but I don't."

The pastor slumped in his chair. A block away, the courthouse clock struck eight times. It sounded like a death knell. He took a sip of coffee but put it down when the cup began to shake.

Jack leaned across his desk. "Just let us find her. Okay?"

Will looked away, toward the windows and the world outside, the world into which his daughter had disappeared. He said nothing.

The lieutenant sat back and continued. "I have a close friend who's an FBI agent in Atlanta. He's coming down this morning as a favor to me. They're not supposed to get involved until Annie's been gone for twenty-four hours, but he's coming anyway. He's also agreed to do whatever it takes to monitor your land line and cell phone."

"They can do that? They can tap my phone lines?"

"Yes, with your permission."

The FBI agent had faxed written releases to Jack for him to sign, authorizing the Bureau to monitor his phone lines and email. He looked down at them and mumbled, "No one's called so far. Not a single call. Not one."

His tone must have sounded pitiful. "I'm so sorry I don't have more to offer yet. Please just sign the papers."

He signed the releases without reading them and pushed them back across the desk. He had an urgent need to do something more than talking with the policeman, but he had no idea what that might be.

Jack stood. "I have to see what's going on out at the fairgrounds. I expect the newspaper and TV people will be swarming soon, and you should be ready for that sort of thing."

At that moment, the security chime on the side door sounded again. Jack stayed in the office, and Will went out to see who was there, expecting a reporter from the Times. Instead, he found Mae.

"Will, I…" she started, but he took her in his arms. "Jack's in there," he whispered. "Come on in."

He followed her into his office, and she greeted Jack. They stood in awkward silence for several seconds before the lieutenant excused himself and left.

After Will heard the outer door close, he took Mae in his arms and held her there for almost a minute. Still holding her, fighting tears, he said, "They don't know anything."

"Surely…" Mae began.

"All of Jack's talk of dogs, and forensic teams, and riding on county roads, and Amber Alerts—it's all just pure filler, Mae. They have nothing. She could be anywhere on God's green earth, and where that is, only God knows."

She broke their embrace and searched his eyes. "You're not a quitter."

He returned her gaze but then looked away. "I used to think that."

Chapter Seven

Tuesday, Wee Hours

When Iblis left the closet under the stairs in the wee hours of Tuesday morning, he flipped off the light switch on the outside wall next to the closet door. He had heard of prisoners going crazy under those harsh lighting conditions, and he assessed it cruel to leave Annie under a lit, one-hundred-watt bulb all night long. Her comfort was of utmost importance to him.

***

Annie panicked when the light suddenly went out, fearful of what might happen next. For a time, a sliver of light shone under the door, but soon it disappeared, too, and total darkness engulfed her. Then, she heard nothing, except for her own, rapid breathing and the movement of her feet on the wooden floor.

She wasn't afraid of the dark, but she hated spiders. In the absence of any light, she was blind to them crawling on the wall or the floor or even on her.

She bullied her thoughts of spiders by busying herself with an effort to force her way out of the chair. Nothing worked; the strap around her waist remained tight, and she gave up after numerous failed attempts.

Her exertions exhausted her, and she fell asleep. Later, she woke up, confused in the darkness. After a while, she heard a scurrying sound. *Is it a spider?* She brushed her hands over her body and the chair as far as she could reach, checking, checking, checking. She touched not a single spider, but the disturbing sounds continued. *Could it be something in the walls? Could it get out?*

After what seemed like hours, she slept again but woke up disoriented. *Is it night or day? Where is Mr. Iblis? What does he want from me?*

She had a pretty good idea of what men like Mr. Iblis might do to girls like her. Several months earlier, her grandmother, Amelia, told her about all the bad things that could happen to girls, even when they were with boys they really liked. She figured that her dad had put his mother up to talking to her, but she didn't let on that she knew. She also failed to mention to her grandmother that she'd already heard most of the stuff anyway.

She knew something else, too. Her dad would save her from this nightmare. He was coming to take her home, and he was on the way right now.

She was asleep again when the light came on in the little room. At the time, she was dreaming that the door dissolved and her father stood there smiling. But instead, when the door opened, her sleepy eyes framed the frightening visage of Mr. Iblis. *It's always him at the door*, a sinking thought.

"Good morning, Annie."

He carried some sort of breakfast on a tray like the ones they used in the school cafeteria. He placed it on her lap, but she didn't want to eat anything on it. The smells made her sick. She pushed the tray away, and he stood there with it, looking at her. Then he left.

"Come back, Mr. Iblis! Please come back!"

She waited forever, but he didn't return. Frustrated, she stomped her feet on the wooden floor. When that failed to bring him back, she screamed and kept it up until she was hoarse. First, she yelled for her father, and then for the dead mother she'd never even met. After that, she shouted "help!" at the top of her voice, over and over again.

***

In a contemplative mood, Iblis huddled with his thoughts at the Formica-topped kitchen table in the house where he kept Annie. Plaster walls surrounded him, all painted bright yellow. Except where metallic trim was necessary, everything else in the kitchen was hospital white. Even the linoleum floor was white with tiny, black specks intended, he supposed, to disguise dirt.

The house once belonged to a woman named Doris Paine, but it was his now. He knew everything about her. For instance, she assigned meaning to colors, and one day, when he was sitting here at this same table, she commented on the colors in the kitchen. She claimed to have chosen them because white was the color of perfection, and yellow, that of madness. Retrospectively, he found those colors quite fitting, as he'd always considered her perfectly mad.

Citing the Biblical story of Abraham and Sarah, she once told him that her parents were 'really old' when she was born. She had no siblings, and when her parents passed away shortly after she graduated from college, they left her their entire estates. It seemed that they were chiropractors known jointly in Catalpa as the 'Doctors Paine.' Their strange equipment still filled much of the small attic adjoining Doris' bedroom on the second floor of the house. It reminded Iblis of some of the Inquisition-like, torture devices featured in old, Vincent Price movies.

After leaving Annie alone the night before, he'd slept in the bedroom on the first floor. As a young boy, he'd spent enough time in this house to know everything about it. Then, as now, the nocturnal noises in Doris' house, especially those seeming to come from her room on the second floor, were quite unsettling at night. Although he attributed them to squirrels in the walls, one could never be sure. That was why he slept down here.

His house guest was locked away in a longish closet under the stairs which led to the second floor. Before retiring for the night, he checked on her one last time. Once again, she demanded to go home, but he refused. He promised to come back to the closet early this morning, and now he had, true to his word. He hoped that his honesty would establish a level of trust that would make everything proceed without incident.

Her breakfast tray with a chicken biscuit, hash browns, and a cup of fruit sat on the kitchen table in front of him. He mistakenly thought Annie might like it. Should she become hungry enough though, she would eat. Now, he considered eating the food himself but threw it out instead. He'd already breakfasted on yogurt and blueberries from the refrigerator.

He left the kitchen for the adjoining dining room with its darkling furnishings of mahogany veneer. Doris chronicled the history of the Victorian pieces as once belonging to her great-grandmother and boasted of their 'heirloom status.' Based on his knowledge of antiques, he thought otherwise.

The day before, he'd placed a lacquered tray on the dining room's mirrored sideboard. On the tray was an unmarked bottle of oblong, olive green tablets, a small, porcelain mortar and pestle, and a tiny scroll of yellowed paper, laminated and tied with a pink ribbon long enough to let the scroll dangle from a person's neck. He liked being prepared, even though he was never a Boy Scout.

As he stood at the sideboard, he felt a slight vibration in the hardwood floor. He guessed it was nothing other than his visitor stomping her feet. His careful research suggested that her frustration was predictable and would dissipate over time. In just a little while, he would have to leave her, but she would be fine until he returned.

The closet under the stairs was just short of being soundproof. Doris once noted that the Drs. Paine lined its plaster walls with thick, cedar boards. Iblis suspected that the boarding was added to quiet the closet altogether for some nefarious, chiropractic purpose other than protecting furs and other fine clothing. As far as he was concerned, the tools and equipment in the attic supported this theory. However, he never would have revealed this supposition to Doris. It wasn't his place to do that.

The thumping ceased, but something else captured his attention. Concentrating, he detected a faint noise coming from the direction of the closet. It might or might not be human; it might or might not have come from inside the house. He was sure that it would be impossible for someone outside the house to determine its nature or its source.

However, he interpreted the sound without difficulty; Annie was screaming. He had intimate knowledge of just how fruitless such a vocal effort might be. When he was a little boy, he'd been locked up in the closet, too, calling out at the top of his lungs. Back then, no one in the house had come to help him either.

Chapter Eight

Tuesday, Early Morning

Soon after Jack left the church, Mae did, too. She and her helper needed to open her business, a bookstore on St. Clair Street, a block off the square. Half an hour later, still at his desk, Will heard his assistant, Callie, come in the side door and head down to the fellowship hall as she did every morning to put her bag lunch in the kitchen's big refrigerator. For all practical purposes, she'd been running the day-to-day operations of the church for years, freeing up ministers for what they were supposed to do. He'd decided early on that she was indispensable.

From others, he learned that her husband had died when their two sons were toddlers, but somehow she held things together through her job at the church. Still attractive in her mid-forties, she claimed that her job kept her too busy to get married again, and from what he'd seen of her work ethic, that was true. Her boys were in college now, both on scholarships, and she confessed to him that she was lonely and at loose ends without them. Rumor had it that she was dating a local man, but she had yet to mention it to him.

When she appeared at his office door, she was wiping her eyes with a tissue. "I saw Lieutenant Carter in the parking lot, and I'm so sorry, Will. It just can't be true, can it? Not our Annie. What can I do to help?"

He left his desk and gave her a hug. "It'll be fine, Callie. We'll get her back."

She stepped away and looked at him. "Yes, of course, we will. Did you know that there's a TV truck setting up out there already?"

"I'm not surprised. Please keep them away from me."

He leaned against the edge of his desk and put his left hand on a stack of correspondence there. "I'll get to these. In the meantime, let the rest of the staff know what's going on. I just don't feel like talking to them right now. I'm sure a lot of our members will want to do something. Please put out the word that I need their prayers more than fried chicken or chocolate cake."

"Forget those letters. I can answer them and sign your name. Will you let me?"

Will didn't hear her question. His head was lowered, his thoughts on Annie again.

She put her right hand on his shoulder. "Will, don't you worry. I'll handle everything for you here at the church."

He raised his head and looked at her. "Thanks, Callie."

She stepped toward the door but turned midway there. "I hate to bring this up, but our janitor is a no-show this morning."

"See if you can run him down. I can't deal with that either."

She left and closed the door behind her. Alone now, he returned to his desk chair and picked up his cell phone to call Mae but didn't. He opened his Bible, intending to read Psalm 46, but closed it without doing so. He couldn't stop thinking about his telephone conversation with Eileen Cuttino earlier that morning. Her questions kept coming back, playing through his head over and over again.

Tell me, Will Rowan, where were you when Annie was talking to some sleazy, carnival type over behind a gambling booth? Just where were you? What in heaven's name were you doing when my only granddaughter disappeared? How could something like this have happened?

Why weren't you watching her? What kind of father are you anyway?

He knew the answers to all of Eileen's questions already. Her interrogation was practically the same when Leah died, and he'd known the answers then, too. Every now and then, even after ten years, the memory of his failings took hold, punishing him with one 'if only' after another, filling his heart with regret. He leaned forward in his chair, put his elbows on the desk, and put his head in his hands. He was still like that when Callie came in a few minutes later.

"I think we have the media under control, but I haven't located Rankin. I'll keep you advised. Are you okay?"

He didn't answer her question but instead looked at his watch and told her he was leaving. He left the church through a discreet, side door and walked across town to the Catalpa Municipal Building, a large, yellow brick structure in the Art Deco style built in the 1930s as a WPA project. A box office and civic auditorium dominated the first floor, and city offices filled the second. The police department and city jail were crammed into the basement, and the main, city fire department was housed next to the building.

The entry to the police station was around back. Special Agent Todd Baxter of the Atlanta field office of the FBI had summoned him here. Jack introduced Baxter and led them back to a small, windowless, conference room stuck off in a corner of the catacomb-like station. They gathered at a table with him and Jack on one side and Baxter on the other.

The agent was a tall, heavy set man with light hair and freckles, dressed in a T-shirt, jeans, and sneakers. His wrinkled, cotton blazer hung on a chair nearby, its sole purpose likely being to hide the pistol and holster strapped under his left arm. Many FBI agents no longer dressed like investment bankers, but his attire took things to a new level of informality.

While Baxter took notes, they discussed Will's background and personal life, including detail after detail about Annie and those who might have come into contact with her since their move to Catalpa. Then, they proceeded to the last few days.

By now, he'd described to Jack and others the events of the day before at least half a dozen times. If he was a suspect, he wondered why didn't they just come out and say so. While the federal lawman reviewed his notes, Will turned to Jack and mouthed the words, "What is this?" Jack shrugged.

At last, Baxter looked up from his work product, smiled, and said, "Let's go through all of it one more time."

So they did. The latest discussion concluded with a new question about the color of Annie's panties. Will pointed out that she'd dressed herself. The agent ignored his response and asked the question again.

"I've already told you that I don't know, and I still don't."

The big G-man glared at him for a full five seconds and then lowered his head and closed his notebook. Will rose to stand, but Baxter motioned for him to sit back down. "Wait. I want to know why you went to the fair on Monday night."

"What do you mean?"

"Why'd you go that night instead of last Thursday or Saturday or whenever?"

"Last week, somebody stuck an envelope addressed to me in the church's mailbox. Inside were two all-ride passes. They were for yesterday—Monday. It was my day off, and my daughter had been asking to go."

"Who left the envelope?"

"I don't know who or when. I assumed they were complimentary passes from the civic club which sponsors the fair. Ministers are always receiving stuff like that."

Will was getting warm in the little room. Droplets of sweat formed under his shirt and ran down his chest.

The lawman seemed skeptical. "You found nothing else inside the envelope? No note?"

The pastor glanced away, thinking. "A note, yes. It was hand-printed. It said, 'For you and your daughter. Have a good time.' I think I threw it away with the envelope."

"Not signed?"

He shook his head.

Baxter wrote in his notebook again. "Okay, preacher. We're just about through. You've said nobody has asked you for money yet."

"No, they haven't." He had already answered the question at least twice. He wasn't claustrophobic, but the close quarters were taking their toll on him.

"Jack told me about the incident this past summer on Tybee Island. It's my understanding that you never called the police. Is that right?"

"Yes."

"And again, why was that?"

"I don't have anything to add to what I told Jack. Calling the police seemed like a useless gesture."

"From what I can tell, this isn't a kidnapping for ransom—" From the hall, running footsteps and a loud yell interrupted him. He looked toward the door and said, "I hope they caught the guy, Jack."

Jack smiled, and the agent turned back to Will. "Is there any money in your family, Reverend Rowan, trust funds or the like?"

"My father's deceased, but he left enough to take care of my mother. Beyond that, you'd have to ask her. My daughter's maternal grandparents appear well-fixed, but I'm not privy to their financial affairs."

"You're a preacher, and preachers aren't supposed to have any money. So unless there's something else out there that we're not aware of, I doubt that anybody would try to do this for financial gain. Am I right?"

"I guess so."

"Of course, who knows what some stupid asshole might do. If you get any overtures, you need to tell us right away."

Will sighed.

Baxter placed both of his elbows on the table and leaned across toward him. "Reverend Rowan, now listen to me. If you try to handle any aspect of this thing on your own, you will lose your daughter. It's that simple."

"I understand."

The agent stared at him again for several seconds without blinking, making him nervous. He felt compelled to say something else, and maybe that was the whole point. "If it's not a kidnapping for ransom, then what is it?"

The G-man looked beyond him, over his head, as if he was trying to remember something. "Two thousand children go missing in the United States every day. Some of them run away, others are taken by a relative, usually a divorced father. Your daughter's case isn't like those. I think the perpetrator had something else in mind. Frankly, it has all the markings of the work of a male pedophile. He could be from anywhere, as far away as New Mexico or as close as across town. There's no way to know for sure whether he was a stranger or an acquaintance, but all indications are that your daughter went with him voluntarily."

Will blanched, suddenly nauseated. He stood as a prelude to bolting out of the room but felt so weak that he had to sit back down. He wrapped his arms around his stomach and lowered his head.

"I have to tell you that with every day she's gone, the odds of finding her go down," Baxter said.

The pastor's head was still lowered when the federal lawman left the room. "Jack, after all I tried to do with my life, it comes down to this?"

"For Annie's sake, don't think about giving up. Just keep on praying."

Will stood, walked out of the room, and left the station. A second later, his cell phone rang. He stopped on the wide walkway in front of the Municipal Building and glanced at the phone's display. It was his younger brother Harry calling from Savannah. He was in the middle of a week-long trial, something about a maritime accident, and he'd stepped out of the courtroom to make the call.

His brother had done everything he'd declined to do. He joined their father's law firm, became a top litigator, and proceeded to enjoy all of the fruits of his practice—the BMW, the power suits, the big boat, and the five-star residence. He wished his father was alive to see what his younger son had accomplished in his life so far, a life that was the antithesis of Will's own.

Harry expressed his deep concern for Annie and promised to keep in touch. While he was doing that, the word 'pedophile' made a brief, imagined appearance on the walkway beneath Will's feet. While his brother was still talking, he abruptly ended the call without saying goodbye. Then he stepped over to a row of shrubbery, leaned down, and vomited.

Chapter Nine

Tuesday, Midday

After Annie shouted until she was hoarse, she gave up. Not long after that, she felt slight vibrations in the floor and wondered if Mr. Iblis was still in the house. She thought she heard a doorbell and voices, but she couldn't be sure.

Hopeless, she lowered her head and went away in her mind on a walk with her dog Pete and her father. The sky was blue, and the fall leaves were beautiful. She was still walking that way when she fell asleep.

Now, after what seemed like hours, she woke and found him standing in the doorway, staring at her. "Earlier, I thought I heard you making noise, Annie. Is something wrong?"

"I have to go to the bathroom now."

"Of course."

Exiting the closet again, he returned with a coiled, metal chain in his left hand. He laid it on the floor and then unstrapped her. After sitting so long, she needed his help to get up. As soon as she was on her feet, he wrapped the light-weight chain firmly around her waist and locked her in it with a small padlock he pulled from his pocket. He held the other end of the chain. She was like a dog on a leash, a situation so upsetting that she began to tremble.

"I'm sorry, Annie. Is it too tight?"

"I don't like it, Mr. Iblis."

"I'm afraid it's a necessary evil."

He led her out of the closet into a short hallway which connected a first floor bedroom on the right with the rest of the house on the left. He motioned her to the right into what he called the 'bedroom where Doris' grandmother slept.' Dark wood and heavy, velvet curtains dominated the room.

"Who is Doris? Does she still live here?"

Ignoring her questions, he guided her into an adjacent bathroom. A white tub on clawed feet faced the door. To the right, she saw a vanity table with a stool and mirror, and in a corner, a free-standing, white sink.

"But where is the toilet?"

He pointed to a door to the left of the tub. It opened onto a little room with a toilet inside. Annie went in and tried to close the door, but the chain prevented its closing all the way. Seeing this, he dropped the chain and returned to the bedroom. From there, he said, "Your privacy is assured, Annie."

The toilet was creepy. The old fixtures and the odor of rusty water and backed-up sewage reminded her of the bathroom in the basement of her father's church, next to the boiler room. Before flushing, Annie closed the lid of the commode seat and climbed onto it so she could see what was on the other side of a small window above it. She pushed back dingy, short curtains and looked out.

The window overlooked concrete steps leading up to what must be the back door of the house. Across an asphalt driveway and a small parking area, an old, white-washed, open barn leaned toward the house. She saw a dilapidated, white truck parked inside it, covered for the most part by a dirty-looking tarp. A large tree to the left of the barn spread over it, and beyond that, tall, dense shrubbery surrounded a small backyard. The same kind of dense shrubbery also framed the yard on the other side of the barn and the driveway. Between the tree and the house, a gray car came into view. She placed her face against the window pane and strained to see any neighboring houses, but the barn and the shrubbery hid them.

She observed all of this in less than half a minute. Afterwards, she struggled to raise the window but found that it was nailed shut. When he called her name, she almost fell off the commode seat. She flushed the toilet and said, "I'm through now." She came out and washed her hands at the sink. Then he picked up the chain.

"Do I have to go back?"

"Yes. Are you hungry now?"

"I guess so."

"Good. I'll bring you something."

When Annie was returned to the closet, she saw the area behind the strapping chair for the first time. An antique table sat against the wall. A large picture of her in an ornate, gold frame hung on the wall above it. It was like the pictures taken at school every year but much bigger. Under it on the table, a pair of pink panties lay on a cloth of blue velvet. *Where did he find all these pictures of me?*

After he removed the chain and strapped her back into the wooden chair, she begged him to leave the light on, and he did. When he was gone, she studied the pictures she could see.

"It's not me. I'm not the girl in the pictures," she whispered.

On second thought, she didn't believe she was the girl in the framed picture above the table either. But the unknown girl *did* look just like her. *Who is she, and why are her pictures all over the walls in this little room?*

Later, Mr. Iblis brought in more food. It was a cheeseburger, fries, and a Coke. He presented the food without comment and then left again. Hungry now, Annie began eating the cheeseburger and drinking the Coke. While she ate, he came back, and smiling, he sat down on the floor with eyes on her. She put the burger down. She couldn't eat anymore, not with him staring at her that way. "Will you talk to me now, Mr. Iblis?"

"Yes."

She gestured toward the walls. "I'm not the girl in these pictures, am I?"

He was silent.

She picked up the Coke beside her chair and took a long swallow. "Who is she? Do you know her?"

He nodded and turned as if to leave.

Her next question stopped him in his tracks. "What happened to her?"

"I'm awfully sorry, Annie, but I don't want to talk anymore right now."

She looked down at her hands. Mr. Iblis told her he wouldn't hurt her, and he hadn't. He hadn't even touched her except when he put the chain on to take her to the bathroom. She hoped he was a kind man, not one used to taking young girls. "Would you bring in the little kitten now? Please?"

He ignored her question and left the closet, carrying the unfinished food and closing the door behind him.

Chapter Ten

Tuesday, Afternoon

After his meeting with the FBI agent, Will returned to the church. At his desk, he closed his eyes, folded his arms on his desk, and put his head down. Soon, he fell into a fitful sleep, dreaming of a grave marker bearing Annie's name. He was still asleep two hours later when Callie touched his shoulder.

"Reverend Rowan? The bishop is on the phone, and I have a sandwich for you. Do you want it now?"

He looked at her with an expression that must have said, "I don't know you, and I don't know what you're talking about."

"It's me—Callie. The bishop is calling." She picked up his desk phone, punched in the correct line, and handed it to him. He took the phone and swiveled his chair around to face the built-in bookcases behind his desk. As he greeted the bishop, his eyes fell on a framed picture of Annie playing soccer. He heard the bishop talking, but he was thinking of her. "Bishop Watson, I'm afraid I missed that."

"I mentioned how sorry I was to hear about your daughter, that you've been in my thoughts and prayers."

"Thank you very much."

"I have chits I can call in from the Governor and the head of the Georgia Bureau of Investigation as well, if that would do any good. Just say the word, and I'll see what I can do."

He hesitated, studying a book on one of the shelves behind him. It was *Unbroken* by Laura Hillenbrand. Annie bought it with her own money and gave it to him for Christmas. Later on, they watched the movie made from it together. It was about the triumph of the human spirit against insurmountable odds. *But right now, my own spirit…*

"Will? Are you still there?" The bishop's voice conveyed genuine concern.

"Yes, sir. It's nice of you to offer, but I hope everything that can be done is being done."

"I take it you've had no news."

"Not so far."

"I'm sure they'll find her. You just have to keep the faith and let God take over."

He was sure the bishop's intent was to encourage him, but he fell short. Will ended the call abruptly with a promise to keep him advised of any developments.

Almost fifteen months earlier, Bishop Watson had talked him into leaving a church that he truly loved to fill the vacant pastorate in Catalpa. He convinced him that the community was growing rapidly and that the assignment would be a 'significant stepping stone in a very promising career.' According to the bishop, he needed to think of Annie, too, pointing out that the position paid twice what he was making now. *If only I'd stayed put*, he thought.

Turning back to his desk, he found a sandwich and soft drink waiting for him. He called Callie to come and get it, explaining he wasn't hungry. Then he tried to get Jack, but his call went to voicemail. Having nothing to say, he left no message, but minutes later, Jack returned his call.

"Do we need to talk, Will?"

"Have you got anything for me?"

"Nothing. You know I would've called you already if I did."

"What should I be doing?"

"Sit tight, and let us find her."

After the call ended, the word, 'nothing,' reverberated in Will's head, and he wanted to scream.

As the day wore on, he paced the halls of the church, catching glimpses of newspaper and television reporters roaming the parking lot. Callie offered them a steady diet of "No news," and "He's not available right now." Somehow, she told Will, a reporter identified the Land Rover in the lot as his, and he noticed a cadre of media types hovering around it.

He suspected she was making up excuses to come into his office, too, most likely her way of checking up on his mental state. Soon though, her faux fortitude began to drag him down, and he plotted to escape. He and Mae had talked several times during the day, and he called her again now and asked her to meet him on the courthouse square.

"Brad's gone for the day, but I'll close early and see you there in ten minutes, Will."

"I forgot that he's not there in the afternoons. Are you sure you can get away?"

"It's almost quitting time anyway, and I'd rather be with you than a stack of invoices."

He left the church using a side exit on the bottom floor and walked to the square undetected. On the way, he considered how close he and Mae had become. They'd first met at her bookstore after he'd gone there at the suggestion of a church member. She was a widow whose late husband, an Army captain, had been killed in Afghanistan several years earlier. Soon after that, he asked her out, and they'd been dating ever since. In the process, she and Annie became close, too. His memory of something she said one Saturday evening when Mae was cooking supper for them was still vivid. She whispered, "Daddy, she's the one." She'd never said anything like that about of any of the other women he'd dated over the years.

On the square, he spotted her in front of the old movie theater. She greeted him with a kiss on the cheek but refrained from asking if he had news. His demeanor must have made it plain that he did not.

"Are you ready to go home now, Will?"

"No. I want to go back to the fairgrounds."

"A customer told me that the carnival folks have already left because of what happened last night."

"I don't care. Going out there is a way of doing something. I just can't stand sitting around and doing nothing any longer."

On the way, she matched his silence. *She doesn't know what to say*, he thought.

The fairgrounds were on the outskirts of Catalpa, adjacent to a county recreation facility. Mae pulled into the parking area, and they walked through the main gate into the equivalent of a ghost town. The afternoon was hot and humid for late September, and wind from the southwest blew dust in swirls along the bleak, main thoroughfare, catching her red hair and exposing fair skin and freckles on her temples. He wasn't at all sure what he hoped to do here, and he just kept walking while she followed close behind.

To their right was a large barn, open and empty. Behind it, permanent, rickety-looking game booths extended along one side of the grounds. A few food service booths, likewise permanent, could also be seen here and there. The place was otherwise an empty shell, all in stark contrast to the bright lights and noisy rides of the night before. The carnival had indeed vacated the premises, taking its fear of litigation over Annie's disappearance with it.

"I have to ask, Will. Exactly why are we here?"

He pointed to a booth and adjacent area that was cordoned off with yellow police tape. It whipped back and forth in the brisk wind. They walked over to the dusty booth and stood there looking at it, imbued with an air of sadness.

She sighed. "What do you hope to find that the police couldn't?"

"I don't know."

He walked around behind the booth to the dirt road that ran along the edge of the fairgrounds, the same one the kidnapper must have used. Thinking of the darkness back here at night and the vehicle that took Annie away made him nauseous. He stumbled backwards and almost tripped over an old railroad tie hidden in a stand of tall, weedy grass. He looked down. When his foot struck the tie, it had moved, exposing a crumpled piece of paper. Wadded up and tossed away, it had come to rest between the tie and the grass. He picked it up and unfolded it.

Mae was at his side now, and they looked at the slip of paper together. It was a receipt for a baseball cap purchased at the Walmart store in Catalpa. Several numbers were on it, but no name.

They glanced at one another and then at the paper again. The receipt indicated that the purchase was made with a Visa card on Sunday at one o'clock in the afternoon, just two days earlier.

"Is this even important, Will?"

"Maybe not, but I guess it depends on whose name is on the Visa card."

"Then it could be…" she started, putting her right hand to her mouth.

He looked at her for several seconds, and then pulled his cell phone from his pocket, punched in a number, and put the phone to his ear. "Jack? I think we found something."

Chapter Eleven

Tuesday, Late Afternoon

After lunch on Tuesday, Mr. Iblis left Annie alone, freeing her from his creepy silence, his unending staring, his mumbled words, and his glazed-over eyes. She ached to get far away from this crazy man as soon as possible.

In some ways, he seemed harmless. Still, she obsessed over what he might do to her. She and her friends laughed about things like rape sometimes. If something that terrible ever did happen to her, she would travel far, far away to another place, a happy one, just like she did every time her daddy took her to the dentist's office. She put aside such bad thoughts for now though, because if she didn't, she was afraid she might go crazy, too.

It was so boring here with nothing to do but sleep and look at pictures on the wall. And for what seemed like the longest time, that's all she did, sleeping, looking at the walls, and wanting to go home.

The young girl in the pictures on the walls was tall, blonde, and athletic looking. She was beautiful, much more so than Annie ever imagined she might be. Her smile beckoned Annie to get to know her. She looked happy, always on the verge of laughter. Even in the pictures, her eyes sparkled with mischief. In many of them, she looked like she was just about to play a joke on somebody. Friendly, likeable, and full of fun, all showed through from the pictures on the walls.

Two boys with dark hair and dark eyes were in a few of the pictures, too. They were about the same age as the girl, but neither was quite as tall as she was or looked much like her. In some pictures, one of the boys was holding the girl's hand. He was okay in a dark sort of way and looked kind of like Mr. Iblis, but the other boy was smaller and already had pimples.

A few of the pictures showed the backyard of the house she was in now, including the old barn and the big tree. *So the girl and boys were right here at this house. Did Mr. Iblis keep the picture children in this closet, too?*

Then, almost as if on cue, he opened the door. He chained her and led her out into the large, main hall, leaving her to stand there for a moment taking it in. Straight ahead, a glass-topped door guarded one end of the hall. Surely it was the front door. To her left, stairs rose to another floor. She guessed that the stairs formed the ceiling of the closet she'd just come out of. Other doors lined the hall, all open except the one in the back of the hall opposite the front door. Where the doors led was still a mystery to her.

Reddish-black stain colored the floors, chair rails, and other woodwork. All of the walls were painted the color of cream which had gone sour after sitting out too long. Area rugs lay here and there, all rose-colored. The ceilings were much higher than those at her house.

"This is your home now, Annie."

"I have a home already. It's on Atwater Street." At the same time, she jerked away, stretching the chain tightly around her waist.

He reined her in with gentle hands and soft words. "Please don't do that."

He opened the door at the rear of the hall and ushered her onto an enclosed back porch. A washer and dryer, yellowed with age, filled the far left corner. An old refrigerator hummed in the corner to her right. Also on the right side, the back door was at the end, and a large, wooden table on rollers dominated most of the wall.

"Let's go outside," he said.

As he led her toward the back door, they passed an open door on the left. Peering inside, she saw the kitchen.

Outside, he motioned for her to sit on the concrete steps she'd seen earlier from the bathroom window and then sat beside her. Being in the wonderful outdoors again overwhelmed her, and she cried.

He patted her knee. "Don't cry, and please don't make any sounds like crying. If you do, we'll have to go back inside."

She brushed away the tears and looked around. The house loomed over her, white and made of something her father called 'clapboard.' From here, she enjoyed a better view of the backyard than through the bathroom window, but the old, white-washed barn and the tall, thick shrubbery still obscured any surrounding houses. Behind them, the sun cast long shadows on the asphalt parking area, suggesting late afternoon. *Even out here, I'm in a prison, but it's a nicer prison.*

She was homesick but determined not to cry again. She glanced his way and caught him looking up toward the sky. She considered pulling the chain out of his hand and running away with it still around her waist. As if reading her mind, he twirled his right hand, wrapping the chain more tightly around his wrist.

This seems like a neighborhood. So *other houses must be on the other side of those bushes.*

As the sun lowered, they sat in silence, listening to sounds of birds and barking dogs and a distant siren. She turned his way and caught him staring straight ahead, like he was in some sort of trance. She agonized over his condition for at least five minutes, afraid that it might be permanent, leaving her chained to him here on the steps forever. "Mr. Iblis?"

He didn't respond, so she called his name again. He turned and gazed at her.

"What is it?"

"Where is this place?" She could come up with no other question to justify disturbing him.

"It's a place far, far away from your father. He's a smart man, and at first, he may want to find you, but it won't be possible even for him."

This news troubled her a lot. She wiped another tear from her right eye and tried to think of anything she might do to help her father find her. If she kept Mr. Iblis talking, maybe he would say something that gave a clue as to where they were. "Why did you bring me out here?"

His gaze turned into a stare again, and she began to shake. After several seconds, he smiled and said, "I wanted to see how it felt to be in the backyard with you."

"How *does* it feel, Mr. Iblis?"

"Good. Very good indeed."

"I want to go home now."

"I'm sorry, but that's not possible yet."

"Okay, but could you please just tell me about the blonde girl in the pictures on the walls? Who is she?"

He developed a pout, turned away, and offered no response. Annie remembered him saying that a relative of someone named Doris had once lived in the house. "Is she named Doris by any chance?"

"No. She's not in those pictures."

"Who is Doris?"

Now he was gazing at the sky.

"This is her house."

"Did she move away?"

"No."

"Then does she still live here?"

He turned and looked at her again. His facial features joined in a weird smile with eyes wide, unblinking, and intense.

It was all too much for Annie. She screamed.

He put a soft hand over her mouth and a firm arm around her waist and got her inside the house. She squirmed and kicked, but he was much too strong. He put her over his shoulder and carried her back to the closet where he strapped her into the chair again. Then he removed the chain and stood in the doorway with his arms crossed.

"I'm disappointed in you, Annie. But if you promise not to act out, I'll bring your supper. It's a sandwich from a restaurant where you and your father go often."

She shook her head. "I don't want it."

He smiled.

"That's fine. Suit yourself. I have to go out for a little while, but I'll be back. I thought that you might have enjoyed going outside, but that didn't work out, did it?"

After he closed the door, she wished that she hadn't refused the supper.

***

Leaving Annie, Mr. Iblis walked to the back porch and stopped before the old refrigerator there, the second of two refrigerators in the house, the newer one being in the kitchen. Doris used this one to chill fresh meat and Coca Colas. He recalled her describing it as "perfectly good, much better than what they make today, even if it is as old as Methuselah." As far as he could tell, she was right.

At present, the refrigerator's temperature gauge was turned down to its coolest setting. Each time he'd opened the door and sniffed, he detected a foul odor, but none of those associated with decaying meat. The old ice box was doing a wonderful job.

Now, donning a pair of rubber gloves, he again opened the refrigerator door. A pleasing blast of very cold air hit him right away, but what he saw there made him wonder just what kind of person he had become. Inside, a human body rested, still quite flexible and life-like as confirmed by his probing, glove-covered hands.

"I am not a monster," he whispered.

Chapter Twelve

Tuesday, Late Afternoon

With the arrival of Jack at the fairgrounds, dark clouds gathered, threatening a thunder storm. He didn't bother to park beside Mae's car in the lot but drove his vehicle right through the gate and up to the booth where she and Will waited. Not only the lieutenant but also one of his deputies, Ted Bridger, got out and joined them.

"What are you doing, Will?" the lieutenant said.

"Nothing. I just wanted to see if coming out here might help me remember something else about last night."

"And has it?"

"No."

Will gave him the receipt and explained where he found it. Jack studied it for a moment and handed it to Bridger. The detective glanced at it and then put it into a plastic evidence bag. Jack frowned and folded his arms across his chest. "Ted, I thought we scoured this area last night and this morning for things like this receipt."

Ted looked distressed. "I promise you we did, Jack. I swear it wasn't out here earlier."

"Maybe somebody dropped it off the Ferris wheel, and the wind blew it over here," the lieutenant said, sounding doubtful.

Will intervened. "If it makes you both feel any better, I wouldn't have seen it if I hadn't stumbled over the railroad tie. It had slipped down between the tie and the grass."

"It doesn't make me feel a bit better. Did both of you touch it?"

Will raised his hand. "Just me. Is it important?"

"Maybe, but we'll check it out. I'm glad you found it, but you and Mae shouldn't be out here in the first place."

As Jack and Bridger roared away in a cloud of dust, the sky opened. They ran for her car, just avoiding a soaking. Behind the wheel, she reached over and squeezed his hand. "Do you want me to take you back to the church?"

He glanced at her but didn't respond. His thoughts were elsewhere.

"Home, Will?"

He nodded. Something important rolled around in the back of his mind, and all at once, it came to the surface. "The man on the beach wore a baseball cap," he mumbled.

"I didn't catch that, Will. What do you want to do about your vehicle?"

"Let's get it later. I don't want to get tied up at the church right now."

On the way to his house, he called Callie and told her that he wouldn't be back until the next day. She mentioned that most of the media had taken off when word got out that he'd left the church.

"They've probably gone to your house, Reverend Rowan."

And so they had. From more than two blocks away, they saw TV trucks and media types, some hunkered down from the rain and others oblivious to it, milling around like guests at an outdoor cocktail party. Mae suggested that they go to her place, but he declined. Not only did he have to feed Pete, but he would have to face the media sooner or later, and it might as well be now.

She snaked her car through the gathering of reporters and TV personalities and into the driveway of the small house with wood siding and stone trim. As soon as she stopped, reporters crowded around it, a few with raised umbrellas.

"I'll just keep my mouth shut, Will."

"Good idea."

They got out and headed to the front door. Along the way, questions came too fast for him to keep up with them. He fielded a few, but halfway to the house he gave up and stopped. He glanced in the direction of Pete, who was barking from behind the backyard fence, and then spoke to the crowd.

"Last night at the Tanotchee County Fair, my daughter, Annie, disappeared. The Catalpa Police are working diligently to find her. If they don't find her today, then the FBI will get involved. She's very smart and independent and knows how to take care of herself. Please pray for her and that she'll be found unharmed."

A blonde-haired woman pushed a microphone at him. "Did somebody take her, Reverend Rowan?"

His response caught in his throat. He nodded and lowered his head, hoping that the rain would hide his tears.

"Has there been a ransom demand?"

"No."

"How old is she?" This came from a black man holding a notepad and pen.

"She's ten. And I'm sorry, but we need to get inside in case there's a call. Please pray that God will bring her back to us."

He led Mae through the crowd to the front door. Once inside, wet and relieved to have made it through the media gauntlet, they embraced.

In the kitchen, she opened the back door to let Pete in. He rushed into the kitchen, his wet, wagging tail thumping on everything he got close to. She tried to dry him off with a dish towel while Will filled his bowl. Soon, the dog was wolfing down his food, spreading bits of it here and there on the kitchen floor.

She offered to get something for their supper and bring it back to the house. They discussed the menu for a minute, and then she left. From the dining room window, he watched her ward off the media with shrugs, open palms, and head shakes.

He had accumulated a considerable amount of voicemail during the day, and he played some of it back now. He listened to those left by well-wishers offering condolence but deleted those from media sources. He was tempted to give the latter treatment to three messages left by Eileen Cuttino, each more strident than the last, but he hesitated. She *was* Annie's grandmother, regardless of how he felt about her.

Eileen's last call had come in right before he got home. She and Phillip had wasted no time in opening their own investigation into Annie's disappearance, and they'd already established a beachhead at a restaurant in downtown Catalpa. According to her, the Police Department refused to tell them anything. She complained that Will wasn't forthcoming either. "Just what are you trying to hide? We've attempted to get you on the phone numerous times today, but you've not accepted even one of our calls. If you don't tell us what's really going on—and I do mean right away—unpleasant consequences will follow."

She was right. He had ignored their calls, but he had nothing to report to them.

Her threat of 'unpleasant consequences' was all too reminiscent of the awful night ten years earlier when doctors at Piedmont Hospital in Atlanta were trying to save Leah's life. Back then, he blew her comments off. But this time was different. Her hateful voicemail had opened old wounds which were never stitched up. They still festered, and she was adding salt.

He sighed and returned her call. Thankfully, he was sent to *her* voicemail. The message he left offered nothing new. He mentioned that he was very tired and would like to meet them in the morning for breakfast. He suggested a time and place, asked them to confirm, and ended his call.

Mae returned a little while later, dressed in worn jeans, tight on her long legs, and a green blouse, matching her eyes. The reporters were gone at last, so he put Pete in the backyard, and she drove him to the church to pick up his Land Rover.

Back at his house, they let Pete in and sat down at the kitchen table to a cold supper of rotisserie chicken, deli potato salad, sliced tomatoes, and iced tea. While they ate, he said little. When they finished, she looked at him and smiled, her eyes lighting up. His attempt to return her smile fell flat, and he sighed and took his plate to the sink. She followed and embraced him from behind. They stood like that for almost a minute, and then he turned and kissed her. When their eyes met again, she smiled, but he did not.

"Will, I know of absolutely nothing you could've done."

"I was talking to old Mr. Tollerson when she was taken. I wasn't watching her. I let it happen."

"You have to..." she said, but a pounding on the front door interrupted her and startled both of them.

Pete barked, and Will grabbed his collar to keep him from charging the front door. *They've found Annie*, he thought, hurrying to put Pete out back and then to answer the door. On the way, his cell phone rang. Jack Carter's name appeared on the screen. He motioned for Mae to get the door and stepped through the dining room into the kitchen, closing the swinging door separating the two rooms. "Have you found her, Jack?"

"No."

"Then you've got something on the credit card receipt from the fairgrounds. Right?"

"No. The bank is giving us the runaround. They're talking about requiring a court order before they reveal the name of the cardholder. Don't get your hopes up anyway. Hundreds of people shopped at Walmart this past weekend, and many of them went to the fair. I'm calling about your janitor, Rankin Turner. Did he ever show up for work today?"

"I don't think so, at least not while I was at the church. Why do you care anyway? Is Rankin involved in this?"

"I don't know. When we checked out your staff, we found out that he didn't come in this morning. I talked to Callie, but she doesn't even know where he lives. When your financial secretary was getting his personal information for payroll purposes, he gave her a P.O. box in Atlanta. He told her he'd rented a place down here but hadn't moved in yet and would have to get the address to her later."

"I'm sorry we don't seem to know much, but he's only been working at the church a little over a week. Tomorrow, I'll get Callie to send you a copy of his job application."

"Do you remember anything about his background?"

"I really don't. We did a criminal background check, and I'm sure he passed. When Callie brought him in, we talked for a few minutes. He seemed nice and strong enough for the job, so we hired him."

At that moment, a shrill, female voice permeated Will's house. It came from the living room, and it was all too familiar. "Jack, somebody's here, and I've gotta go."

"Wait..." he heard Jack say as he clicked off.

He steeled himself and pushed through the swinging door into the dining room. There, he stopped and eavesdropped on Eileen's grilling of Mae.

Mae's voice was calm, and her responses were direct. "You have the wrong idea about me, Mrs. Cuttino. I don't live here, but I did bring over dinner tonight. Will and I were just finishing it when you arrived."

"How long have the two of you been an item?"

"I'm not sure what you mean by an 'item.' We met shortly after he and Annie moved to Catalpa last year. She's an outstanding young lady, and I've enjoyed getting to know her. In fact, we've become quite close."

"You don't say. Of course, she has mentioned you, but she didn't seem to know all of the details. Are you divorced from Mr. Shaw?"

Will could take no more. He barged into the living room and answered her question himself. "Mae was married to Raymond Shaw. They met in Washington while she was working in Senator Neely's office, and he was an Army captain assigned to the Pentagon. After they married, he was reassigned to Afghanistan and killed in a fire fight there. He was awarded the Distinguished Service Cross posthumously."

Eileen frowned, raised her eyebrows, and looked at the silent Phillip sitting next to her. He leaned forward as if he might say something, but she shoved him back with her right arm and spoke again. This time, her tone was even more strident than before. "Well, well. I'm glad you decided to join us, Will. I must say that Phillip and I are deeply dissatisfied about your stonewalling over the true circumstances of Annie's disappearance. Be honest, if you can. What's going on? And do they really expect to find her?"

"The two of you know everything I know. The Catalpa police and the FBI are doing all they can to find her, but in the meantime, they're keeping me in the dark to a great extent."

She snorted and shook her head, looking at him and then, at Mae. "When I heard about Annie, I couldn't help but think about what happened to our poor Leah. You probably don't even know it, but one of her teachers—Henry somebody—helped us set up a perpetual scholarship in her name. When he got in touch with us about it, he was still upset, thanks to you, over all of her personal papers being lost when she was assaulted. It's like this, Will—your negligence in connection with both tragedies is palpable, and I'm afraid that you won't find us letting it go this time around. What do you have to say about that?"

He glared at her. Being civil to her had eaten all of his reserve. "I have nothing more to say, nothing at all. I think it's time for you to leave. I promise that I'll be in touch with you as soon as I know anything."

He stood and so did Mae.

"You can't just send us on our way, Will."

"Yes, I can."

"We have a right to know what's going on. If need be, we'll enforce our rights by legal means."

"Do whatever it is you feel you have to do, but right now, just please go."

After Eileen mumbled something about "our only grandchild," they left. Will and Mae returned to the kitchen to finish dealing with the supper dishes. Several minutes went by before either of them spoke. She broke the silence. "I can't believe that you've put up with them all these years."

"They're Annie's only blood connection to her mother."

"A disconnection is in order."

"Mae, I can promise you that Eileen will never talk to you again like she did today, not while I'm around."

"Well that's good news."

He put his arm around her, and they got quiet again. He was trying to remember everything that he could about Rankin Turner, his background, his hiring by the church, and his time on the job. He was still reflecting on the janitor's brief stint at the church when she spoke again.

"I've never said much about Raymond, and you haven't said much about Leah. I know that she passed away in the hospital after some kind of serious injury and that Annie was delivered on the same day. But that's really all you've ever told me. Regardless of what happened to Leah—and it truly must have been awful—I can tell that you've never put it behind you. It's obvious that Eileen still blames you for what happened. I wish you could have seen the expression on your face when she did. It wasn't good. Would it help you to talk about it?"

"No."

"I disagree. You can't blame yourself for everything that happens to the people around you. You weren't responsible for Annie's disappearance. I know that. I have to think the same applies to what happened to Leah. Let's talk about it."

He regarded her but said nothing.

"I'm waiting, Will."

He shook his head. "I can't, Mae. I just can't."

After that, they stood in silence for what to him seemed a long time. Then she left the kitchen, and seconds later, he heard her open and close the front door. She drove away without saying another word.

Chapter Thirteen

Tuesday, Night

After opening the door for Pete, Will began an aimless wandering through the house with the dog on his heels. He ended up at the door to Annie's room. After the police detectives rummaged through early that morning, her room was left in a state of mild disarray. Its condition would have upset her because she had a place for everything.

Before straightening up, he did some searching of his own. He found nothing to suggest that she might have come across someone who would kidnap her. He was not sure whether he was disappointed or relieved.

That done, he carefully returned each item in her room to the place where she would have kept it had she been looking over his shoulder. Doing so, he had a terrible thought. *What if she* is *looking over my shoulder?* He shuddered at the thought.

She used a small, antique table for a desk. He bought it for her during the summer before she entered the fifth grade. He imagined her sitting here now, engrossed in her latest writing project, her blonde hair falling across her face. She was already an excellent writer, much better than he, just like her mother.

In the middle of the table, her digital tablet sat in the sleep mode. He opened it and found an article entitled, 'Hair Braiding Made Easy' on the website of *Glamour* magazine. The police must have examined it and finding nothing, restored it to whatever she'd looked at last.

Along with several framed photographs on the left side of the desk, he noticed a paperback book entitled, *Soccer IQ: Tricks of Smart Players.* A complete set of Laura Ingalls Wilder's *Little House on the Prairie* books occupied another corner, along with an array of pens and pencils jammed into a large Atlanta Braves plastic cup. Nearby, an open spiral notebook contained a list of 'Things to Do—Tuesday.' Number three on the list reminded her to give Pete a bath.

He moved to her closet and ran his fingers over her clothes. His hand stopped on a white dress, and he took it out. His mother bought it for her to wear at her church confirmation. She and the day were beautiful. "Jesus, help me," he whispered.

On the shelf above her clothes, a stack of scrapbooks caught his eye. He returned the dress to her closet and took down one of the books. Thumbing through it, he came to a page entitled, 'Churches.' Three pictures were on the page. The first showed him holding Annie at three months old in front of his first church in Harris County, the one he hoped would help him to leave the death of Leah behind. It hadn't. The next photo, taken four years later, pictured him and Annie standing together at the altar of his second church. They loved that church, and neither of them was happy when he was reassigned to Catalpa First Methodist after its pastor retired. Friendships were close at their second church, and the goodbyes were tough, but under the Methodist system, when a minister was needed to fill a pulpit elsewhere, defying the bishop wasn't an option. The last picture was a large, color photo appearing on the front page of the *Catalpa Times*. It was taken in June of the year before, on the day they arrived in Catalpa. They were standing on the steps of the church, and by now, Annie looked like a young woman. She wasn't at all happy about being here, but she managed a beautiful smile anyway. *Our churches, our lives*, he thought, returning the scrapbook to the shelf.

At her desk again, he sat and picked up a framed, professional head shot of Leah, her wedding announcement photo, the best picture of her that he had. A photo of him and Annie sat beside it, her favorite of them together, taken two summers ago. They sat at a white, wrought iron table in the garden behind his mother's Savannah townhouse, both tanned from long mornings on the beach at Tybee Island and afternoons cycling on island roads. He couldn't believe how beautiful she was. Through the years, she asked him over and over again if she looked like her mother, and his answer was always the same—exactly. It seemed so important to her to look like Leah; it provided the only real bond with the mother she never knew.

As he was putting the picture back on Annie's desk, one of the *Little House* books fell to the floor. An envelope slid partway out of it, unnoticed before. Chiding himself for not leafing through all of her books for wayward papers, he removed it from the book.

The envelope, addressed to 'Reverend Will Rowan,' looked familiar. He opened it and found the handwritten note that came with their passes to the county fair. He thought it had been thrown away, but she must have kept it. An obsessive scrapbook maker, she always saved stuff like it, mostly memorializing things they did together. In her mind, this note would have been prime scrapbook material, a reminder of something fun she did with her dad.

He studied the note as if seeing it for the first time. Neat, block printing suggested that someone was trying to disguise his or her hand. In every respect it was typical of notes of its type.

Could they find the author's fingerprints on the note? He took out his cell phone and called Jack. His call went to voicemail, so he left a message. He put the ticket envelope and note on his dresser for safe-keeping until he could get it to Jack and then returned to Annie's room.

He thumbed through the rest of her books and found only one other thing. It was an appointment card for her upcoming annual check-up with her pediatrician, Dr. Lundie Taliaferro. They'd gotten the reminder card at the desk following a visit to his office one cold afternoon in January. When the receptionist handed the card to him, she took it out of his hand, insisting that he let *her* have it. "It's for me, not you, Daddy," she'd said at the time. Will had already put the date in his cell phone calendar anyway, so he agreed.

Why had she made such a fuss about the appointment card? He hadn't given it much thought then. But recalling the day now, he understood. It all came back in a rush.

***

That afternoon was a perfect mess. Annie was to try out for her school's cheerleading squad, something of utmost importance to her. Will arranged for the mother of a friend to take her to the try-outs, because at the same time, Bishop Watson was to arrive at his church to meet with him prior to his speech that evening at a gathering of representatives from all of the churches in the district. But right after he learned that the bishop was on his way from Atlanta, he got a call from the nurse at her school. Annie was running a high fever. It was flu season, and he needed to take her to the doctor right away. He agreed, assuming he could do that and return to the church long before the bishop arrived.

From the time he picked her up, each of them was at the other's throat, a rarity in their relationship. She blamed him for missing the cheerleading try-outs, and he reminded her of the importance of the bishop's visit to his career.

Antsy, sick, whining children packed the doctor's office. With few available seats in the waiting room, he had to stand against a wall. Their walk-in status put them behind those with appointments. After close to an hour, a nurse came out and said that Dr. Taliaferro's associate, Dr. Wycke Randolph, could see Annie so they wouldn't have to wait. Dr. Randolph wanted him to know that dealing with the flu was beyond routine and that a minister had more important things to do than spending his afternoon with mothers and coughing kids. The nurse insisted, even though they were waiting for Dr. Taliaferro. So, Will left Annie in the care of one of the mothers from his church and followed the nurse on back to Randolph's office. Although he'd never met the doctor, he was sorely tempted by his offer. But he declined because he knew how much Annie liked 'Dr. Lundie.' As it turned out, it was after five o'clock before they finally got to see Dr. Taliaferro, and Annie missed her practice.

***

He put the appointment card back where he'd found it. Annie had insisted on keeping it herself because of what he'd seen in her many times over—a need for control of her own life. It was something that cropped up fairly often, and later in life, it would likely be an issue for her, a child who couldn't control the loss of her mother. She wanted to keep the card, so she could be absolutely sure that she wouldn't have to wait like that again. She, and she alone, would make sure of that, and she trusted no one else to do it, not even him.

By this time, the searching and remembering had exhausted Will, and he sat on the edge of her bed, still thinking about her nature. She was smart, and she was savvy. She would never have followed a total stranger to a car parked behind the fairgrounds. She wouldn't have gone back there with someone she knew either, not without first telling him. *Unless.* Unless the circumstances compelled her to do it because at the time she thought it was the right thing to do.

Next to her bed, a framed poster decorated the wall. At a yard sale the previous spring, she had taken one look at it and insisted that he buy it for her, calling the words on it 'the truth.' The poster, a painting by Bob Henley, depicted a house wren perched on the worn handle of an old door. A verse from *Psalm 91* appeared in large script at the bottom.

Will read it out loud. "He will cover you with His feathers, and under His wings you will find refuge."

"She believes that," he whispered.

He took one of her stuffed animals to his chest and lay back on her bed. It was the pink rabbit that Leah's mentor, Henry Pylant, had given Annie almost ten years before. From the start, they had always called it 'Henry.' Its connection to past regrets wasn't lost on Will now. With his arms wrapped around it, he fell asleep on her bed, still in his clothes.

Chapter Fourteen

Tuesday, Night

Annie was really hungry now, and she wished she hadn't refused the sandwich Mr. Iblis offered her. Her father once told her that whenever she wanted something she should use sugar not vinegar. She guessed he was right.

Tonight, if it *was* night already, the slight vibrations in the wooden floor under her chair told her that Mr. Iblis was still in the house. She hadn't been very nice when he brought her back to the closet, but maybe if she promised to behave, he would relent and let her out of the closet again.

She looked at the girl in the pictures on the wall for probably the millionth time. The girl looked so happy and carefree, but she couldn't say the same for herself. Nothing good could ever happen in this little room.

It was unfair that she should have to spend one minute of her life locked up like this when, like the girl on the wall, her Catalpa friends were having fun with boys. She studied the pictures, trying to concentrate on going inside them to sit on the grass beside the girl and the two boys. She knew the whole idea was ultimately ridiculous, but she'd seen it done on an old episode of *The Twilight Zone. Why not give it a try?* She was still trying to get into the picture when she fell asleep, and in her dreams it *did* work. She and the girl who looked like her held hands and giggled and talked with the boys.

***

When Iblis' cell phone notified him that the time had come, he was sitting at the kitchen table reading *The Sot-Weed Factor* by John Barth. Barth was his favorite novelist, and he'd read the book several times. He found it most intriguing, but he put it aside now. Trembling with anticipation, he stepped into the dining room. At the mirrored sideboard, he removed the bottle of green one milligram tablets from the tray, opened it, and shook one tablet into the porcelain mortar. He then crushed it with the pestle into a fine powder. With that done, he took the mortar to the kitchen and placed it on the table. He took a can of cola from the refrigerator, opened it, and through a plastic funnel, added the powder from the mortar. He stirred the cola with a thin, glass rod he'd acquired just for that purpose. He then stuck a colorful straw into the can.

The green tablets were flunitrazepam. Obtaining them was relatively easy, even though the drug wasn't available legally in the United States. He'd assumed the name and license number of an internist from the State Medical Board's website, and citing a need to treat a patient who suffered from a severe case of insomnia, he purchased a small supply of the tablets from an online distributor in China. But the brochure included with his order, being in Mandarin, was useless regarding dosage.

His research indicated that reactions and other experiences related to use of the drug varied among different people and that arriving at the proper dosage was quite tricky. In addition, he found nothing satisfactory in the literature regarding dispensing it to a young girl. Although overdoses of the drug were rarely fatal, instances of surfeit dosages resulting in coma and related death were documented in the literature. He found this quite frightful. If Annie died during the process, all of his careful planning would be for naught.

In the early stages of his dealings with the drug, he pondered at length over its proper usage. In the end, he resolved it through controlled testing. Even now, one of his tests brought a pang of mild regret for what he'd done to a dog named Buddy, a calm golden retriever who lived down the street from him. He'd always liked the dog, whose weight seemed close to that of a young girl such as Annie.

As a test, he gave the compliant canine two green tablets and observed the effects. He would never forget the look in Buddy's eyes as the dog watched him pour the drugged, chicken broth into a doggie bowl. Before his untimely death, the poor animal lay in a comatose state for over thirty-six hours, hidden away in Iblis' utility room. Disposing of him was quite a challenge indeed. *Too much flunitrazepam*, he thought.

In time though, he learned enough from his experiments to satisfy himself as to the safe dosage for Annie. Keeping her alive and unconscious until the conclusion of his project was essential. Making certain that she remained so was a balancing act, the implementation of a calculated risk, something he thought doctors exposed their patients to day in and day out.

Now, with the can of cola in his left hand and the laminated scroll in his shirt pocket, he proceeded to the closet under the stairs. He tapped lightly on the door and entered.

***

Annie was asleep when she heard the tapping. She hoped Mr. Iblis had forgiven her tirade and come to let her out. She sat up and said, "Come in." He came through the door smiling, a good sign.

A can of cola with a straw was in his right hand. "Are you hungry now, Annie?"

She nodded.

"I'm glad you're hungry, but let's start with this. You must be thirsty, too." He handed her the cola can. "I've already opened it for you."

"I am so thirsty. Thank you, Mr. Iblis."

She guessed that he was waiting for her to drink the cola because he stood in the doorway, smiling and watching. When she'd finished drinking the sweet drink, she held the empty can out it to him, and he took it.

"Annie, I'm in the middle of preparing dinner for you, and I need to attend to that. In the meantime, why don't I leave the door open to let some air in here? If you need anything, just give me a holler."

He left, and she heard him doing something in another part of the house. She wished he would hurry because she was so very hungry. After several minutes though—she didn't know how long—her head felt heavy, and her eyes begged for closure. At about the same time, her whole body went limp, and she wanted to go to sleep. *What's happening to me? Why am I so tired?*

Just then, he returned and stood in the doorway, staring at her. He was waiting for something, or so it seemed.

"What have you done to me, Mr. Iblis? I don't feel right!" Her voice was shriller than she would have wanted, but she couldn't help it. She was terrified by the way she felt. All she wanted to do was go to sleep. She fought it, afraid that she was about to die or even worse, that he would do something to her after she passed out.

She was saying a prayer to Jesus when her head fell straight down onto her chest, and everything went black.

***

Before Annie's eyes closed, the way she looked at Iblis caused him to think of the dog Buddy again. This made him sad because he had no intention of hurting Annie, not in the least. He wished he could remind her of that now, but she was sound asleep.

Chapter Fifteen

Tuesday, Night

Pete's barking jerked Will awake. Groggy, feeling like he'd been asleep for hours, he rolled off Annie's bed and put his feet on the floor. As he roused, he heard another sound. Someone was tapping on his front door. He stood and headed in that direction. On the way, he looked at his cell phone. It was only eleven o'clock.

Mae was at the front door, holding an overnight bag, and smiling.

"Has something happened? Why are you here? Where's your car?"

"I know how you preachers are about propriety, not to mention that your former in-laws are probably watching your house with some kind of drone thing. So, I left my car on the other side of the block."

"I don't understand."

"It's a first, Will. I'm staying with you tonight. I thought you might need some company after all that's happened."

"You're spending the night with me?"

She nodded. "Just so I can support you; just so I can hold you close. That's all. Okay?"

He picked up her bag, and she came inside. When the front door was closed, he put his arms around her. "There's no way I can sleep, Mae."

She kissed him. "You need to, so let's give it a try."

Later, after he *had* slept for a while, he woke up and sat on the side of the bed with his head slumped over. She roused, too, and slid over beside him, pulling his head to her chest. "It's not the end, Will. I know they'll bring her home to you."

"A little bit of my soul is dying with every minute she's gone. I'm down in a pit, and I don't think even God can pull me out of it."

She gently turned his face to hers so that she could see his eyes. "You're the last man I'd ever expect to lose his faith."

He left the bed, went over to a window, opened the curtains, and looked out. He spoke again without turning around. "I have to do something. I can't just continue to sit around."

Mae got up and joined him at the window. They stood side by side, each in the arm of the other.

"What if it's already too late?" he said.

"There's no reason to think that. The police and the FBI are out there looking for her right now. You've got to trust them to find her."

They stood there for several minutes looking out at the front yard, the sidewalk, and the street beyond. Except for the dim glow of an overhead light down the street, everything was dark and empty of any sign of life.

"Come back to bed, Will. If you don't get some rest, you won't be any good to Annie or anybody else."

Will didn't move. He continued to look up and down the street, hoping to see Annie on the sidewalk, coming home. When he spoke again, his voice was so quiet that Mae told him she couldn't understand him.

"I'm beginning to feel exactly like I did after Leah died, when I couldn't shake the depression. For years, I hid it with phony smiles, and artificial optimism. It was exhausting, but effective, I guess. I was like an actor on a stage, and I was so good at it that my parishioners never knew how low I'd sunk. They loved me. They always asked the bishop to send me back for another year at their churches."

"Who could blame them? I would have wanted you back, too."

"My mother wasn't fooled, but she wasn't around me all the time either. She was five hours away in Savannah, and because of the distance, I could keep her at bay. She urged me to go to counseling, and I said I would, but I never did. She also asked me to return my father's pistol. She had given it to me right after Leah died. This was when Annie and I were still living in Atlanta, and after Leah's death, she was concerned for our safety. I never returned the pistol, and I bet she lay awake at night wondering if I would use it on myself. I was that bad off."

"So you still have it?"

He nodded.

Her expression evoked deep concern. "I wish you would just talk with me about Leah. I think it might help."

"Since I left Atlanta, I've haven't talked with anybody about what happened, not even Annie."

She put her face very close to his and whispered, "Let me be the first, the virgin listener."

After he studied her face for several seconds, his cracked with a smile, and then they both started laughing. When they settled down, he turned to the window again and nodded. "Okay, I will talk about her. Maybe you're right. Maybe sharing it would make a difference."

She kissed his cheek, and still standing there, looking out at the street, he told her about Leah.

"We met at a reception on the Emory campus—at the Carlos Museum. I don't even remember what the occasion was. We both came with someone else, but our dates had wandered off. I was looking at an ancient Egyptian artifact, a child's coffin or something like that, and Leah came up and asked me a question about it. She thought I worked there. A year and a half later, we were married."

A wave of sadness engulfed him, and he paused, lowering his head.

Mae put her arm around him. "Maybe I was wrong to ask you to do this. Let's just get back in bed."

"No, you were right. I do need to talk about it."

So he told her about the day Leah died and the days after, and when he'd finished, Mae's eyes were filled with tears. "I don't know what to say other than I'm sorry. Sorry for Leah and for you and for Annie."

"For the longest time, I was obsessed with the identity of the man who did it, and the fact that he'd never been punished. My desire for vengeance, my regret, my guilt—all of them ruled every day of my life until Annie brought me out of it. I remember the day, cold and gloomy, around the end of December. Christmas had come and gone, and Easter was months off—a period known in clerical circles as 'the inglorious in-between.' At the time, she and I were at a Walt Disney movie. The intent of the movie was humorous, but I wasn't reacting to it at all. It was like I wasn't there. After a while, I realized that she was looking at me. I thought she might want some of my popcorn, but she put her hand on my arm, leaned over, and whispered, 'Daddy, why don't you laugh at the funny parts? Everybody else does.'

"All at once I couldn't hold back the tears, and I turned away. It was as if God had taken me by the collar, jerked me up to the ceiling of the theatre, and made me look down at what I'd become. I wiped my tears, and turned to face her. I put my arm around her, leaned down close, and told her that sometimes I just forgot to laugh.

"Her question was the catalyst that got me straight. For the most part, the darkness receded, and I could see the future again, and it was good. I had lost Leah, and I would never forgive the man who murdered her. But I did have Annie, and that was more than enough."

Mae leaned on him. "You can't forgive the man, but have you forgiven yourself?"

He turned and took her into his arms. "Maybe I had...before Monday night."

"Let's get some sleep, Will. I'm looking for good news tomorrow."

In the light coming through the window from the street, he could see the doubt in her eyes. She looked away, hiding it.

"Mae, I'm sinking into the abyss again. I don't know if I can crawl out this time."

Chapter Sixteen

Wednesday, One a.m.

Everything was ready now. Annie was sedated, but stable, her breathing deep and regular. Her old clothes, neatly folded, were in a shopping bag tucked away in a corner of the dining room. Her new clothes were waiting for her in the closet under the stairs.

With great care, Iblis picked her up, placing his left arm under her back and his right arm under her legs. He was wearing a new pair of soft, white, cotton gloves because he didn't want to harm her in any way as she lay sleeping. After all, the whole idea was to save her from harm.

He took a deep breath. Leaving the closet, he carried her through the dark hall, across the back porch, and out the back door into the clear, September night. As he proceeded along the asphalt driveway beside the old house, he held her in outstretched arms, a starlit offering to the gods. She could have been a bouquet of long-stemmed flowers. She was that light, that delicate, and that beautiful. She was limp, too, but that was expected. As he walked, her hair trailed down, lightly brushing his thigh through his trousers. It was quite a pleasant sensation.

At the end of the driveway, he stepped onto the concrete sidewalk fronting Methvin Avenue. He looked both right and left, like a good little boy, he thought, and seeing no one, he began walking in the latter direction down the sidewalk, not stopping until he reached the intersection of Methvin and Oglethorpe Street. As anticipated, the entire neighborhood was down for the night.

He was shaking, a condition brought on more so by anticipation than by nerves, for he'd looked forward to this night for well over a year. Tonight, he would make things right at last, shedding the heavy guilt that had haunted him for almost forty years.

At the intersection, he hesitated for a moment, listening, but he heard no approaching vehicles. Disappointed, he went forward with his plan anyway. Oglethorpe was the main artery leading into Catalpa, and surely at least one big tractor-trailer would travel on the street over the next hour. Otherwise, all of his year-long, painstaking planning and preparation would be for naught.

Nearby, at the northwest corner of the intersection, a vacant, two story, brick house faced Oglethorpe. The boxwood shrubbery surrounding the house was tall, uncut, and unruly. To the right of the house, a big, old dogwood tree graced an unkempt lawn. It had all begun under that very tree. Iblis trembled just thinking about it, and he almost dropped Annie onto the sidewalk at his feet.

He slowly turned away from the house and looked toward Oglethorpe Street. All at once, he was overwhelmed with fear, not for himself, but for Annie. *What if...?* An instant later though, he regained his composure, refusing to let the thought of failure consume him.

From the sidewalk, he carried her down a low, grassy incline and across the curb into Oglethorpe Street. He stopped in the middle of the street and left her there on her back, just to the right of the yellow centerline. Then he walked away.

Chapter Seventeen

Wednesday, Early Morning

At five o'clock on Wednesday morning, Will was wide awake, still engaging in virtual self-flagellation. His inattentiveness had laid the foundation for the taking of his only child, and he saw no way forward, no way to cope with that. In his own mind, he was a flawed loser of a parent and a faithless pastor.

Next to him, Mae stirred, moving closer to him. He couldn't understand why she failed to see his fault in Annie's disappearance and why she continued to think of him as a fit parent and a potential spouse. *How could she love* me*? What makes me think that I deserve* her*?*

In the darkness of his bedroom, painful images of Annie filled his head. In all of them, she was either lying dead in a shallow grave, pale and dirty, soon on the menu of maggots, or if not dead already, then cowering alone in some miserable hovel, hungry, thirsty, and cold, dying a slow death and waiting for help that would never come. He even found himself wishing that she *was* dead. At least that way, if she was suffering, it would be over.

In this hopeless mode, he deemed himself unfit to serve as a minister any longer. He was on the verge of cursing God for what had happened to Leah and now Annie, uncaring of whatever wrath the Almighty might bring down on him.

He slid out of bed, careful not to wake up Mae, and headed for the kitchen. There, Pete met him with a wagging tail. After he let the dog out, he pulled a legal pad and pen from a drawer, sat at the table, and began drafting a letter to Bishop Watson.

He'd made up his mind. This would not be a request for a temporary leave of absence or a sabbatical. Instead, he intended to notify the bishop that he was quitting his pastorate at Catalpa First Methodist and tendering an outright letter of resignation of his ministerial position in the North Georgia Conference. The bishop had no choice but to accept it. It was odd, but the idea of drafting the letter was the only positive thought he'd had in the last twenty-four hours. At least, he was doing something.

He was staring at the legal pad, having written nothing more than a salutation, when he heard a car door slam out front and Pete barking in the back. He went to the living room, looked out, and saw Jack heading for the front door. He cringed and then opened the door, unable to imagine any news but the worst.

Somewhere behind him, Mae said, "Who is it?"

He ignored her question and held the door open.

"Jack, what's happened?"

He didn't respond at first, stepping inside and looking over Will's shoulder. Mae was standing in the hall doorway, wearing nothing more than the dress shirt Will had worn the day before. She gave Jack a little, smiling, embarrassed wave. He nodded in return, and then his eyes returned to Will.

"Let's get you some coffee. Then I have news. Okay?"

He nodded, and Jack followed him to the kitchen. While Jack made the coffee, he retrieved the note about the fair tickets and envelope they came in and gave them to him. The lieutenant studied them, touching only the edges. Then he asked for a zip-lock bag. Will found one, and he dropped the envelope and note inside and sealed it. He was upset that his people had neglected to find the letter when they'd scoured Annie's room. "Some of our guys couldn't find a clown in a three-ring circus. I'll make sure Todd Baxter gets these."

By the time the coffee was ready, Mae was dressed and joined them in the kitchen. Jack poured the coffee, and they sat around the table drinking it. "Did you get any sleep, Will?"

"I have a bad feeling about why you've come this early in the morning."

He clasped his hands together and spoke quietly. "Annie is still alive."

Will and Mae were both speechless.

"Around one o'clock this morning, Annie and the man who took her were over on Oglethorpe Street, a few blocks away from this house."

Will couldn't stop the tears. Overcome, he left the room, mumbling something about washing his face. When he returned, the others were talking in quiet tones, and neither gave him eye contact. "I'm sorry about that. I promise I'm okay."

Jack nodded. "I would have cried, too."

"Where is she now? Is she all right?"

"She was alive at one o'clock this morning, and she was here in Catalpa. That's all we know so far."

Mae poured more coffee for Will, but he let it sit. He was so shaky that he was afraid he would spill it if he picked it up. For the first time, he noticed that Jack had brought a large, brown envelope with him. He opened the envelope and took out several sheets of paper and two compact discs. He placed them on the table.

"I'm getting ready to share some things with you that I shouldn't. If the chief finds out, he may fire me. If anything comes up about it, I'll say I was doing it because I thought you might recognize someone or something in what I'm about to show you. I'm only letting you in on it because you're my friend, and you deserve to know what's going on. Do you have a computer here at home?"

"I've got a laptop. It's in the den."

Mae volunteered to go get it. When she came back, Jack asked her to put it on the table in front of Will.

"About four hours ago, I interviewed a man named Lester Pitbone. In a moment, I'll let you read a copy of the transcript of the interview. Although it was videotaped, the chief has the only copy of that disc right now, so the disc wasn't available to me.

"I did obtain a copy of a security video which shows Pitbone before his interview, and I'll play that disc for you just to see if you recognize him. I also brought a copy of another disc for you to look at. It was made from a video which Pitbone took with his cell phone. I don't have permission to show that to you, but I'm doing it anyway.

"Pitbone has a history with our department. It includes driving under the influence and a few other misdemeanors. When we questioned him, his blood-alcohol level was zero point eight. In other words, he was intoxicated. When he witnessed what he described to us, his BAL was probably much higher. I'll talk with him again when he sobers up, but I don't think his statement will change much if at all."

Under the table, Will's legs were shaking.

"First, I want to show you what Pitbone looks like." He inserted one of the discs into the laptop's slide-out tray. After the disc was downloaded, he played it back. Will leaned forward to watch it, and Mae took up a position behind him so she could see it, too.

The camera was focused on a skinny, scruffy-looking man with greasy, long, blonde hair. He was sitting alone at a conference table, slumped over and seemingly asleep. Jack came in and sat across from him. He reached over and gave the man's shoulder a push. The man jerked his head up and looked around as if he didn't know where he was. Then he looked at Jack, and the camera caught his face in full. "Oh, yeah, you wanted to talk to me, lieutenant."

The playback stopped. "Do you know him, Will?"

"No. Is he the man who took Annie?"

"He's not the man. Have you ever seen him before?"

"No."

"I've never seen him before either," Mae said.

Will was getting impatient. "Why don't you just go on and tell us what the man said?"

"I want to give it to you in sequence in case something *does* tweak your memory."

"Let's get on with it then."

He picked up the sheets of paper he'd placed on the table and slid them over to Will. He took them and began reading. As he finished a page, he passed it to Mae.

Interview

This is an interview of Lester Abercrombie Pitbone, Jr. a.k.a. Skanky Pitbone, conducted by Lieutenant Jack Carter at the Catalpa Police Department, Catalpa, Georgia, on the date and at the time set forth in the transcriber's certification following this transcript.

Carter: My name is Jack Carter, and I'm a lieutenant with the Catalpa Police Department. I am interviewing Mr. Lester 'Skanky' Pitbone in the Department's conference room. Present are Mr. Pitbone and Officer Jane Melson, who is transcribing this interview. I am now showing Mr. Pitbone a copy of the Waiver of Rights he signed prior to this interview relating to his right to counsel, his right to remain silent, and his other related rights. Is that your signature on the Waiver, Mr. Pitbone?

Pitbone: Yes, sir.

Carter: State your name please.

Pitbone: Lester Abercrombie Pitbone, Junior. Some people like to call me, 'Skanky.'

Carter: What's your date of birth, your address, and your place of employment?

Pitbone: I was born on February 18, 1979. I live at 86 Salbado Avenue, Catalpa. I work at TowelCraft, Old Peach Orchard Road, Catalpa.

Carter: Before you arrived at the station tonight, had you been drinking alcohol?

Pitbone: I had a couple of beers at home after I got off work on Tuesday afternoon. I think yesterday was Tuesday. Wasn't it? Then, I went out to the Tip Top Bar and Grille up on the Old Atlanta Highway to get me some supper. I guess I drank quite a few beers out there.

Carter: Are you intoxicated right now?

Pitbone: No sir, I ain't drunk, not now, just tired.

Carter: What time did you leave the Tip Top?

Pitbone: Well, let me think. I was still there after midnight but not up to one o'clock yet when I seen Frank starting to run his long tape. When he does that, I know he's getting ready to close it down. So, I slipped out the back door. If I hadn't, Frank would've thrown me up against a wall, took my keys, and made me ride with Uber. He's done that before, and it's really a pain in the ass to get somebody to take me back out there the next day for my truck.

Carter: Tell me about your truck.

Pitbone: I drive a 2010 Chevy Silverado that I bought from my ex-wife's brother last year. He's letting me make payments on it.

Carter: When you left the Tip Top were you in your truck?

Pitbone: Yeah, I was driving it. You already know what kind of fix I was in, drinking and all. I didn't want to get myself pulled over, so I headed onto Oglethorpe right through the middle of town. Y'all don't always hang out down there late at night, do you? I remember what was on my radio—'Way Down Yonder on the Ole Tanotchee.' I think I was singing along with it, too.

Carter: I don't care about your music, Lester. Did something happen on Oglethorpe Avenue that you want to tell me about?

Pitbone: I got to about where the top of the courthouse comes into view on Oglethorpe, and I seen something down there in the middle of the street. Even with tree tops and all, the street lights are pretty bright, so I could see something sort of white and shiny-looking in the street up ahead. When I first saw it, I was about half of a football field or maybe a little better away. Honestly though, my vision was sort of blurry about then.

Carter: How fast were you going?

Pitbone: You got me there, but when I got closer to that thing in the street, I decided I'd better put on the brakes. A second later, I could see what it was. Right then, I slammed on the brakes and said something like, "Holy shit!"

Carter: What made you start cussing like that, Lester?

Pitbone: Because by then I could see it was a little girl lying there in the middle of the street. She was flat on her back. She had blonde hair sort of all spread out, and she was naked. All at once, a man came running into the street. I think he came out from behind the bushes over to the right next to that old brick house. He was hauling ass. He picked up the girl and moved her. My brakes locked, and my truck went into a skid, and it kept on skidding right down the middle of the street. It was smoking, and the burning rubber was stinking to high heaven. I stopped right about where that girl would've been if he'd left her there. I would've run right over her.

Carter: How long was it from the time you first put on the brakes until you stopped?

Pitbone: Hell if I know, lieutenant. I was just thinking about that little girl, and to be honest, I was scared shitless. My cell phone was there on the floor. It'd flown off the seat. I picked it up and looked at the man. He was just a few yards over to the right, still in the street, just standing there with his back to me. All of a sudden, he did something crazy. He held up that little girl high over his head like he was showing off a trophy or something. Can you believe it? After I seen that, I had to do something, so I hit the video button on my phone.

Carter: What did the man do with the girl then?

Pitbone: He carried her off into the dark, right up the sidewalk on Methvin where it runs off Oglethorpe. I thought of following him, but my truck wouldn't start. I'm not sure I'd gone after him anyway. The whole thing was too weird. If they got in a car up there on Methvin, I don't think I heard it, but I might have.

Carter (holds up cell phone): Let me show you this phone. Take a look at it. Is it the same phone you just described—the one you hit the video button on?

Pitbone: Yes. It's a new phone. It's costing me a lot, but everybody's got to have one, don't they? I gave it to you, and you marked it with those white letters, 'JC.' Those letters are still on it, and it's my phone.

Carter: What did the man look like? What was he wearing?

Pitbone: He was wearing a baseball cap, but I couldn't tell you a thing about his face. The cap hid it, and then he turned his back to me. His hair looked kind of dark, and he had on dark—maybe black—clothes. A sweater? I don't know. It seems like I remember running shoes or basketball shoes. I maybe could of whipped him, but he looked pretty strong. I was afraid of what would happen to that girl, too.

Carter: Lester, I want to show you a picture of a girl. It has my initials on it, too, 'JC.' Is that the girl you saw in the street tonight?

Pitbone: The girl in the picture looks a lot like the girl I saw, but I can't be sure. It was all so fast. Lieutenant, I wasn't scared for me. I just didn't want to see that girl hurt. When I couldn't see the man and the girl anymore, I called y'all. I was tanked, but I thought, what the hell? Whatever that man was doing with that little, naked girl, I can tell you this—it just wasn't right.

Carter: Thank you, Lester.

End of Interview

Will was dumbstruck. He made a sound, but it wasn't a word. He stood up and moved toward the kitchen door as if he was about to bolt from the room.

"Hold it, Will. There's more. Please just sit down."

He collapsed back into his chair at the table, still mute.

"Jack, how can you be sure she was alive?" Mae asked.

Without responding, he removed the first disc from the laptop and inserted the second.

"This is a copy of the video Pitbone shot with his cell phone. It's not the best quality, but it'll show you why we think that Annie is still alive."

Something else was on Will's mind. "Why was she naked, Jack?"

Jack shook his head. "I don't know."

He played Pitbone's video. It had been shot through the windshield of his truck. It showed a dark-haired man wearing a baseball cap and dressed in dark clothes walking away with a girl in his arms. The girl was Annie, and she was naked. Her head and hair, her shoulders and drooping arms, and her legs and feet were all visible.

Will's heart was pounding, his blood pressure soaring. *She's either unconscious or dead.*

Jack froze the video and said, "Look at her mouth. It's closed all the way." He started the video again and said, "Now watch this."

As they watched, Annie's mouth opened and she was moving it. Then it closed again.

"Did you see her mouth, Mae?" Will said.

"Yes!"

But that wasn't all. They watched her clinch her right hand into a tight fist and then let it go.

"She's still alive!" Will whispered.

Chapter Eighteen

Wednesday, Early Morning

As Iblis thrust Annie to the sky in triumph, he noticed for the first time that the little scroll was gone. It no longer dangled from her neck on the pink ribbon. The ribbon was gone, too. He'd tied it around her neck with a bow knot before they left the house, but somehow, it came loose and slipped off.

He mourned the loss of the scroll which he'd kept for all of these years. It was an important part of the staging, too, making it seem almost real. Of course, nothing would ever be exactly the same, but still, in its own small way, the scroll had helped.

Regardless of its loss though, the guilt that had dogged him for almost forty years was fading from his troubled psyche. After he brought Annie back to the old house, he was euphoric. Along the way, he checked again and again, but neither the truck driver nor anyone else followed them. Furthermore, the dark and chaotic scene made it impossible for the driver to identify him. *Was it too early to call the reenactment a smashing success?*

In the closet, he dressed her with care, helped her to the bathroom, and then strapped her into the chair again. After that, he watched her sleep for a few minutes before changing into pajamas to wait for the police to come. When they pounded on the front door an hour later, he hesitated and let them knock two more times before he responded, feigning surprise at their visit. His wrinkled pajamas and his sleepy performance fooled them, as did his promise to let them know right away should he see or hear anything strange in the neighborhood. When they asked for his name, he simply said, "Iblis." They took it as his last name, calling him "Mr. Iblis" for the rest of their visit and thinking no more of it. If anything came up about it later, he would claim that it was a nickname.

After the police left, he returned to the kitchen. The lights were still off, but enough moonlight streamed through the windows to heat some milk on the old gas stove. He sat at the kitchen table drinking it slowly. Soon he dozed off into a light, troubled sleep, but an odd sound woke him up. *Did it come from the direction of the closet?* He went to investigate.

***

Annie stirred and lifted her head. She slowly opened her eyes and said, "Daddy?" Confused, she looked around, unsure of where she was. She had a headache, too, and moving her head and eyes made her disorientation even worse. As her eyes adjusted, she realized she was in a little room.

She tried to say, "Where am I?" but it came out as, "What...I...am?"

She wasn't sure why, but she needed to get out of here as soon as possible. Her legs and arms felt odd and weak. She tried to stand up but couldn't. It wasn't just that her arms and legs wouldn't move like they were supposed to. Something was holding her back. A leather strap confined her to the chair where she sat.

The light in the ceiling hurt her eyes, so she lowered her head to her chest. Then she noticed her clothes. They didn't feel or look right. She had on funny-looking sneakers with glitter on them and jeans that were too big in the legs. The T-shirt she was wearing depicted a teenage boy with long hair, holding a microphone, surrounded by a starry sky. The writing on the T-shirt looked cursive like a signature, but from her position, the lettering was upside down, so she couldn't read what it said. She tried to pull the

T-shirt off, but it was held fast under the strap around her waist. She jerked and pulled the shirt to the side until she could just make out the writing. "Shaun Cassidy?" she asked out loud. At the same time, she reached for her locket, but it was gone! So was the gold chain!

When she raised the T-shirt, something came into view, too. Under the waistband of the big jeans, something pink peeked out. She pulled on the lacy fabric, and then to her dismay she realized what was under there. She was wearing some other girl's panties.

By now, she was overwhelmed with dread and a real, black, physical fear. She pulled at the strap around her torso again and again, straining against it, but it wouldn't give way. The strap held her fast to the chair, and the chair was stuck to the floor.

She panicked, stamping her feet and yelling as loudly as she could, "Help! Help! Somebody help me!"

Seconds later, the door to the little room flew open, and a man hurried in, closing the door behind him. She tried to see his face, but her eyes wouldn't work right.

"Are you all right, Annie?"

Her vision slowly cleared, but her mind went blank. She studied the man for almost half a minute, as he stood staring at her, not moving. He had dark hair and wore light blue, long-sleeved pajamas and bedroom slippers. At last she remembered where she was and who he was. Then she wanted to scream again, but she didn't. Instead she asked a question which came out sounding like an accusation. "What have you done to me, Mr. Iblis?"

He placed his hands behind his back and leaned forward as he spoke. "Nothing. I've done nothing to you. I swear I haven't touched you in a bad way."

"I don't believe you. Where is my locket?"

"I'm so sorry, but I don't know anything about your locket. Have you lost it? All I've done is to give you a mild sedative. Nothing more."

All at once, she was overtaken with dizziness, on the verge of throwing up. She put her head down toward her knees in an effort to quell the nausea. It didn't work.

She raised her head.

"Do you remember anything at all about tonight, Annie?"

"What do you mean? What are you talking about?" she whispered, and then she left that terrible place and slumped over into a blissful state of unconsciousness again.

***

In the kitchen of the old house, Iblis was too wired to fall asleep again. The night's events had been exciting, and the warm milk hadn't helped much. He was a little worried, too. As the euphoria wore off, concerns crept in. Two things were troubling him.

His face was obscured from the truck driver by the hat and the way he kept his back toward the man most of the time. Still, determining just what the driver did see was essential. He may have noticed something even if it was less damning than his face. Regarding his identification of Annie, that was likely a given. The police would already have photos of her to show him.

The other concern was the unexpected loss of the laminated scroll. He supposed it would be found, and he wasn't certain that he'd wiped both sides of its surface clean. Vexing him more than that though was just the prospect of being without it. The little scroll had been with him for forty years, and he wanted it back.

Sitting there in the moonlit kitchen, his paranoia gave way to a vivid memory of the night he first laid eyes on the scroll. It played out now on the yellow, kitchen wall like an old movie. The stars were Doris Paine, her daughter, Desdemona, and her daughter's friend, Ravenel Monroe. The two boys, Doris' son and his friend, were no more than bit players.

***

Before that night, Doris had never let either of her children have a friend sleep over at her house on Methvin Avenue—this house—but on that occasion, she relented.

Desdemona's guest, her classmate, Ravenel, was a dark-haired beauty admired by all of the boys at school. Her father was a surgeon, and they lived in a large house on Honeysuckle Circle, Catalpa's most exclusive neighborhood. Her son's invitee was an older, neighborhood friend, who spent most of his waking hours at Doris' house and knew her very well indeed, especially how and when to avoid her ire.

After supper, the boys and girls gathered in Desdemona's bedroom. They were gossiping about classmates when Doris announced that it was time for everyone to go to bed.

In the son's bedroom, the boys lay awake, straining to hear the girls talking across the hall. Soon the enticing sounds of scampering feet and unrestrained giggling became too much for them to bear. They got out of bed, tiptoed into the hall, and headed for the other bedroom. Along the way, soft snoring sounds coming from Doris' bedroom at the other end of the hall emboldened them.

At Desdemona's door, the boys got down on all fours and peered inside. The girls were kneeling on the bed facing one another. The sheet covered them, but the light from a small flashlight moved up and down their bodies from one girl to the other, revealing their shadows. Crawling on their stomachs, the boys moved closer.

"Yours are so much bigger than mine," Desdemona whispered.

"Don't worry, in time they'll grow," Ravenel advised. "Gosh! Just look at your mother's boobs. They're gigantic."

Moving downward, the light stopped on Ravenel. "I want a black one like yours, Ravie. Mine's not dark enough," Dessie whined.

"Then dye it!"

An immediate burst of giggling ensued. Hearing this, the boys moved even closer, by now almost touching the bed.

"I promise I'll always be your friend, Ravenel, just like you said in your note." Under the sheet, she was holding something up. "I've still got it. See?"

"Oh, that. You mean the stupid note I gave you at school last week?"

Suddenly, Doris' booming voice filled the room. "That's it! That's enough, you little, Sapphic sluts! I heard all your nasty talk of female breasts and pubic hair. You should be ashamed of yourselves!"

It seemed she'd slipped into the room behind the boys, seeing and hearing everything. She was a fearsome sight, standing with her feet spread wide apart, her arms crossed on her chest, and her big, auburn hair all aglow in the soft light from the hall.

The boys cringed and sought refuge in a far corner of the room with their hands over their heads as protection from the coming barrage. On the bed, the flashlight went out, and the girls were motionless and quiet.

Doris marched forward and ripped the sheet off them. They both assumed fetal positions, attempting to cover and protect their exposed bodies. Desdemona was quick to pull her gown over her head, but Ravenel was transfixed. From the boys' secure corner, it was an unforgettable sight.

"Put on your gown, young lady," Doris ordered.

Trying to cover her nakedness with one hand, she fumbled for her gown with the other, but she couldn't find it. She fell off the bed trying to locate it. Doris walked around the bed and looked down at her with disgust. "What kind of girl are you anyway?"

Ravenel didn't answer. She was a pitiful lump on the floor.

"Here's your gown," Desdemona whispered.

She reached up for it and put it on, but she didn't stand up.

Doris grabbed her elbow, jerked her to her feet, and pushed her toward the door. "Miss Monroe, you'll be sleeping elsewhere for the rest of the night. I don't want your sort in the same bed with my little girl."

As Doris pulled her through the door, Ravenel turned and looked back at Dessie and the boys. Her eyes were filled with fear and panic. She mouthed the words, "Help me." Of course, they couldn't.

The other children got quiet. They could hear Doris struggling to get Ravenel down the stairs, then dragging their friend across the hall on the first floor, and then opening a door and slamming it closed.

Dessie moaned. "Poor, poor Ravie. Mother put her in the closet."

It was so sad that they didn't sleep after that. Doris had locked Dessie and each of the two boys in the closet at one time or another. It was her ultimate, most dreaded form of punishment.

Much later, they sat next to one another on the floor in Dessie's dark bedroom. As tears came for the plight of her friend, Desdemona reached down inside her gown and pulled out a small roll of white paper. It dangled from her neck on a pink ribbon.

"I keep it here, under my clothes, so mother can't ever see it."

"Why don't you want her to see it?" her brother asked.

"I'm afraid she'll take it away. She's an evil bitch and a witch. She hates me because I'm pretty."

She turned away from the boys and unrolled the paper, but they both looked over her shoulder. In the low light coming through one of the bedroom windows, the words on the little paper, written in neat, cursive script, were clearly visible.

***

Now the words on the scroll disappeared from Iblis' mind, and the kitchen wall turned blank again, like a movie screen when the film suddenly breaks and the reel starts clicking as it goes round and round. In this instance though, the clicking sound came from his troubled tapping of a teaspoon on the old kitchen table.

That night, he'd wanted to leave the boys' bedroom and go to Dessie's. There, he hoped to hold her and comfort her and tell her how sorry he was about Ravenel, but he was afraid of what terrible things Doris might do if she walked in on them.

He put his head down on the table. As he drifted into sleep, he thought of Dessie and even now just how much he missed her.

Chapter Nineteen

Wednesday, Early Morning

At Will's house, he and Mae watched Pitbone's short video for the third time, studying the man in the ball cap as he disappeared into the darkness on Methvin Avenue.

"You can't tell much from the video, but do you recognize him?" Jack asked.

"I just don't know…" Will's voice trailed off.

Jack leaned over his shoulder to look at the video. "We still can't locate your janitor, Rankin Turner. Could it be him?"

Will gave him a blank look and turned back to the video. "I guess it could be, but how can I be sure? I can't see his face."

"I agree," Mae said. "It's so dark. We're seeing his back, and he has that cap on. I couldn't even tell you the color of his hair."

Will restarted the video for the fourth time. "She looks like she's been drugged."

"With nothing to go on but the video, we couldn't tell. And by the way, I forgot to mention something else. One of our people is adept at reading lips. He thought Annie said the word, 'Daddy,' twice."

Will put his hands on the table and looked down at them. He tried not to cry again, but his effort failed. A tear rolled down his right cheek and fell onto his lap.

Jack removed a piece of paper from his pocket and placed it face down on the table. He started to say something, but Will interrupted him. "What did he have in mind when he put Annie in the street? If he wanted her run over, why did he put her there and then rescue her?"

"Of course, we didn't see him put her in the street, but we assume he did. Even so, there's no logical explanation for what's going on. We're dealing with a man who's very disturbed, a man with an agenda only he understands."

He turned over the sheet of paper he'd placed on the table and pushed it toward Will. "Does this mean anything to you?"

He looked down at the sheet without picking it up. It was blank except for a copy of a much smaller document in the middle of it. The smaller portion was about the size of a sticky note. Writing appeared on it in a neat, cursive hand. As he read the words, his lips moved:

Dear Desdemona,
Please be my best friend forever.
Love, Ravie.

"Will, do you know anybody named 'Desdemona' or 'Ravie?'"

Puzzled, he studied the sheet again. "No."

Jack sighed. "You're looking at a copy of something we found at the scene, right near the spot where Annie was lying. We don't know how long it'd been there or if it has anything to do with this. It was a little piece of paper, maybe pretty old, but hard to tell because it's laminated. It was rolled up like a tiny scroll and tied with a pink ribbon. We opened it and copied the note, and then we sent it up to Atlanta to the crime lab."

Will looked at the note again but said nothing.

"We couldn't find any prints on the ribbon or the scroll, but the crime lab will check them again. We don't know yet if they are even connected to Annie's disappearance."

Will got up and emptied his coffee cup in the sink. He spoke without turning around, his voice halting.

"He took…her clothes off. What else do you think he's…done to her, Jack?"

"Our main concern is getting her back alive. After that, we'll deal with everything else."

He sat at the table again. "Annie could be anywhere. The man could have taken her to Florida by now."

"That's right," Jack said.

Mae put a hand on Will's shoulder and said, "Jack, I was wondering whether anybody in the neighborhood saw anything."

"Right after Pitbone told his story, our folks knocked on a lot of doors. I'm not aware of any instance in which someone didn't respond. Almost one hundred percent of the occupants looked like they'd just gotten out of bed. No one saw or heard anything."

Jack looked at his watch. "Turner remains a mystery, but everybody else is checking out. In Catalpa, all employees of transient, entertainment enterprises like carnivals are required to have background checks. They might've looked as sleazy as could be, but they were all clean. Your church employees were clean, too. We've interviewed all of them except Turner. Without exception, they painted Annie as being a sweet, smart, young girl and you, as a fine man. They couldn't recall anyone associated with the church ever acting in a suspicious manner, including Turner.

"We also checked the names you gave us of everybody who's worked at your house since you came to town. All clean. At her school, background checks are routine, and no suspicious persons turned up there, either. Her regular pediatrician, Dr. Taliaferro, has been out of the country for the last ten days. That rules him out, and Annie never saw any other doctor at his office.

"Meanwhile, where is Rankin Turner? The timing of his disappearance bugs the you-know-what out of me,

Will. The DMV sent me a copy of his driver's license. He's not a big man, five-eight and a hundred and forty pounds. He has dark hair and brown eyes. Does that sound about right?"

Will was lost in thought when Mae said, "Is that a good description?"

His expression was blank. He looked at her and then nodded, saying, "It could be him. He could be the man in the video."

Jack stood to leave, but hesitated. "There's one other thing I guess I need to mention. It's about the Wal-Mart receipt you found at the fairgrounds. I got a fax from the bank early this morning. Rankin's credit card was used to purchase the ball cap."

Will stood, too. "Then it *was* Rankin, wasn't it, Jack?"

"I've got to run now. We'll talk soon."

Before he reached the front door, Will called him back. "Can you arrange for me to talk with that FBI agent again?"

"I've already gotten in touch with him. He'll be here in an hour or so. What do you want to talk with him about?"

"A day has gone by. I want him to tell me what Annie's chances are now."

Chapter Twenty

Wednesday, Early Morning

Annie woke up in total darkness. At first, she thought she might be dead, but then she realized she wasn't floating like an angel. She still had her regular body, and she was still strapped in the chair like a baby in a car seat, weak and helpless. She was hungry and thirsty, too, and she needed to go to the bathroom.

She yelled, "Help!" Then she stomped her feet on the wooden floor until they were numb. At last, light poured in, revealing her little prison. She squinted into the light and saw Mr. Iblis in the doorway. The chain was in his left hand.

After helping her to the bathroom, he sat her at the kitchen table and locked the chain around a table leg. It was a useless gesture on his part because she felt so weak she had little hope of getting away from him. She lowered her head.

"Won't you let me go home, Mr. Iblis? My daddy needs me." Her voice was so soft she couldn't be sure he heard. When he didn't reply, she raised her head. He was taking a baking sheet out of the oven. Whatever was on the sheet smelled good, and she was so hungry.

"They call these things 'breakfast burritos.' I got them at the grocery store on Sunday. They'll have to cool before I can give them to you."

He sat across the table from her. She moped again, her head on her chest, thinking he might feel sorry for her. She knew all about breakfast burritos and didn't like them, but she was so hungry she could have eaten a roach burrito. She wondered if she would ever leave this place, if he would keep her here for the rest of her life.

She closed her eyes and tried to conjure up a mental video of her father throwing a ball to Pete, happy and laughing in the backyard of their house on Atwater Street. She missed her dog almost as much as she did her father. But instead of that joyous scene, another image came to mind and then faded. It was her father, sad and crying, tears of blood streaming down his face and splashing onto the long, white robe he sometimes wore on Sundays. Once, she saw a similar scene in a horror movie at the house of friend, a movie her father would never have allowed her to watch. It was gross.

"I have something new to ask you, Annie."

She looked at him. "What?"

"There's a word I want to ask you about. The word is 'reincarnation.' Do you know it?"

Her mind was on the breakfast burritos which were cooling on the other end of the kitchen table. Their odor was driving her crazy. She thought she might have to answer his question to get the burritos, so she responded as best she could. "I think I do. It's when somebody dies and comes back to life as a bird or a dog."

He nodded and smiled. He seemed pleased with her answer. "You're on the right track. You and I have known each other for a long, long time. We knew each other before you were born, and we will know each other again even after we die. We will always be together."

He paused. She thought he was trying to give her time to take this in and agree with him. But she sat mute, watching him, waiting for what came next. Before continuing, he leaned across the table toward her and placed his right, open palm to the side of his mouth, as if he had a secret to tell. Then he whispered in a conspiratorial tone. "Last night, while you slept, I laid down my life for you. I took a great risk to save you. I am your hero, your savior."

Her eyes met his. "My savior? Like Jesus?"

"Yes, just like Jesus the Christ."

"My daddy taught me not to say things like that, Mr. Iblis."

"As long as we're together in this house, it's okay. That's because it's the truth."

This last remark troubled Annie a great deal, even more so than the sacrilegious implications of what he said. "Where else would we be together besides here in this house?"

He ignored her question and placed the burritos on a plate in front of her, along with a large glass filled with orange juice. She wolfed down the burritos and drank all of the juice. He watched her from across the table until she finished.

"Please don't put me back."

"I have some things to do this morning."

"I may die if you put me back."

He smiled, unhooked the chain from the table, and took her back to the closet. After he removed the chain and strapped her into the chair, he stood in the doorway looking at her.

"What are you looking at, Mr. Iblis?" She looked down. "Is it the clothes you put on me? What are they for? Where did they come from?"

"It's a matter of hygiene, Annie. You can't wear the same clothes every day. You never did that at home, did you? You seem unduly agitated this morning. Are you feeling all right?"

"Yes…no…I don't know. Why? Have you done something to me?"

"Of course not, Annie. I would never do anything to you. I've told you that already."

He moved very close to her, leaned down, and spoke, his words soft and measured. "I have lost something very dear to me. Last night, I put a pink ribbon around your neck. A little scroll was attached to it. Do you know what happened to it? Did you pull the ribbon off and throw it down at some point?"

She shook her head, wondering why he didn't ask about the locket, too. His question alarmed her. The pink ribbon and the clothes were proof that he *had* done things to her the night before, things that she knew nothing about. She began to cry.

***

Ignoring Annie's tears, he used the flashlight on his cell phone to check every nook and cranny of the closet, the hallway, and the back porch, but he didn't find the scroll. He sighed and gazed through a window on the back porch. It was still rather early. He considered whether it would be safe to check the driveway, the sidewalk, and the street this soon after the incident with the truck driver. He doubted that the police would still be out and about investigating the area, but one never knew.

He went out and examined the back steps for the scroll, finding nothing but a big, black, lubber grasshopper. He stomped it and kicked its carcass into the bed beside the steps. Then he headed along the driveway with his eyes on the ground, but it wasn't there. When he reached the sidewalk on Methvin Avenue, he glanced up and down the street, checking for police activity. Seeing none, he strolled down the sidewalk toward Oglethorpe Street with his hands in his pockets, glancing here and there along the way. The scroll wasn't there.

As he reached the corner of Methvin and Oglethorpe, still looking, he noticed a sedan parked in front of the vacant brick house on his left. He heard voices of two men before he saw them. They were thrashing about in the foundation shrubbery surrounding the house. One of them, a black man, wore a navy blazer and a red tie, and the other, a white man, looked scruffy in a T-shirt, coat, and jeans. Both were bent over, pushing the bushes back, looking in them and under them, right near the exact location where he stood the night before. *Cops.*

Neither of the men noticed him, but just their investigation of the bushes was disturbing enough. *Did the driver see me come out of the bushes, too?*

He turned and rushed up the sidewalk on Methvin. By the time he reached the back steps of Doris' house, he was shaking.

Chapter Twenty-One

Wednesday, Morning

Mae left not long after Jack, and now Will sat alone at his kitchen table with the incomplete draft of his letter to Bishop Watson in front of him. He didn't feel like working on the letter again, so he went out back and sat on the steps where a cool, autumn breeze was bringing in the new morning. Pete rooted around in a stand of bushes in the far corner of the yard, and when he saw him, he ran over and bounded onto the steps, almost knocking him backwards. He put his arm around the dog, and they sat together as the sun rose behind them, sending bright, straight ribbons across the grass.

As he watched the light of the new day fill the backyard, he said a prayer, "You know my heart, God, and I'm asking: Please help me bring her home."

He stood, and Pete leapt off the steps onto the grass, ready to play. He left him there though, returned to the kitchen, and picked up his cell phone. He made the most difficult call first, but it wasn't answered. Instead, a rasping, female voice said, "It's not convenient for us to come to the phone right now. If you think you've called the right number, please leave a brief, clearly expressed message. We won't return your call if we can't understand you." In response, he said, "Eileen, there's still hope for Annie. That's all I can say right now. We don't have her back yet, but we're working on it."

His cell phone buzzed almost as soon as his call ended. When he saw Eileen was calling, he let it go to voicemail.

Next, he called his mother. He told her that something had happened the night before that gave them reason to hope, but that the police asked him not to give out any other details. When he finished, he could tell that she was crying.

"I'd like to come on up to Catalpa. I can stay in Annie's room until she comes back."

He knew it would make him feel worse to see his mother upset because his anxiety would feed off hers and vice versa. He saw that play out when his father was dying, and it was the last thing he wanted to deal with right now. He begged off again, citing his continuing need to work with the police and the FBI, pointing out that having a house guest would just add to his stress.

"Please stay in Savannah until I have her back. I know I'll need you then."

"Is Mae taking care of you?"

"Yes."

"Okay. I'll stay out of the way for now. But please call me the minute you have any news. If I don't hear from you again in a day or so, I'll be heading your way."

His last call went to Callie. She'd just arrived at the church. He told her he hoped to meet with the FBI agent soon and planned to come by the church after that. He asked her to have the associate pastor stand by for the Sunday service if he couldn't handle it. He also asked her to pull Rankin Turner's résumé and see where he'd worked before the church hired him.

She reported back in less than a minute. "We have no résumé."

"What about his application? Did it include his work history?"

"I've got it right here in front of me. On the work history line, it says, 'See attached sheet,' but none is attached. Do you have it somewhere?"

"No. I don't remember discussing his prior employment. I didn't even look at his application. He seemed intelligent and strong enough to do the job, and we were desperate at that point for help."

Only two weeks before they hired Rankin, the man who'd served as the church's janitor for many years died in a freak accident. While taking a shower he fell and cracked his skull on the side of the bathtub at home. A neighbor expecting a ride to town found him the next day. The shower was still running, and water pooled everywhere. This horrific mishap led to the hiring of Rankin.

"Please tell me that we *do* have a background check in the file."

"Yes, sir, we have the state, but not the national. We never do the national. I'll get what we have to Lieutenant Carter."

Then he told her that Annie and the man who took her had been spotted in Catalpa the night before, but still honoring Jack's request for secrecy, he omitted any details.

"Oh, Will, I already know a little bit about what happened last night on Oglethorpe Street. It all sounds so strange. I mean the circumstances—lying in the middle of the street—naked. What kind of man would do a thing like that?"

Her comments astounded Will. *Who told* her *about it?* His concern roared to the surface. "Callie, how did you know about what happened last night?"

Callie paused for at least five seconds before she spoke again. "A friend—a doctor—heard people talking about it early this morning. They took the truck driver to the hospital for a blood test, and he was telling everybody about what happened. He even said he'd taken some kind of video of Annie. My friend knows my connection to you and wondered if you'd already said something to me about it. He wondered what the video showed. I had no idea it was supposedly a secret. If it's all just gossip, I hope you'll forgive me for even talking with him about it."

"I don't mean to sound irritated. It's just that the police assured me they hadn't shared it with the press or anyone else. They asked me to keep it quiet. By now, I'm sure that everybody in town knows about it anyway. I'll be in touch."

After the call ended, Will headed to the other side of the house to get cleaned up. He'd just gotten out of the shower when the front doorbell rang and Pete barked from the backyard. He wrapped a towel around his waist and headed toward the door. Through a sidelight, he saw Jack and Todd Baxter waiting. He cracked the door and asked them to come in and give him time to dress.

A few minutes later, he joined them in the living room. They went over the events of the night before. The FBI agent wanted to make sure that he hadn't omitted anything from what Will had already told Jack. He also mentioned that they would continue monitoring his cell and landline phones as well as the church phone.

"Should I be concerned about the confidentiality of my conversations with church members?"

"Look, your daughter is in great danger here. Can't you just forget about clergy privilege for the time being? For all we know, it was a member of your church who took Annie. If you're worried about your conversations with Mrs. Shaw, we'll ignore them altogether."

"How did you know about Mae?"

"Reverend Rowan, we know pretty much everything there is to know about you. We have to if we want to get your daughter back."

"I understand."

Pete's barking from the backyard was disrupting their meeting, so Will let him in. The dog sniffed his way around the room, first checking the FBI agent before moving over to the police lieutenant. Seemingly satisfied that their presence wasn't a cause for concern, he flopped beside Will's chair and lowered his head.

Jack spoke up then. "When I was here earlier you mentioned that you wanted to talk with Todd about something. What was it?"

Will glanced at him and nodded. "Based on the video, we know Annie was still alive last night. Right? If so, does that mean the man intends to keep her?"

Baxter frowned. "We have profilers for this sort of thing, but I know a little bit about it."

"I would appreciate anything you're willing to share with me. Mainly, I'd like to know what you expect the man to do with her."

The agent eyed Jack, but he returned his glance with a blank expression.

"Okay, preacher. Based on the episode at Tybee Island last summer and what happened last night, it's obvious that this wasn't any spur of the moment thing. Turner or whoever took Annie—it sure looks like it *is* Turner—had been planning to do it for a long time. We can't be sure why he chose her rather than some other little girl. He may have known her from somewhere, maybe from one of your churches or one of her schools. It may be that he knows you and harbors a grudge against you, or against preachers, or against the church in general. Or it could be that your daughter's appearance was the important factor in his selection of her. She may remind him of somebody he knows or knew in the past. The last factor— her appearance—seems the most likely reason he chose her."

Will was leaning forward. He wished that he had a pad and pencil, so he could make notes.

"I have no clue as to what was going on last night on Oglethorpe Street. It has all the markings of some kind of ritual. Whether or not it served its purpose, I don't know. If it did, then the man may not need her any longer. On the other hand, whatever he was doing with her out there last night may have sealed her place with him in some kind of a long-range plan. It may have validated her so to speak."

Will thought 'validate' in this context sounded evil. He remained silent, waiting for more, losing hope by the minute.

"The fact that Annie was seen here last night indicates to me that the man has some connection with Catalpa. Of course, your church janitor may fit into that category. We're running down his birth certificate now."

"Why would he risk discovery by putting Annie in a public street and then hanging around afterwards?"

The G-man placed his right hand on his chin, removed his hand, and raised his right index finger. "I've considered that very thing. What was the reason for his taking such a substantial risk? I think it had something to do with that particular location. In his own mind, Oglethorpe Street and nowhere else was where it must be done. As far as I'm concerned, it offers further evidence of his connection to Catalpa."

"Well, what is it?"

"That's what we're trying to determine."

Having heard all this, Will withdrew, looking down at his hands folded on his lap. The stink of his failure to keep his only child safe permeated the room, only slightly diffused by the inability of these policemen to bring her back. He turned to Jack. "The truck driver told everybody in the emergency room about Annie lying naked in the street last night."

"All of our people have been told to keep their mouths shut about last night. They did take Pitbone to the hospital to check his blood-alcohol level. Who told you that anyway?"

Will mentioned his telephone conversation with Callie and then unloaded. "Imagine how Annie will feel when we get her back. Everybody in town—all of her friends—will look at her and think about her being naked in the street. How could you have ever let Pitbone put out that sorry detail?"

Jack ignored his question. "Are we finished here? We need to get back to work."

"No, not yet." Will turned to Baxter. "Do men like this always end up killing their victims? How long are they usually kept before that happens?"

"I'm not sure I want to go into all that, Reverend."

"You've got to understand that it's the uncertainty that's eating away at me the most. I want Annie to live. You know that. But if that's not going to happen anyway, I need to know that her terrible suffering will come to an end soon, one way or another."

The agent paused, glanced at Jack, and then answered Will's question.

"Okay, it's like this. Your daughter might escape on her own, but something like that is exceedingly rare and not even worth discussing. I hate to tell you this, but unless we recover your daughter soon, it's unlikely that she'll be found alive. The only exception to that pattern is where the kidnapper knows the victim can't identify him, either because of her very young age or because he always wore a mask or other disguise, or because the victim has, in effect, lost his or her mental faculties over the whole experience.

"As far as knowing how long this man might keep her, no hard and fast rule comes to mind. Men like this sometimes keep their victims around for a very long time. The only reason we know that is because some of the victims escaped or were rescued after many, many years in captivity."

A wave of despair engulfed Will. After an awkward period of silence, Jack asked him if he had anything else on his mind.

"What about the note that came with the fair tickets?"

Baxter answered, "Nothing so far. We couldn't lift any prints on the note other than those we believe to be yours and your daughter's, and I doubt we'll get anything else from it. The paper and envelopes are available at most of the big box stores."

Will frowned. "Then what about the pink ribbon and the rolled up paper?"

Jack sighed. "The crime lab confirmed that no prints at all were on the ribbon or the scroll. They may have some value, but it's not apparent yet."

Will's scintilla of hope—based on knowing that Annie was still alive—was fading fast, and a mental picture of her lying on a cold, black, concrete floor, waiting to die, was gaining ground on his troubled spirit.

Chapter Twenty-Two

Wednesday, Mid-Morning

By the time Mr. Iblis returned Annie to the closet after breakfast, she was more frightened than ever. It wasn't just what he did to her the night before, drugging her, changing her clothes, and whatever else he did. It was his claim that he was her savior, like Jesus. That was the scariest thing of all.

He was crazy, and crazy people did bad things, sometimes things they didn't even know they were doing.

While she ate the cardboard-like, breakfast burritos, she had come up with a plan. Before he began to strap her into the chair, she would push her stomach out and arch her back as far away from the chair as she could. The over-sized T-shirt he'd put on her would hide this activity. If her plan worked, the strap would be loose, and she could slip out of it. She hadn't decided what she would do after that, but she had a vague notion of waiting until he returned to the closet again and then hitting him over the head with the large picture of the girl which hung over the table behind her chair.

All went well when he brought her back to the closet. She begged him to leave the light on, and he did. She arched her back, loosening the strap, and he didn't notice.

But as soon as he left her, she went to sleep again. She woke up not knowing how long she slept and surprised that she'd slept at all. She blamed that on breakfast and the lingering effect of the drug he'd given her which must've been very strong. Maybe that was what he had in mind all along. He would keep her drugged, so he could do strange things to her over and over again.

She sighed and looked at the pretty girl in the pictures on the wall. She thought the girl might have winked at her. She took that as a sign that she should go ahead and try to get out from under the strap.

The idea for her plan had come from a book she read in Miss Gentry's fifth grade class at Marley Breen Elementary School. It was a book about Houdini, and she wrote a report on it. In the last chapter, the author claimed to reveal how the magician did some of his tricks. According to the author, one of Houdini's methods was to contort his body so that chains or straightjackets weren't fixed tightly around him. That way, he could escape from almost everything. But a concern popped into her head. *Houdini never got away from being strapped down to a chair in a little room. He used a key sometimes too, but a key won't help me. Is this a stupid idea?*

The leather strap around her waist was much looser than it had been. Before, her torso was held tightly to the chair, but now, after she'd arched her back, the strap was not tight around her middle. Under the loosened strap, she could move up and down pretty much with ease, and she thought it just might be loose enough for her to slide out of the chair.

She didn't even try to move her body upwards. Her hips wouldn't allow her to go that way. So she pushed her torso down as far as she could, and soon her rear end was hanging off the edge of the seat. Her stomach and chest made it through the strap, but try as she might, she couldn't get her shoulders out from under the strap even with her arms stretched high above her head. She pulled and stretched, but she could go no farther in the chair.

It was then that she remembered Miss Gentry commenting that Houdini could do all sorts of wonderful tricks because he was in great, physical shape. The implication was that the children in her class weren't in great shape and should get that way as soon as possible.

But Annie *was* in great shape. She and her dad had run eight laps around the high school track together just the week before. But maybe her shape wasn't quite good enough. "Help me out, God…Houdini…whoever!" she said out loud.

Her plan to slide out feet first wasn't working. The whole idea was foolish. She gave up and tried to go back the other way, struggling to pull her rear end back onto the chair and herself into a sitting position. She tried and tried, but her chest wouldn't go back through the strap again. She tugged, she pulled, and she stretched. Nothing worked. For the first time since one of her girlfriends had told her how much boys liked boobs, she wished that she didn't have the beginnings of them. "I can't get back up!" she yelled, wriggling and sliding back and forth.

It was no use. Her hips still hung off the chair, and her lower back was fixed at a painful angle against the edge of the chair seat. She was terrified of what Mr. Iblis might do if he found her like this.

While she waited for him to return, she began to moan.

Chapter Twenty-Three

Wednesday, Morning

After Jack and Agent Baxter left his house, Will's head was still filled with images of Annie in the arms of the dark-haired man in a baseball cap. Pure anger was slowly beginning to join his despair.

He headed for the church but parked two blocks away, hoping to arrive undetected. Entering through a back door, he spent five minutes with Callie and left again the same way. On the sidewalk, his cell phone rang, displaying Jack as the caller.

"Where are you, Will?"

"I just left the church."

"Come over to my office. There's something I need for you to look at."

Will made the five-minute walk to the police station where an officer ushered him back to Jack's office, a small, windowless, claustrophobic room somewhere in the middle of the station.

"I apologize for the air in here. It's not always of the best quality. I'm insisting on two large windows if we ever get into a new building."

He offered Will a seat in front of his desk.

Now that they had a partial description of the man who took Annie, detectives were comparing it to that of sex offenders who filled out state-required, public registrations showing a Catalpa address. "It's hard to believe how many dark-haired perverts of medium height are living right here," Jack said.

"You aren't satisfied that Rankin took her?"

"Are you, Will?"

"Callie told me that he's not at work again today."

"That's not good. He told your people that he had a place in Catalpa but hadn't moved in yet and didn't know the address. I'm thinking he's been living up in Atlanta. That's where his P.O. box is. If we can find out where he lives up there, we'll get a search warrant and take a look."

"Let's not forget that the man who took Annie may not even live in Georgia, Jack. What else is going on? What do you want to show me?"

Jack picked up a small bundle of papers, neatly stapled together, and pushed it across his desk toward Will. He gave it a cursory thumb-through. "Hundreds of names are on these sheets, Jack. Who are they?"

"The FBI is flat out amazing. After I told Todd about the incident on the beach last summer, he got the Bureau's resident agent in Savannah to check hotel guest registers on Tybee Island. In short order, they accumulated a list of every person who had a hotel room on Tybee Island on the night last summer when the dark-haired man tried to grab Annie."

"That doesn't seem possible."

"Tybee doesn't have that many hotels, plus it wasn't that long ago. They even got records from some of the bed and breakfast establishments, too. Of course Tybee's not far from Savannah. Checking hotels there will tell a different story entirely."

Will held up the sheets. "What am I supposed to do with these?"

"I know it'll take a while, but I want you to look at every entry on the list. If you come across any name that you know, it might be important. That person's presence on Tybee that night might be more than a coincidence. By the way, Rankin isn't on the list, but that doesn't mean anything. He could have used a phony name."

"Okay, but do you really think this will get us anywhere?"

"It's something."

The phone on Jack's desk rang, and he picked it up, listened, and spoke into the phone. "Okay." He stood, explaining that he needed to meet with Baxter, and promised to get back to him later in the day.

Back on the sidewalk, Will folded the stapled sheets and stuck them in his coat pocket. It was much too early for lunch, but he headed to Mae's bookstore anyway. He was crossing the square in that direction when someone behind him said, "Preacher!"

He turned and acknowledged a woman coming toward him on the sidewalk. She was white-haired and tall, dressed in a conservative skirt and blouse, and a green, cardigan sweater. It was Janie Stewart, a member of his church, whose stature and eyes had always reminded him of Vanessa Redgrave. "Good morning, Miss Janie."

"I feel so terrible about what's happened. Hannah has just put one of her pound cakes in the oven for you, and I want to get it to you while it's still warm. Should I just drop it by the church?"

Food was the last thing he wanted to think about. "Thank you so much, but please do take it to the church. I don't know when I'll get back to the house."

"I'll leave it with Callie. I wish I could do more, but at my age, delivering cakes and such is about the extent of it."

"The cake is really appreciated, but your prayers and concern will mean even more to me and Annie."

She nodded, and he gave her a hug and began to walk away.

"Will, wait."

He stopped and turned around.

"I heard that something happened on Oglethorpe Street last night. That sort of thing always seems to get around Catalpa pretty fast." She paused, perhaps to wait for his reaction, but when he remained silent, she continued.

"There's something I need to tell you. It may not even be important, but I haven't been able to get it out of my head since I heard about poor Annie being left in the street."

He held his mouth closed; otherwise, it would have dropped open. He was amazed that she already knew all about what had happened less than twelve hours before.

"Do you have time to hear what I have to say, preacher?"

"Of course, I do."

They were abreast of the only coffee shop on the courthouse square, so he suggested they sit and talk at one of the alfresco tables near the entrance. She declined his offer to get her a cup of coffee.

"Miss Janie, you do live on Methvin Avenue, don't you?"

"Yes."

"Did you see anything last night?"

"Last night? No, I've already told the police that I didn't. But I do remember that something happened on Oglethorpe Street years ago. It was in the early fall of the year, right at the same spot where Annie was seen last night. I think it was about forty years ago, and I'm afraid that many of the details are no longer with me."

He sat up. "Please go on."

"I've been thinking about it ever since I heard about the truck almost hitting Annie. Doris Paine's daughter got hurt in the middle of the night in the same spot on Oglethorpe Street. Her son was also involved. She only had those two children, but I don't recall their names. They were twins. And the little Turner boy was in on it, too. I do remember his name. How could I forget it? It was 'Rankin.' He practically lived at Doris' house, and it seems like he might've even moved in with them at one point."

"Wait a minute. Surely you don't mean the same Rankin Turner that's the new janitor at the church. *He* was involved in what happened back then?"

Her confusion led him to continue. "Miss Janie, not long ago we hired a man named 'Rankin Turner.' He's the janitor at our church. Did you know that? Was he the other child with the Paine twins that night?"

"Now that you mention it, yes, I guess he was. I heard that we'd hired him, but I haven't seen him at the church yet. Who else could it be but the Turner boy?"

"Please tell me what went on that night." He was on the edge of his seat.

She wrung her hands. "I'm trying to remember. I know that Doris Paine's little girl got hurt at that intersection. Something happened, but I don't recall exactly what. And the boys were out there, but they were all right."

"What were the children doing?"

"I'm upset because I just can't bring up the details."

A woman who appeared to have been working out at the fitness center a few doors down from the coffee shop waved to Mrs. Stewart as she got into her car. Returning her wave, Ms. Stewart said, "I couldn't imagine exercising in public at my age, but it doesn't seem to bother her. She's pushing eighty."

"I can't think of any good reason why you shouldn't be doing it, too, Miss Janie. Now, we were talking about Doris Paine. Does she still live on Methvin Avenue?"

"Oh, no. She died early on, several months after what happened to her daughter."

"What about Mr. Paine? Where is he now?"

"Oh, I wouldn't know about that. He left before the twins were even born. His name was something other than Paine. I'm not sure I ever knew it."

"Would anyone else remember any of this?"

"Maybe, but most of them are gone now. I guess I could ask around."

"I would really appreciate it, if you would, Miss Janie. What about the newspaper? Would it have been in the *Times*?"

"Back then, the paper only came out twice a week, and it would have been very unusual for them to print an item about something like that. Doris' family had been in Catalpa for generations, and it would have been an embarrassment for her. Her great-grandparents—dead now, of course—were the ones who built the house on Methvin. Later she lived there with her mother and father; they were chiropractors. They're dead, too, both succumbed to some kind of food poisoning when Doris was in her twenties. They left her the house and a considerable fortune."

A waitress appeared and offered to take their order. When they declined, she frowned and went back inside the shop. As soon as she was gone, Mrs. Stewart continued.

"Doris was on the strange side. After her parents died, a man best described as swarthy, some kind of salesman—plastic cemetery flowers, I believe—moved in with her. It was sort of scandalous really. He left town before the twins were born. Later, she claimed they'd been married, but he'd obtained a Mexican divorce. No one believed any of that.

"A few weeks after the salesman moved out, she appeared at Catalpa General and gave birth to twins. She had no prenatal care, and no one in town even knew she was pregnant. It was rumored that she didn't know either.

"After the twins were born, she kept them at home most of the time. I wish I could recall their names, but I just can't. I do remember them being as different as night and day. She enrolled them in public school, but otherwise she kept them isolated in that house."

"Which house? Where did they live?"

"It's on Methvin, the second house on the right coming up the street from Oglethorpe."

He got quiet. He was trying to figure out what all of this had to do with what had happened to Annie. She reached across the table and touched his arm. "Are you all right, Will?"

"Does anyone in the Paine family still live in the house on Methvin?"

"To tell you the truth, I've been wondering who does own that house. If anybody lives there, I haven't seen them. The daughter was hurt, but after that, I just don't know. And then, Doris died. I think the little boy was adopted by a couple from somewhere else. He never came back to town as far as I know. But what happened to the little girl? Did she die, too? O, my…my memory is not what it once was. Do you understand that, preacher? It was forty years ago."

Will looked over at the courthouse across the street. Two deputies escorted a prisoner in cuffs and chains out of the building. Seeing the prisoner like that brought to mind the man who took Annie. "Miss Janie, was there a man in the street with the Paine children that night?"

She gave that some thought. "I don't think so. The Turners lived right there at that corner in the brick house, but they drank a whole lot. I imagine they slept through the whole thing."

"Are they still around?"

"They left town years ago, and the bank ended up foreclosing on their house. It's vacant now. I couldn't tell you whether the Turners are dead or alive. Maybe Rankin knows something about them."

"Miss Janie, are you sure that nobody ever told you what was going on that night?"

"If they did, I don't remember it. For the life of me, I don't have the slightest idea what those children were up to out there."

Chapter Twenty-Four

Wednesday, Morning

Will rushed back to the police department with Janie Stewart's revelation. Jack listened in silence and then promised to check out her story. Will offered to see what he could find out about the prior incident, suggesting that he might talk to other homeowners in the neighborhood or go to the newspaper, but his suggestion brought another rebuke from Jack.

"Will, I know how hard this is for you. I really do."

"But Jack…"

"No. Based on what Miss Janie told you, it's beginning to look more and more like Rankin may be involved in this somehow. She was right when she said that he grew up in Catalpa. This morning, the FBI tracked down his mother through the bank that had a mortgage on the brick house at the corner of Methvin and Oglethorpe. After the bank foreclosed on the house, she moved to Valdosta, and she's still down there. When Rankin was in high school, the State removed him from her home. The last time she heard anything about him, he was a student at Georgia State. The university says that he graduated, but they don't know what happened to him after that."

This astounded Will. "You're telling me Rankin had a college degree? What was he doing working as a janitor?"

"We've asked ourselves the same question. Maybe he made a lot of money in some other job and just wanted to do something mindless."

He was doubtful, and his expression confirmed it, while Jack continued. "Of course, there's another possibility, it could be he wanted proximity to Annie's father for whatever opportunities that might bring. I hate to say it, but that seems most logical. The truth is, though, we know nothing about him except that he's a college graduate, works at a church, owns an old, white truck, and says he's moving here but doesn't know the address yet."

"I can't believe we hired him. There are layers and layers here, and we don't have time to peel them off one by one."

On that note, he left and walked over to Mae's bookstore where he found her working behind the counter. The store was otherwise empty. He suggested they get an early lunch.

Her helper, Brad Dixon, was out running an errand. He was part-time, and his day usually ended around noon. An Army lieutenant colonel who took a job to supplement his retirement checks, he'd moved to Catalpa because he served alongside her husband in Afghanistan and heard him talk about visiting it with Mae.

While they waited for Dixon to come back, Will related his conversation with Janie Stewart, as well as Jack's reaction. She suggested that she might look into the prior incident herself, even if the lieutenant told him not to. "Several years ago, they began putting everything on microfiche at the newspaper, but searching for an article can take quite a while unless you know how to go about it. I have a friend who works down there, and if an article exists, she can find it for me in no time at all."

He frowned. "Please don't. As hard as it is, I need to follow Jack's directive."

She shrugged.

He sighed and reached for her hand, but she pulled it back. "I've got to find her, but I don't have a clue about what to do or where to start. It's like I'm letting her down because I'm not out there looking for her. It's not right."

"I feel exactly the same way. I want to do something—anything—and going down to the newspaper office is one thing I *can* do."

At that moment, the colonel returned. He headed straight for Will, offered his hand, and patted him on the shoulder. "I'm so sorry about all of this, Reverend Rowan, but I don't need to tell you that God's on your side. I'm sure He will bring her back to you."

Will considered Dixon unctuous, and he had no desire to discuss his missing child with him. He thanked him and suggested to Mae that they go on to lunch. She agreed and stepped to the back of the store to freshen up. Dixon took this as an opportunity to mention Annie again, revealing that he, too, knew all about the incident on Oglethorpe Street the night before. "I've never had the privilege of meeting her, Reverend. She was already in school when I came to work here, and I only work mornings. Mae tells me that she's an outstanding young lady. Have they made any progress identifying the 'evil man' who removed her from the street?"

Will hesitated. He was about to explain that the police had asked him not to talk about the case when Mae returned. She gave brief instructions to her helper about handling the shop, and they left.

To avoid media exposure in the downtown area, they got a take-out at an Italian restaurant located in a shopping area a few miles away. She went inside to get the food while he waited in her car. In the few minutes that followed, two different sets of his parishioners saw him and stopped by the car to offer encouragement. It seemed that they, too, had heard that Annie had been spotted the night before.

On the way to her condominium, Mae said, "You're too quiet, Will."

"I've been thinking about Colonel Dixon. Right before we left for lunch, he tried to get me to talk about Annie almost to the point of being offensive. He seemed to know all about what happened last night down to the smallest detail. It wasn't in the paper this morning, and it wasn't on TV. Did you mention it to him?"

"We've talked about her a few times, but that was only because he seemed to know a lot already. This is Catalpa. You should understand by now that no secrets are kept here. You don't need reporters to tell you what's going on."

"I don't like everybody knowing everything, especially the part about her being naked in the street."

"There's not much I can do about that, Will."

"You can stop talking to your employee about it."

Inside her condo, they sat at the kitchen counter and ate in silence for a while, before she brought up the subject of her assistant again. "There's a lot of dead time at the store, and he and I end up talking about things. But you're right. I won't say another word to Brad about Annie. Trust me on that."

He glanced at his food and slid some of it around with his fork. "Jack wants us to keep it quiet. He must have a reason for it. If I can't trust his judgment…"

"I was wrong, and I've said I was. It won't happen again."

He nodded, put down his fork, and pushed his plate away. "Can we go?"

She ignored his question, continuing to eat. With her eyes still on her plate, she said, "I'm concerned about you, Will."

"I've never been at such a low ebb. I don't feel fit to serve the church or do much of anything else. If I don't get Annie back, I don't expect that to change…ever."

If she wanted him to explain further, she was disappointed. He avoided her eyes, saying nothing else.

"I hate to see you like this. How can I help?"

He was still silent.

After she finished eating, they left. As they drove away, he mentioned that he wasn't ready to go back to the church. "I want to see the house that Miss Janie told me about—the one that the Paine woman used to own. Go over to Oglethorpe, and turn left up Methvin Avenue."

She complied, and he asked her to park on Methvin in front of the second house on the right. It was a white, two-story, frame house with brick steps leading up to a front porch. The porch was rounded to the right, and except for the wide entrance on the left, it was protected by a wooden railing with ornate balusters supporting rounded columns. A driveway ran beside the house on the right from the sidewalk to an old, white-washed barn. Some sort of vehicle sat inside the barn, but a large tarp obscured its identity from passersby.

Mae sighed. "When you're around people raised in the sixties, have you ever heard them use the phrase, 'bad vibes?'"

He nodded, never taking his eyes off the house.

"Will, the place is giving me a load of 'bad vibes,' but I couldn't begin to tell you why." The longer they sat in front of the house, the antsier she appeared. "Come on, let's go. Even if no one has lived here for a while, I feel uncomfortable just sitting in the car and staring at it. Somebody may be in there, somebody with a gun."

"That's what I'd like to know—whether anybody lives here now. The house Rankin grew up in is empty, but I don't know about this one. I just want to go up there and see if anybody comes to the door."

"I wish you wouldn't," she said, but he ignored her. He left the car and set off up the walkway. The house was well-maintained, but the same couldn't be said for the grounds. The grass and shrubbery begged for attention.

He climbed the brick steps to the wide front porch. If the house was occupied, it wasn't apparent here, where leaves, dust, and similar detritus cluttered the porch and its green, wicker swing and other outdoor furnishings. He crossed over and stood before the black, sturdy-looking, front door. To its left, a small letter box was stuffed with weathered circulars. A curtained, glass pane was set into the door's top half, and in the bright, afternoon sun, no light or movement was visible inside.

He knocked but got no response. He knocked again with more force this time and waited. Again, nothing happened. Even with his face up against the glass portion of the door, he couldn't see anything through the sheer curtain on the other side. Disappointed, he turned to leave, but right then, he heard a sound. It was a muffled pounding, not a hammer, but something else too faint to identify. He waited but detected no other sounds.

The thumping sound could have originated from either inside or outside this house. Stepping off the porch, he studied the adjoining houses. He walked across the grass to the driveway and looked down toward the barn. He saw no activity and heard no more sounds.

He returned to the car perplexed.

"Was there anything?"

Without answering her question or looking her way, he said, "I've changed my mind. I'd like to go back to the church."

She left him at the church, and he sneaked through a side door on the lower level. According to Callie, the news people and TV trucks were still coming and going in the parking lot, all hoping for a statement. This brought more negative thoughts. *Sooner or later, none of this will matter. Annie's plight will be old news, and some other tragedy will grab the headlines.*

After he sat at his desk, he asked Callie to come in. "Something came to me a little while ago," he said. "You're from Catalpa, so you must have known something about Rankin before he came to work here."

She looked toward the bank of windows to her right. "He grew up in Catalpa, and I knew who he was, but that's about it. I was kind of surprised when he applied for the job, I guess, but I couldn't tell you why exactly. He was on the wrestling team with my older brother, so I heard things about him because of that."

"What kind of things?"

"That he was kind of odd. That his parents drank a lot. While we were in high school, I'm pretty sure he ended up in foster care because of their drinking."

"Why odd?"

"He was a good student but not part of the 'in' crowd, if you know what I mean. He was an outsider; he didn't seem to fit in for some reason."

Will waited, thinking she had more to say.

"You weren't aware of this, but when the church hired the last janitor—the one before Rankin—it took us forever to find one. I'm talking months. When we needed a janitor again, I didn't want us to have to wait like that. We'd already gone a couple of weeks without one by the time he applied, and I was afraid that no one else would apply. I was reluctant to say anything about him because I didn't really know him that well."

Will left his desk and sat in the chair next to her. "Callie, for all I know, Rankin may be involved in what happened to Annie."

She put a hand to her mouth. "Oh, Lord, Rankin did it?"

"They don't know. He's disappeared, and I hoped you might have some background information which would help us find him."

"Before he showed up here, I hadn't even thought about him at all since high school. I don't have any idea what he's done since then."

"That's okay. One other thing—what about the Paine twins? Did you know them? They lived over on Methvin Avenue with their mother."

"No, I don't think so. Which house did they live in?"

"The second house on the right going up from Oglethorpe."

"Oh, that house. It's vacant, isn't it? There are some old rockers on the porch, and somebody has the grass cut every now and then. But as far as I know, nobody has lived there since I was a little girl." She stood to leave his office. "With all of this coming up about Rankin, I need to tell you something else. One day last week, I smelled alcohol on his breath. I should have mentioned it already, but I wanted to see if it happened again. I didn't want him to get fired the first week he was here."

He sighed and got up, too. "Okay. Thanks. I'm going on home now. By the way, please take Miss Janie's cake home with you. I really don't want any of it."

He left through a back door and went home. No media types had yet migrated to his house for the evening, and for this, he was grateful. He fed Pete, let him out again, and sat on the back steps while the dog chased a ball in the backyard.

Annie had been gone now for less than forty-eight hours. *Has she been 'validated' now or is she no longer needed?* Either way, her life might very well be over, and so might his.

Chapter Twenty-Five

Wednesday, Early Afternoon

What seemed like hours had gone by, and Annie remained stuck. Her neck craned in an unnatural position; her shoulders were scrunched up against the back of the chair; her back snaked up and down like a roller coaster; her legs were still bent at the knees, holding up her rear end, with her feet on the floor. After a while, her muscles cramped and ached from her neck to her toes, and she feared rubbing herself raw as she tried to sit up straight over and over again. She couldn't remember ever suffering such pain.

At last, the door opened, and he was standing there.

"Oh, Mr. Iblis, I'm so sorry for this. Please, please help me," she whispered.

And so he did, in the kindest and most gentle manner she could ever have imagined. "Thank you. That's so much better."

"I brought us something to eat. I think you'll like it. Let me take you to the bathroom, and then there's something special waiting for us in the dining room."

She hesitated, her eyes searching the closet.

"We won't need the chain this time, if that's what you're looking for. I'll trust you not to do anything, and I'm hoping that my trust will be contagious."

This last was said with a smile as he guided her out of the closet. After she visited the bathroom, she followed him to the dining room. There, an elegant, white table cloth covered a large, round table set with fine china, crystal, and silver flatware. An arrangement of cut, fall flowers created a colorful centerpiece. On a sideboard to her right, a platter of barbecued, baby back ribs, and serving pieces filled with

French fries, coleslaw, and Brunswick stew promised a wonderful feast.

"Do you feel up to serving yourself, Annie?"

She nodded, wiped a tear, and took a plate. When she turned to the table with a mound of food, her hands were shaking under its weight.

"Iced tea, Coke, or water?"

She asked for Coke and sat quietly while he poured it. He served his own plate and sat across from her. Polite to a fault, she waited for his cue to begin eating, but he sat in silence, staring at her through the beautiful, floral centerpiece. At last, he spoke again. "I suppose your father always asked the blessing at your house."

"I did, too, sometimes."

"Would you mind if I asked it now?"

"No."

She bowed her head, waiting.

"Great One, please let us sup forever on Heaven's dew and earth's rich bounty of grain and new wine. Amen."

While they ate, he told a strange story. "Once, there were two little boys who lived near one another in a small town. They were friends. Before one of the boys was even born, his father left and never came back. His mother was not a good person either. She smothered the boy, not with a pillow, but rather with a distorted type of love. She died while he was still in middle school.

"The parents of the other little boy stayed drunk all the time. Lucky for him, he was removed from their home before they could do him harm.

"Being without parents, both boys were turned over to the Tanotchee County Department of Family and Children's Services, and each of them in his own way thrived and enjoyed a pleasant life after that. The first boy was adopted by an attentive, older couple of limited means. The second boy was placed with loving, foster parents who helped him get a college scholarship."

For reasons she didn't fully understand, his story disturbed her. When he finished, she had trouble making eye contact.

"You said the first little boy's mother died. Was she sick?"

He was quiet. Annie could feel him looking at her even though she kept her eyes fixed on her plate. After a minute or so, he answered her, his voice even and his tone flat.

"She was a very attractive woman, but she died from a malady of the head."

"Do you mean like cancer?"

"She *was* the cancer."

At that point, she raised her head and looked at him. His eyes were glazed over, just like she'd seen a girl at school look right before she suffered what her teacher called a 'grand mal.' This worried her, but after several seconds his eyes were normal again.

He stood and circled the table to stand beside her. He placed his hands on her shoulders. "Annie, the moral of the story I've just told you is this: a child can feel loved and be happy even if the child's father is absent and the child's mother is dead or might as well be dead as far as the child is concerned. Sometimes a child is much better off under those circumstances."

She nodded although both his story and why he'd told it mystified her.

"It's a pretty day. Let's go outside."

After he led her out, he directed her to sit on the concrete steps at the back door, and he sat beside her. The effect of whatever he'd given her the night before had worn off, and being outside again lifted her spirits. He surprised her, taking her hand and holding it in his, but she didn't object or resist. "Where are my clothes, Mr. Iblis?"

"You have them on. If you don't like what you're wearing today, I suppose I can find others."

She looked down at the picture of the long-haired boy on the T-shirt she was wearing and ran her hand over the knees of the funny jeans. "Would the clothes you might find look and fit like these?"

"More or less. They're difficult to locate now, although some Sunday dresses of that era are available online."

"Will you always keep me at this house?"

"Please, please don't say that I'm *keeping* you. I'm not *keeping* you anywhere. You're not an animal in a zoo. You're *staying* with me right now, that's all. Furthermore, I hope you'll want to continue to stay here with me until we have to leave."

She thought about that for a moment, his answer puzzling her. *Want to stay? Could I leave any time I wanted to?* She was afraid to voice her confusion though. "If I have to stay with you, Mr. Iblis, I want it to be right here. It's not very far from my father's house, is it?"

He sighed and pulled his hand away.

"Annie, from now on, just like the first little boy in the story, you won't be seeing your father ever again. You need to understand that he let me take you away from the fairgrounds, and he did nothing to stop me. He's already given up on finding you. I looked into it, and I know it's that way. Your father is planning to marry Mae Shaw very soon, and they'll have another little girl to take your place. They'll pick up and move to a town far away from here, too. You know ministers have to do that. And we both know that your mother is dead. You don't need your father or your mother now because you have me. It's as simple as that."

Tears streamed down her cheeks, but she refrained from crying out. "Are you telling me the truth about my father, Mr. Iblis?"

"As long as you've known me, have I ever lied to you?"

She was silent. She was thinking. *How long* have *I known him? It seems like forever, but how long has it really been?*

"Have I always been honest with you, Annie?"

"Yes."

He took her hand again, and they sat for a while, hand in hand, until he stood and announced that it was time to go back inside. Instead of taking her back to the closet though, he told her he wanted to show her 'Doris' house.' She was happy to do anything that kept her out the closet, and she told him so.

The few rooms she'd seen earlier and those he showed her now were all completely furnished, as if the owners had just stepped out for a moment and would soon be back. It was a lot like walking through a museum where everything is in perfect order but dusty. The tour included his commentary on each room, but only in terms of what 'was' and 'once was.'

Two parlors flanked the front hall of the house. As they faced the front door, he referred to the parlor on the right as Doris' and that on the left as her mother's. A lectern stood in the one on the right. It was made of oak and reminded her of what Sunday School teachers stood behind at her father's church. He told her that this was where Doris lectured her two children after school each weekday.

"Why did she do that?"

"Her children had very few friends. They weren't normal like you are, and neither was their mother. After school they were subjected to what she called 'booster classes.' A child from the neighborhood wanted to take part, but he wasn't allowed to do so. All he could do was watch."

He pointed to a low, brocaded settee on the far side of the fireplace, facing the lectern. "The children sat together over there on the settee with the girl to the right of the boy. With the benefit of an oversized, unabridged dictionary, their mother expounded on topics ranging from Adam and Eve to the Georgia Guidestones, and everything and everybody one might imagine in between. She introduced the children to role playing, too, which soon became one of their favorite, academic methods. They were especially fond of the story of the birth of Rome, including their roles as the twins, Romulus and Remus, and Doris' role that of the mother wolf. Her reenactment of the death of Socrates was no less electrifying. She starred in the title role with her daughter and son playing Xenophon and Plato, respectively."

"I'm not sure that I know all of those people, Mr. Iblis."

If he heard her comment, he didn't acknowledge it.

"These activities and others had the effect of isolating her children and causing them to spend most of their waking hours together, all to the extent that their relationship began to blossom into something not akin to that of normal siblings. Of course, this was her intended purpose all along."

Annie was having trouble following much of this.

"Did she ever take them to church?"

He chuckled. "Oh, yes, whenever the doors were open. She was what one might call a hypocrite. Do you know what that means?"

"She wasn't honest?"

He laughed again and then led Annie upstairs.

Three bedrooms were on the second floor. The first was decorated in dark colors. It reminded her of her father's bedroom at home. A tennis racket was in one corner, and two model airplanes sat on a small desk against one wall.

"You mentioned a boy. This was his room, wasn't it?"

"It was."

Two other bedrooms were across the upstairs hall from the first. They stopped at the door of the one on the right. The Venetian blinds on the windows were closed, and the room was so dark that she could hardly make out the bed. When she headed inside, he restrained her. "No. Not Doris' bedroom."

"I don't understand."

He offered no explanation, guiding her into the adjoining bathroom. A large, white, cast iron, porcelain bathtub with claw feet dominated it. "When you feel like you need a bath, you are welcome to use this."

The very thought upset her, but she didn't let on.

"On hot, summer afternoons, Doris used to fill the tub with cool water, and she and her children would get in together. It was like a swimming pool, so big that the children could almost swim in it. Sometimes the neighbor child would come, and she let him watch, but he was never allowed to get in. He was excluded from many of their other familial activities, too."

"Why?"

"His people were not of 'first water' according to Doris. She wasn't either but spent her days ignorant of her own lowly status."

This explanation failed to enlighten Annie, but she kept it to herself.

He sat on the edge of the tub and let his right hand dangle down, as if the tub were filled with water. His mind seemed elsewhere, his eyes gazing at something far away. After a moment, he licked his lips and resumed. "One afternoon, when Doris had gone to town, the girl got in with the boys…" he began but never finished. His tone was wistful.

The last bedroom, directly across the hall from the first, was done up entirely in shades of pink. She supposed it was pretty but found it cold. The room lacked any items of a personal nature, and aside from its color, nothing suggested that it might be the room of a young girl. Annie saw no clothes, no dolls, no scrapbooks, no hair brushes, no soccer balls, nothing. "I guess this is the girl's bedroom, but where's her stuff?"

He leaned against the door jamb and frowned. "Doris called it 'junk for the junkman.' After her daughter was gone, she threw out all of her things—her dolls and toys, her books, her clothes, and her other personal items, even her toothbrush. She stacked them in the street near the curb in front of the house. One day a city garbage truck came and took everything away. But she didn't find some things."

"Where did her daughter go?"

He glanced her way but was quiet. He took her back into the hall and over to the top of the stairs. He turned toward her and smiled. "If you like, the room we just left can be your own, very special room, Annie."

She blanched and moved to go down the stairs.

"Wait," he said, but she didn't.

He grabbed her, put his arm around her waist, and lifted her up. "Annie…"

"You lied, Mr. Iblis! You said you didn't want to keep me. But you do! You want me to live here. You want to keep me right here in this house forever!"

She pulled at his arm, trying to get away.

"Please don't jerk like that. It will bruise your stomach."

"Leave me alone!"

She continued to resist, but he was too strong. He carried her downstairs and returned her to the closet. There, she stomped her feet so furiously that the floor vibrated. He *was* going to keep her. He would keep her until it was time to skin her alive or eat her. A boy at school had told her about a man who did those things to children and then made lampshades out of their skin. "Please, Jesus, help me," she whispered.

She was still praying when she fell asleep. Much later, she woke to find not Jesus, but Mr. Iblis, standing there with a tray of food, a sandwich and something in a bowl, maybe some kind of soup.

"Supper," he said, presenting the tray with outstretched arms.

Still upset, she kicked the tray with her right foot as hard as she could. The mayonnaise laden sandwich flew against the wall, and the soup splashed onto the floor. Some of the food landed on him, staining his clothes. "Oh," he said and hurried out of the closet carrying the now empty tray.

After he left, and to the extent that she could while strapped down in the chair, she rocked back and forth, imagining that she was in a rocking chair in the lap of her daddy.

***

In the kitchen, Mr. Iblis sat at the table with his head in his hands. Things were not going the way he'd hoped they would. He lost the scroll, the truck driver might have seen too much, and Annie kicked her supper all over him. For the first time since he was a young boy, he thought of harming himself.

***

Not long after Mr. Iblis left the closet, he returned with a spray bottle of cleaning liquid and paper towels. Annie could tell that he'd changed his clothes. Without speaking, he got on the floor and cleaned up the mess that she'd made of her dinner. She felt sorry for him and apologized again and again for what she'd done. He glanced at her but remained silent. When he'd finished, he gathered up the used towels and stood next to the door, staring at her.

After his staring went on for a while, she said, "Mr. Iblis?"

He shook his head and said, "I'll take you to the bathroom, and later, I may go away for a time, but I'll be back." He took her to the bathroom, and then returned her to the closet without another word.

She felt badly. *What else could I have done but apologize?* It was obvious that he wasn't happy with her, and she considered just what 'a time' meant. *Was it an hour? All night? A day? A week?* In the closet under the stairs, it was impossible to tell how long anything lasted. Time was like forever. When her father preached at the church, sometimes he talked about eternity. Now she knew exactly what he meant.

Waiting for him to return, she slept off and on. Whenever she woke up, she was hungry, and very, very thirsty. *Is he still so upset that he isn't coming back? Do I miss him? What if he never comes back?*

The more he was nice to her and didn't hurt her, the more confused she became about how she really felt about him. *How could I miss a weird man who kidnapped me?* No, she didn't miss him like she missed her father. It was being alone hour after hour in this little room that was upsetting. She was a popular girl in school, and she'd never been lonely until now.

At least he left the light on in the closet. "I've come to understand how the dark upsets you," he said, sounding just like the ultimate creep.

She was so glad to have the light because the dark *was* so scary, especially when she woke up and was still sort of asleep. Mostly, the light allowed her to see that no spiders were crawling on her legs. It gave her more time to look at the pictures on the wall, too. Her father talked all the time about Jesus being the 'Light of the World,' and God being the 'Father of Light.' "Now I have light, but where is God?" she whispered to herself, looking around the little room.

She had already studied every picture on the walls of the blonde girl who looked just like her except the one behind her that she couldn't quite see. She imagined them being great friends and doing all sorts of fun things together. She could tell that the girl was happy and would make a terrific friend. She wanted to get to know her.

But the girl on the walls seemed caught in another time, a time before Annie even existed. It wasn't just her clothes and shoes. It was mostly her hair, and the type of pictures. Nobody took those kinds of pictures anymore either; they just used their cell phones.

If one of the boys in the pictures was Mr. Iblis, then the girl on the wall must be old now, too. *Where is she today? Did she marry Mr. Iblis or the other boy in the pictures? Did she grow up and have a little girl like me? Could they be pictures of my own mom Leah when she was younger? Is that what this whole thing is all about? Did he know my mother when they were growing up?*

The tears flowed then. As she cried, she begged, "Daddy, please come get me," over and over again. She said other things, too—to Jesus. She didn't stop crying until her T-shirt was soaking wet.

Chapter Twenty-Six

Wednesday, Evening

After dozing off sitting on the back steps of his house, Will woke with a start, stood, and went inside with Pete following close behind. He checked his cell phone, finding no missed calls from unknown numbers, or emails or texts from the man who took Annie. Her kidnapper had made no effort to get in touch with him, and by now, it was obvious that he never would. He wanted her, not money.

Outside, no media people milled about. In a way, their absence was a good thing, but at the same time, he saw it as a bad omen. Annie was moving to the back-burner. He retreated to a chair in the small den at the rear of his house, and Pete lay down at his feet, seemingly happy in his relegation to the kitchen. Mae had offered to come by after work and fix his supper, but he'd declined, citing exhaustion. The offer was typical of Mae. She was that sort of person, full of grace and caring, not to mention that she was beautiful.

Before he moved to Catalpa, almost all of the women he dated expressed concerns about the prospect of being married to a minister, and most of their comments lacked subtlety.

I'm not much on prayer meetings and Bible studies, Will.

Do they really still have those tacky, covered dish suppers?

I can't believe that you have to pack up and move to another town whenever the Bishop snaps his fingers.

What's it like being on call twenty-four hours a day?

What do preachers do for fun anyway?

And so forth.

But Mae was different. She never expressed any reservations about his profession vis-a-vis their relationship or anything else. She seemed to like what he did for a living. *Was it just her giving personality or really the way she felt?* He couldn't be sure. Regardless, it would be wrong to call her now and take advantage of her good nature, especially after his sullen behavior at lunch.

So, he had no one to talk with about Annie, and he was weary of discussing his problems with a dog. Her absence had taken on an appendage-like quality, like the other half of a conjoined twin, inseparable and attached at every waking moment.

Solitude was an age-old predicament for the clergy. People put them on pedestals, thinking that they were pure, Christ-like, holy, and wholly unlike the good old boy down the street. Parishioners tip-toed around them, rarely being open and honest, ever fearful of being judged and coming up short. No one seemed to know exactly how to relate to them, even in social settings. Usually, it was downright awkward.

As a result, ministers were some of the loneliest people around. They had few close friends aside from their spouses and others in the profession, and in many cases, no one with whom to share their own troubles. It was ironic, really; they were helpers who had nowhere to go for help unless one counted God.

Exhaustion took hold again, and he fell asleep. Almost an hour later, he woke with a start, disturbing Pete, who jumped up and began barking.

In the kitchen he made a sandwich but couldn't eat it. Pete was glad to get it. While the dog wolfed it down, he dropped his cell phone into his pocket and grabbed a leash from a peg in the laundry room. It was pink; Annie had picked it out. He leashed Pete and led him through the back door, locking it before heading to the sidewalk.

Without any real purpose in mind except getting away from the house and its crushing memories of Annie, he moved at a brisk pace along Atwater Street toward downtown. Some distance ahead, but within easy sight of his house, a dark, older model sedan was parked on the other side of the street, partially hidden under the shadow of a tall, draping elm tree. He'd never seen it in the neighborhood before, and he slowed as he neared it. He couldn't see much, so he crossed the street and came abreast of the car. In the murky interior, a man sat behind the wheel, obscured by tinted glass. *It could be one of Jack's people, or it could be…him!*

Emboldened with the big dog at his side, he knocked on the closed window. Pete growled as it rattled down an inch at a time, and a burly, pock-faced man with thinning hair came into full view. Taking a step back, Will said, "I don't think I've seen you in this neighborhood before. Can I help you?"

"I'm just selling Bibles. Want to buy one?"

As if to prove it, the driver reached over to the passenger seat, grabbed what was a brand-new Bible, and showed it to him.

When the man picked up the Bible, something else on the passenger seat caught Will's eye—a shiny, black handgun. Seeing it birthed a higher pitch in Will's voice than was usual. "I've got all the Bibles I can use right now. I'm a preacher."

"I know who you are. I know all about you."

He made a show of returning the Bible to the seat, but his hand stayed there, inches away from the gun.

Although Will wanted to take off running down Atwater Street, he couldn't let himself do that. This might be the man who took Annie. *What is he doing here?* He closed his hand over his cell phone in his pocket, wondering if he should go ahead and dial 911 right now.

"You don't want to do that, Reverend Rowan."

"What?"

"Call somebody."

He took his hand out of his pocket, leaving his cell phone behind. Shaking, his voice quavering, he asked, "Okay then, but who are you? Are you the man who took Annie?"

The man chuckled. "Hell, no. I'm a private detective. Your relatives hired me. Didn't they tell you?"

His face went blank. *Did my mother hire a detective? Did my brother?*

"Eileen and Phillip hired me. You know—the Cuttinos. They wanted me out here in case someone shows up with your daughter or without her. Whatever. I'm supposed to watch your house when you're inside and follow you if you leave."

"Well, I'm leaving right now."

"Where are you going?"

Will turned and dashed down the middle of the street with Pete leading the way. The very last thing he wanted to do was to give the Cuttinos the satisfaction of knowing his every move, and not only that, he didn't want their detective messing up the investigation of Annie's kidnapping. Behind him, he heard a car start up and leave the curb. He knew the man would have to make a U-turn before heading back up Atwater, so he left Atwater and cut through two backyards, ending up on Oglethorpe Street. From there, he and Pete raced up the sidewalk until they reached the courthouse square. He pulled the dog into the alcove forming the entrance of the Alhambra, an old movie theater on the west side of the square. Years before, it had been converted into a nightspot, and it usually buzzed with patrons coming in and out.

He flattened against the alcove wall, catching his breath, watching Oglethorpe Street as it joined the square, and hoping for a glimpse of Eileen's man as he drove by. In the meantime, he took his cell phone from his pocket and called Jack.

"Will? Why aren't you in bed? I am."

"Annie's grandparents have hired some detective. He's been parked on the street down from the house. He has a gun, and I'm afraid he'll do something to foul up what you're trying to do."

"Okay, thanks. They've been calling me all day long, too. I talked to them the first time, but since then, I've been avoiding them. I'll send an officer over there to check out the detective right now. Why don't you try to get some rest?"

He didn't follow Jack's advice. Instead, he stayed where he was, waiting. Numerous cars passed in front of the old theater but not the detective's sedan. Minutes went by, and he speculated that the man had gone the wrong way or gotten lost. Alhambra patrons came and went, most of them eyeing him and his dog. As he watched the street, he even heard a woman behind him say, "Look! It's Reverend Rowan. What's *he* doing at a bar?" He turned around to offer an explanation, but her group had already gone back inside.

He glanced at his watch. It was almost midnight. *Maybe I should head home.* But just as he inched toward the sidewalk, an old, white truck rumbled across the square, right in front of the theater. A man in a jacket with the collar turned up, wearing a baseball cap over dark hair, was behind the wheel. Shadows hid the man's face, but Will recognized the truck.

He was so shocked, he dropped the leash. At the same time, Pete put his nose to the sidewalk and shot down Oglethorpe in the opposite direction to that taken by the truck. He ran down the sidewalk after him, caught him, and turned back toward the square. By then, the truck was nowhere in sight.

Holding the leash in one hand, he grabbed his cell phone again and thumbed in Jack's number. When the lieutenant answered, Will yelled into his phone. "Jack! I just saw the truck on the courthouse square. It's on Oglethorpe, going south!"

"Blast it, Will! What are you doing? And what in the devil are you talking about?"

"Rankin Turner's truck! I just saw it going across the square!"

Chapter Twenty-Seven

Thursday, Wee Hours

Jack directed Will to "get home," assuring him that the police would be looking for Rankin's truck all over Catalpa and its environs within minutes. With some reluctance, he set off for his house. A block away, he noticed the detective's car parked on his street again. He ignored it as he passed by, pleased that the man inside had no idea where he'd been.

He hoped to stay up until he heard from Jack, and while he waited, he opened his email. Ninety-nine percent of the messages he read were expressions of concern for him and Annie, almost half saying, "please let us know what we can do." Some were encouraging, others close to fatalistic. They came from around the block, from Atlanta and other Georgia cities, and even all the way from Boston where a Yale classmate had read about the kidnapping on the internet. After reading twenty or so of these, he closed the app. The messages were too much like condolences.

Outside, a car door slammed. As Will headed to the front of the house to investigate, blue lights flashed across the windows. He opened the door and looked out. A policeman was talking to the Cuttinos' detective. This lasted for about a minute, and then the officer returned to his vehicle and drove off, but the detective's sedan didn't move.

Will went back inside. He was fading fast. In his bedroom, he put his phone on the night stand and flopped down on the bed fully clothed. He intended to relax for a few minutes, but soon he fell asleep, unaware that Pete had joined him.

At 5:45 a.m., the ping of an incoming text message woke him. Groggy, he sat up and stared at the dog stretched out beside him. The text was from Jack: *Meet me at Jordan's for breakfast—6:30.* He was anxious to know if the lieutenant had something to report, but his call back to him went to voicemail.

"Well, shit," he said and headed for the shower. Thirty minutes later, he was on the way to the courthouse square.

Jordan's was an institution in Catalpa. For over a hundred years, it had been owned and operated by the Jordan family in the same prominent location on the square. Its specialty was barbecued pork with sides of coleslaw and Brunswick stew.

He found Jack at a table near the back. Only one other customer was in the restaurant at this early hour. The policeman was looking at his phone. He put it down and smiled when Will joined him. "As far as we can tell, you're the only person in Catalpa who saw Rankin's truck last night. Are you sure it was his?"

"Yes."

"And how do you know?"

His challenging question threatened to set the tone for their entire meeting, and it annoyed Will. "Have you ever seen a *Perot-Stockdale '92* bumper sticker before? If you find his truck, you'll see one. What's going on? What do you have for me?"

"Nobody wants to find her more than I do, you know that."

"I do know that, but why did you want to see me this morning?" He hadn't noticed the waitress standing nearby with a pad and pencil. He asked for coffee, and Jack ordered bacon and eggs and biscuits.

"You don't want breakfast?"

He shook his head. "Not hungry. Why am I here?"

The waitress nodded and left before Jack answered.

"You're my friend, and I'm concerned about you. That's the main reason I wanted to see you. You probably aren't eating like you should, and I hoped to buy you some breakfast, so I could see you eat."

Jack was right. Lunch yesterday was the last time he'd eaten much of anything.

"Mae's been taking care of me. Now, what are we doing to get Annie back?"

"Practically every man in the police department is working on this. If Turner's still in town, we'll find him. If he's taken off, the FBI will find him. We've also reopened the investigation into the death of the janitor who worked at your church before Rankin came on board. We're wondering if Rankin may have had something to do with that, too."

"I never considered that he might be involved in what happened to the other janitor. If he would do that..." His voice trailed off.

Jack was quiet, but the pity in his eyes spoke volumes.

"Where is Rankin, Jack?"

"If that was his truck you saw last night, and if he was driving it, he may still be here somewhere. I have trouble believing that he's dumb enough to drive right through the middle of town, but desperate people do dumb things sometimes."

"What makes you call him 'desperate?' Is it because he's afraid of getting caught?"

"Now that Rankin's got her, maybe he doesn't know what to do with her. We found his house in Atlanta. The FBI sent an agent to check it out. There's a 'For Sale by Owner' sign out front, and it appears empty. The Atlanta P. D. has agreed to stake it out. We still don't know where he's renting here, but we'll find it."

At that point the waitress brought coffee and food to the table, and their conversation ended. Without asking,

Will took a buttered biscuit from Jack's plate. "The detective hired by the Cuttinos was still parked on my street when I left this morning. He's probably followed me up to the square."

"He has a business license and a carrying permit for his weapon. He was parked on a public street. He wasn't breaking any laws that we know of."

"If there's nothing else, Jack, I guess I'll go to the church."

Jack sighed. "One other thing. The FBI found out where Turner worked before he took the job at your church. After he graduated college, he was a fifth grade teacher at Angelou Elementary School in Atlanta. In the Georgia system, a teacher can retire after putting in thirty years, regardless of age. He retired last June at the age of fifty-three."

This news was more than Will could bear. He'd been taken in by a man who'd spent thirty years ogling young girls just like Annie. He abruptly pushed back his chair and stood. "Sorry, but I've got to get to the church," was what he said. *I've got to live with being duped by the man who took my child*, was what he thought.

As he headed to the door, he heard Jack say, "When you get there, say a prayer for me, too," but he left without acknowledging him.

Outside, the darkness was just beginning to recede. He got into his vehicle but didn't leave right away. Through the restaurant's windows, he saw Jack, drinking coffee and talking on his cell phone. His friend was doing his best, but it wasn't good enough.

He eyed the old theater on the corner. He was standing right there under the marquee the night before, five yards from the street, when the truck came by. He was sure it was Turner's, and for all he knew, Annie was in it, too, tied up on the floorboards. He pulled away from the restaurant and drove back and forth through town, thinking he might spot the truck again. He saw quite a few trucks but not the janitor's.

He had nowhere to go except the church, nothing to do but wait. If his hope for Annie's return hadn't reached its nadir, it was awfully close.

The sun was just spreading bright on the horizon when he pulled into the church parking lot. He planned to escape long before the media types arrived, so he wasn't concerned about hiding his SUV. Only one other vehicle was parked in the lot at this time of day. It was the small, church bus sticking far out of a parking space down to his left. Passing the bus on the way to his own space, something caught his eye. He glanced back that way, and what he saw almost caused him to wreck his Land Rover.

"Rankin's truck!" he shouted.

He braked his vehicle and jumped out. Dashing over to the truck, he threw open the passenger door. An empty water bottle, a sports magazine, a few candy wrappers, and a fast food container greeted him but nothing suggesting that Annie was once inside. The same could be said for the litter behind the seats. He leaned back out of the truck, lowered his head, and waited for the wild beating of his heart to subside.

But a moment later, something in the truck bed grabbed his attention and set his heart in raging motion again. A long-handled shovel with a muddy blade lay across a bag of cement, a bale of pine straw, and several pieces of lumber. And as he examined the bed further, the hint of a foul odor wafted up and magnified his angst. "Oh, Jesus," he whispered.

Now he had no doubt about what had happened last night. After driving here, Rankin had parked on the other side of the bus so that his truck wouldn't be visible from the street. His eyes shot toward the church buildings which harbored his last, vain hope that Annie might still be alive. *If Rankin is in there, let her be with him!*

He ran across the parking lot and up the walkway to the side door nearest his office. He punched in the security code, his heart still pounding. Slowly opening the door, he went inside and stood there, listening, hearing nothing but the whirring of the air conditioning system. He gazed up and down the empty hall, afraid to call out the janitor's name for fear he would grab her and take off through another door.

He pulled out his cell phone, called Jack, and got sent to voicemail. For a second, he considered calling 911 or the police department landline but hesitated. Endless questions about his identity and why he was calling would follow. By the time it was over, Turner would've heard him and run, taking Annie with him. Immediate action was required. He couldn't wait for the police.

He exited the building and applied the security code to another outer door. It led under the sanctuary to the filthy boiler room where the janitor often hung out. He wasn't there. Back outside, he bolted across the walkway and gained entry into the Sunday School addition. Inside, he leapt down the stairway to the bottom floor and dashed across the wide fellowship hall to the kitchen and the maintenance closet behind it, both occasional haunts of Rankin. But again, futility marked his search.

Next he rushed through the two upper floors of the addition, ending up in the hallway adjacent to his office again. Breathing hard, he paused there, panicked by the thought of the numerous other rooms, closets, and hiding places in the facility. Annie and Rankin could be anywhere, and if he didn't find them soon, it might be too late.

The original church was laid out in an inverted 'U' and now he stood in the hallway on the north side of the 'U.' The later addition, including both his office and Callie's, was behind him. He hurried down the hall into the older part of the church, stopping for fruitless searches of the baby nursery and the small chapel. Along the hall spanning the front of the old building, he glanced into the ladies' lounge and a utility room and after finding both empty, he ended up in the narthex.

The sanctuary occupied almost the entire south side of the 'U.' He saw little chance that the janitor would be hiding there, but he had to look. He pushed through the leather-covered, double doors on the right hand side of the narthex and headed into the sanctuary. A few yards down the right hand aisle, he slowed; one step after that, his legs gave way, and he grabbed the nearest pew for support. His eyes shot from the aisle to the ceiling and back again.

Then, he fell to his knees. "God help me! I can't believe it!"

Two feet above the aisle, midway between the narthex and the altar, Rankin Turner dangled from the end of a long rope.

Chapter Twenty-Eight

Thursday, Early Morning

The taut rope around Rankin's neck was tied to one of the massive rafters bracing the ceiling high above him. His face was white, contorted, and incongruously splashed with rainbow colors dappled by the morning sun through stained glass windows. Fighting an urge to vomit, Will stood and slowly inched down the aisle for a better view.

The janitor's face was swollen almost beyond recognition, and his tongue protruded at an unnatural angle. His khaki pants were stained below the crotch. Near the janitor's feet, he saw a turned over stool which he recognized as coming from the ladies' lounge.

Overwhelmed by the visual impact, he was reluctant to get much closer. For him, no tableau could ever be more horrifying than that of Leah lying in a pool of blood on the kitchen floor of their house in Atlanta. But this was a close second.

He turned his back on the disgusting scene and called Jack. This time he answered. "It's Rankin. He's here at the church—dead. He hanged himself."

"What? How about Annie? Is she…?"

"I don't know."

"Have you found her?"

"No." He looked around the sanctuary. "I need to. I'll start looking for her again right now."

"Wait! Don't do anything else until I get there. And don't touch Rankin."

He didn't respond.

"Did you hear me, Will?"

"I'm going now," he said, ending the call.

He returned to the side door adjacent to his office and propped it open for the police. Then he went back to the sanctuary and, careful to avoid Rankin, he looked through all the pews, and then the choir loft, and after that, the balcony. He even pulled down the ladder to the belfry and scrambled up there. He didn't find her.

He was still frantically rummaging around through closets and anterooms when Jack arrived. "Will, go to your office, sit behind your desk, and wait there until we're through. Does the church have any security cameras?"

"There's been talk of getting some, but no, we don't."

While Will was waiting in his office, Callie arrived. After hearing about Rankin, she burst into tears.

"But what about Annie?"

He just shook his head.

This brought more tears. He left his desk chair and gave her a handful of tissues from his credenza.

"Don't go down to the sanctuary, Callie, and when the others get here, keep them away, too. And I don't want to see anyone right now. Please tell them that."

She nodded and left his office, blotting her eyes and closing the door behind her.

He sat at his desk, staring through the windows. The import of Rankin's death had begun to sink in. He would never find Annie now. *God has forsaken me; He has no compassion for me; He has crumpled my soul and tossed it into the wind like so much Biblical chaff. I am Godless.* As he waited for Jack to return, he just sat and stared, numb and blank of mind except for the constant whine of three questions. *What has Rankin done to her? Where is she? How could I ever have let this happen?*

After an agonizing, interminable wait, Jack appeared at his office door. He was surprised when Mae came in, too. He hadn't even thought of calling her. *Why would Jack have asked her to join them unless he had terrible news?* He set his mouth, lowered his hands to his lap, and clasped them together. It was an act of pure resignation. They were here to tell him that Annie was dead.

Jack had brought some sort of cloth bag. He sat across from him and placed the bag on the floor. Mae came around his desk and stood beside him, her left hand on his shoulder. It all seemed rehearsed somehow.

"I asked Mae to come over. I wanted her here when we talked."

She leaned down and spoke softly. "I don't know any more than you do yet."

His eyes fell to his desk. *Here it comes.*

"Annie is not in the church. We've been through every inch of it twice, including the belfry and the crawl space over the sanctuary ceiling."

"So he didn't bring her here. She must be locked away somewhere. How can we find out where she is?"

Jack sighed. "I don't think she's locked away, Will."

"Well then, where is she?"

Jack ignored his question. He removed a pair of latex gloves from a coat pocket and put them on. "We've been through the truck and Rankin's pockets, and I want you to see some of what we found. I didn't bring the baseball cap from Walmart. It was in the truck, behind the driver's seat."

I know. I saw it there.

Jack reached into the cloth bag beside him and removed a small, plastic bag. He opened it and let the contents fall out onto the desk. It was a delicate, gold locket and chain. The chain was broken. "Please don't touch them, Will."

He moved his hands to his lap, fighting an urge to reach for the locket and chain. He leaned over and looked at them, having no doubt about their origin. One tear fell from his right eye, staining his desk. He sighed. "Annie started wearing it about a year ago and never took it off. It has Leah's picture inside. Where did you find it?"

"It was in the crease of the front seat on the passenger side of Rankin's old truck."

Will wiped his right eye with the back of his hand.

The policeman returned the locket and chain to its bag and reached into the cloth bag again. This time, he removed another much larger, plastic bag which appeared to contain a colorful object. He opened the bag, took out a tennis shoe, and placed it on the table.

Will reached for it, but Jack stopped him, and he pulled his hand back. "It's her shoe. She wore them all the time. She was wearing them Monday night. She loved them."

"I took her to get them," Mae said, wiping tears. "They're Van's. She wanted the ones with the printed pictures on them. She was so happy that day…"

Will interrupted her. "Jack, I looked through the truck. I didn't see her shoe. Where did you find it?"

"It was in the truck bed. Under the shovel."

Will lowered his head, shaking it slowly. "What else do you have in that bag?"

Sadness filled Jack's face. "Rankin left a note."

"A suicide note?" Will dreaded the answer, but he had to ask.

"I'm afraid it may be one. We'll be testing the original. I asked Callie to make a copy of it for you to look at." He pushed a piece of paper across the desk. It sat there waiting for Will to pick it up.

He glanced at the piece of paper and saw a handwritten combination of cursive and block printing, and then he quickly turned his head away. "I don't want to read it."

"Then I will," Mae said.

She reached over him, picked it up, and read it out loud. "I am so sorry for what I have done. It took hold of me. It would not let me loose. I deserve to go to hell. But she will rest in the arms of the Good Lord forever and ever."

Her hand trembling now, she put the note back on the desk in front of him.

He stared at it and then turned it face down. Mae tried to embrace him from behind, but he leaned away from her and put his head in his hands. "I did this to her. I let it happen, and I can't just leave her out there. I've got to bring her home. Can't you understand that?"

Jack stood and put his hand on his shoulder. Then he retrieved the items he'd brought with him and left his office.

Chapter Twenty-Nine

Thursday, Morning to Afternoon

It took all morning and a large part of the afternoon for the police team to remove Rankin's body from the church and complete their investigation of the premises. Will wondered out loud if they would need to get somebody in to clean up a mess in the sanctuary, but Jack said not. "We'll handle all that before we leave."

The search of Rankin's body and church haunts had revealed one oddity—his keys to the church couldn't be found. After Will explained that a person could enter with nothing but the security code, the missing church keys no longer seemed all that important.

Jack was in and out, but Mae remained in his office most of the morning. Neither of them mentioned the fact that Annie was likely dead. They skirted the issue by only expressing the hope that the police would find her. She offered to get lunch for him, but he declined, claiming a need to catch up on things. After staying with him for several more hours, she departed without having any lunch herself.

The news of Rankin's suicide by hanging and all of the circumstances surrounding it soon saturated the town. As word got out, people came to the church in droves, most wanting to pay their respects but some just to gape. Callie related that many of them were not even members of the church. The entire staff, save Will, was engaged in greeting visitors, answering questions, and explaining that he wasn't available.

With the kidnapper dead and his victim resting 'in the arms of the Good Lord,' nothing was left for the media to hype. When it became apparent that Will would give no interviews, the reporters and tall-pole television vans began to thin out. He speculated that media coverage would now focus on where Annie might be found with her death being implicit.

Earlier, Callie had moved his Land Rover from the parking lot to a residential area three blocks away. He stayed at the church until he couldn't stand it any longer and then left, avoiding media stragglers by sneaking out a back door and walking to his vehicle.

At home, he found his front yard deserted. Annie's story was no longer one of hope. Most people didn't want ugly things like kidnapped little girls brought to their attention over and over again. This was especially true of dead little girls. Tonight, Rankin's hanging would still be news, and law enforcement types like Jack would offer guarded opinions based on crime lab results and the like. The story would dwindle to nothing after that. When Annie was found, coverage would no doubt resume for a period, the length depending upon whether she was dead or alive. After that, she would be forgotten altogether until years later when filler was needed and the anniversary of her kidnapping was coming up. *Where Is She Now?* or *Ten Years Ago Today* would be the expected, depressing headlines.

The food parade began shortly after he got home, offering further proof that his only child had been written off after the suicide of her kidnapper. Within an hour, two chocolate cakes, a pan of lasagna, a baked ham, and a pea and asparagus casserole were delivered to his front door along with remarks like "you've got to take care of yourself, too, Reverend Rowan," and "we're all thinking about you," and "we love you, preacher." It wouldn't be long before some parishioner trotted out, "she's in a better place."

Hope fast turned into despair. *When might I expect the "so sorry about your loss" comments to start? How long will it take the populace to decide collectively that Annie must be dead? Would it be tomorrow, several days, a week, two weeks? How long can a child survive without food and water?*

Before long, the bell ringing became so frustrating that he sat down at his computer and prepared a sign in bold letters which announced: **Reverend Rowan deeply appreciates your concern, but he's not receiving visitors at this time. If you've been kind enough to bring food, please make arrangements to drop it off at the church. Thank you.**

After posting it on the front door, he heard more visitors, but an hour or so later, the caring onslaught ended. In the calm and quiet that followed, he considered everything that had happened since Monday night. He detailed it all on a legal pad, point by point, much the way that he prepared his sermons every week.

He began by outlining the case against Rankin. The church janitor's effort to take Annie began last summer. When grabbing her on the beach didn't work out, he determined to get closer. He killed the former church janitor and took his place. During the few days he worked at the church, he didn't see Annie, but he arranged for her presence at the fair with his gift of tickets. The risks associated with grabbing her there were many, similar to those he experienced on Tybee Island, but he wanted her badly enough to take them. The Walmart receipt put him at the fairgrounds at the same location where she disappeared. Even though Annie had probably never laid eyes on him before, somehow he convinced her to follow him into the alley. He took her away, keeping her only God knows where. On Tuesday night, he drugged her and made her the focus of a bizarre ritual of unknown significance but similar to something which occurred at the same location years earlier. While he transported her, perhaps more than once, she lost her locket and chain in the seat crease of his truck. At the end, he put her in the 'arms of the Lord,' and killed himself. Being in the arms of the Lord meant only one thing.

Next, Will indicted himself. He failed to call the police after the incident on Tybee; he hired a college graduate and elementary school teacher to a janitorial position without really checking him out; he was duped by Rankin's free fair passes; he took his eyes off Annie at the fair; he instilled in her the idea that kindness and civility were good things; and he neglected to grasp the significance of the janitor's absence from work. *Forgive me, Annie! I put you into the man's truck as surely as if I, myself, opened the door and shoved you inside.*

Finished, Will thought of taking down the three bottles of Scotch from the high cabinet and getting stinking drunk. Before the week was out, that seemed like a strong possibility. *These three things I know: short of a miracle, Annie is dead or has been left to die; either way, I will never see her alive again; and the evidence of my own culpability is damning.*

While he engaged in this virtual self-flagellation, a New Testament passage from Matthew came to mind. It was the one where Jesus tells Peter that he should forgive his transgressors seventy times seven. Will understood why Jesus had said that to Peter, but he could no longer bring himself to live by it. He would not struggle with the concept of forgiveness anymore. He would never forgive Rankin for what he'd done to Annie, not seven times, not seventy times seven, not ever. Nor would he ever forgive himself either.

He thought of his father's pistol, the one his mother gave him. Now, he had no use for it. Mr. Tolley's question about preachers and killing would go unanswered. The man he needed to kill was already dead.

He felt a wet nose on his knee and got up to fill Pete's bowl and change his water. Someone knocking on his front door interrupted him. He headed in that direction still holding the bowl with the dog barking at his heels.

The sidelight revealed a man standing on the stoop. He opened the door and found the private detective hired by Phillip and Eileen Cuttino. He smiled at Will and said, "Remember me?"

He glared at him, saying nothing.

"This is for you, Reverend." He shoved a large envelope in Will's direction. He did the natural thing and took it. He didn't have to ask what was in the envelope; he'd expected its arrival ever since the news got out about Rankin's suicide note.

"Good luck," he said, turning and walking away.

After watching the Cuttinos' flunky saunter down the street to his car, he returned to the kitchen, placing Pete's bowl on the floor. At the table, he opened the envelope and pulled out a document with the heading, 'Complaint for Damages.' A red stamp on the first page indicated that it had been filed just hours earlier in the Superior Court of Tanotchee County. The Cuttinos had sued him so many times over Annie's custody that he knew right away where to find the bottom line of their lawsuit. It would be on the last page or so. He flipped through the complaint until he reached the end and read what their attorney had written there.

Wherefore, Plaintiffs Phillip and Eileen Cuttino demand:

(a) As to Count One, that this Court enter a judgment finding that the gross inattention and negligence of Defendant William Fournier Rowan caused the wrongful death of Plaintiffs' only grandchild, Leah Anne Rowan; and that for such willful and negligent acts, this Court should further enter judgment awarding Plaintiffs a sum to be determined by the jury equivalent to the full value of the life of their said grandchild; and

(b) As to Count Two, that Plaintiffs be awarded their reasonable attorney's fees and all costs of litigation herein; and

(c) That Plaintiffs have such other and further relief as to this Court may seem just and proper.

He threw the complaint across the kitchen. It fluttered up and came down to rest in the dog's bowl. Pete stopped eating, sniffed the complaint, and turned and looked at Will with questioning eyes.

Chapter Thirty

Thursday, Afternoon

After Will calmed down, he called the office of Sam Franklin, an attorney who belonged to his church. He arranged to drop off the Cuttinos' complaint and visit with Franklin the next day. The lawsuit didn't trouble him, but it demanded the filing of defensive pleadings, a routine with which he was well-acquainted thanks to his former in-laws.

As the afternoon dragged on, he obsessed over the idea that with the death of Rankin and the likely death of Annie, too, efforts to find her would lose their urgency. He wanted reassurance that the search for her, or her body, was still of utmost importance, a major undertaking involving multiple law enforcement agencies, civilian volunteers, and media sources, and continuing as long as it took to find her.

He called Jack, but his call went to voicemail. Instead of leaving a message, he tried again, twice. A voice he didn't recognize at first answered his third call. "Jack, is that you? Let's talk about what's being done to find Annie."

A long pause followed. "I'm right here."

"At your office?"

"No, no. I'm at my house. After what happened today, I came on home. I guess I needed…"

Something wasn't right. "Is Maggie there? Why don't you hand the phone to her for a second? I have a question for her."

"No, she's not here. She took the boys to a Cub Scout meeting."

"Have you been drinking, Jack?"

"Yeah, but I'm mainly just tired."

"Why don't you hang up and go make some coffee. Call me back when you feel like talking about the search for Annie."

The policeman paused again. "You woke me up, but I want to talk now. I want to get it over with."

"What do you mean by that?"

"We're friends, Will. You've been a very good friend to me."

"And you, to me, Jack."

"I could tell you that there's a chance she's still alive, locked in a room somewhere, or tethered to a tree, or buried in a fiberglass box like Barbara Jane Mackle, drawing air down through a tube."

"Then why don't you?"

"Because I don't believe any of it, and I suspect you don't either. No child who isn't dead would 'rest in the arms of the Lord.' Days, weeks, or years from now, some dog, or hunter, or boys romping in the woods may find her, but she won't be alive."

Jack had never sounded like this before, and Will considered getting off the phone. But instead, he was determined to stick it out, regardless of how painful it might be. He wanted to hear the truth, and Jack might need this conversation just as much as he did. "We still have to look for her, don't we? Can't the FBI help you out?"

"Help me? Hell, no. Todd Baxter and his boys blew in from Atlanta this morning, but they left again before lunchtime. They had nothing else to do. The perpetrator hanged himself from a rafter forty feet up and left a note saying that his child victim had gone to her heavenly reward. They offered help with follow-up 'if needed.' Otherwise, it was hello and goodbye, FBI."

"So what happens now? Who will help with the search if the FBI won't?"

He couldn't be sure, but he thought he heard a sardonic chuckle.

"What search? I doubt if the chief will even authorize much of anything. Oh, there'll be an investigation all right. Rankin's body was sent to the state crime lab for an autopsy. A handwriting expert will examine the suicide note, comparing it to any available, known samples of Turner's handwriting. The forensic team will comb through the church, Rankin's truck, the clothes he was wearing, and his home in Atlanta and the one in Catalpa if we can find it. We'll canvass neighbors, family, and friends of Rankin. In due time, his work records, school records, and the like will be obtained and studied. The file will be left open until all of this has been completed. In the end though, not one bit of it will make a scintilla of difference. We all know what happened already. Rankin Turner took Annie Rowan. Now he's dead, and she's probably gone, too."

All of this rendered Will speechless. He wanted to say something else, but he was torn between feeling bad for Jack and being mad at him. He kept quiet, and Jack spoke again, filling the void.

"Annie was like part of our family. Maggie and I loved her. Losing her has brought me to the brink. Up until now, my work has been a source of pride for me and my family. I'm just thirteen years out of college, and I've already made the second highest position in the Catalpa Police Department. I've gotten there in spite of my race, and people tell me I'm respected within and without the law enforcement community. Black folks look up to me. But as of this morning, all that has changed. I tanked completely when it came to the handling of the most important case of my career, all because I didn't focus on Rankin Turner from the start. So much evidence just sat there, but I missed it all. I need to quit."

Will wanted to say that he intended to quit, too, but he didn't. Instead, the preacher came out in him. He consoled Jack, telling him that nothing was his fault, praising him, encouraging him to stay in the job, reminding him that Catalpa needed him. Ironically, it was the same sort of thing that Mae had said to him the day before at lunch. Then it was time to let Jack rest. He urged him to go back to bed and suggested that they talk again in the morning.

When the call ended though, he was more determined than ever to find Annie even if he had to do it alone.

Chapter Thirty-One

Thursday, Mid-Afternoon

The man who took Annie wasn't Rankin Turner, and he was far from dead. The night before, Iblis had handled the morbid business of hanging Rankin at the church and had jogged back to Methvin Avenue without a hitch. After that, he'd gotten a well-deserved, good night's sleep in the downstairs bedroom at Doris' old house.

On Thursday morning, he'd greeted Annie with a smile, let her freshen up, and taken her to the kitchen for breakfast. There, he served her poached eggs, fruit, and buttered toast. The eggs had been a little runny, but she didn't seem to mind. When she'd apologized again for her petulant behavior of the night before, he'd patted her on the back, assured her that it wasn't a problem at all, and returned her to the closet.

After that, he'd left the house and devoted all of the time to his job that was expected of him. Now, he was heading back to Methvin Avenue with her supper. She'd been by herself for most of the day, and she would be lonely, hungry, and compliant.

These were days of 'firsts' for him. Hosting a young girl for the very first time, he wondered what he should say to her, what books would interest her, and what she would prefer to eat. It was all guesswork, and he'd spent weeks guessing his way through stacks of *Girl's Life* magazine and a clothing section on eBay called, 'Vintage Pre-Teen Girl.'

Before this afternoon, he'd never been inside a pizza parlor either. Somehow though, he conquered the 'toppings' conundrum, so pizza and a large soft drink were on the dinner menu tonight. He had tomorrow's breakfast all planned out as well. But by the time he pulled into the driveway at Doris' house, he was on the verge of gagging from the unpleasant odors of pizza and the sacked breakfast food. Inside, he refrigerated the breakfast food and set the kitchen table with flatware and a linen napkin, as well as a handful of colorful, gerbera daisies, cut and arranged in a small vase.

After taking a moment to admire his handwork, he went to the closet under the stairs, and for some reason, perhaps as a matter of courtesy, he knocked before he entered. Annie was overjoyed to see him. After escorting her to the bathroom, he led her to the kitchen. She loved the pizza and the Coke and the big cookie that came with it, and she kept saying, "Thank you, Mr. Iblis."

When she finished, he offered to let her take a nap on a bed upstairs, and she jumped at the chance. He took her to Desdemona's room and watched her doze off from a chair nearby. *She could be her*, he thought, and then, *she is*.

As a boy, he'd spent hours in this room, often at this same time of day, when Doris' add-on lessons were over at last, and he and Desdemona were left to their own devices until supper. And now, the sleeping child on the bed and the warm, afternoon sun streaming through the blinds kindled memories which had once stoked a lifetime of guilt and regret but, praise to the gods, no longer did so, not since the wee hours of the day before.

On many an afternoon, Rankin Turner had been in this bedroom, too. Intelligent, naïve, and trusting to a fault, that was his childhood friend. Along with decades of remorse over the death of Desdemona, Rankin was gone now, too. In the life of Iblis, some things gave him no choice, and the fate of his boyhood friend was one of them. Sitting there while Annie slept, he carefully reviewed his activities over the last forty-eight hours or so and still had no qualms about what he'd done. It had all started quite early on Tuesday morning, just two days earlier.

***

When the doorbell rang, Iblis was in the dining room of the old house. The sound of the bell was unusual. After acquiring title to all of Doris' property fifteen months before, he'd seldom been here, and even then, visitors were rare. Its ringing was especially disturbing today as he feared that the police, having just visited only hours before, might be returning.

He stepped from the dining room into the dark hall and studied the front door. In the bright, morning light on the porch, he made out a thin, familiar-looking man. At the same time, he was confident that the visitor couldn't see him because of the sheer curtain which covered the glass pane set into the entire, top half of the door. He stood very still and whispered, "Who are you?"

Stepping toward the door, he tried for a better look. Meanwhile, the slight man turned around to face the street where an old, white truck hugged the curb. Curious now, he opened the door, and the visitor turned around.

The dark-haired man smiled at him and said, "Chalker?"

Iblis froze. No one had called him Chalker since the day after his eleventh birthday, the same day his adoption was final and his name was changed forever. Suddenly woozy, he placed his right hand on the marble-topped chest next to the door for support.

The man kept smiling. "Chalker? It's me, Rankin Turner."

Rankin! He hadn't given him a second's thought for close to forty years, never once wondering where he was or what he was doing. Nor had he cared. Now he was so taken aback and upset by the presence of his visitor that a denial seemed appropriate. "You must have me confused with someone else, Mr. Turner."

"Oh, no, you're Chalker Paine."

Why deny it? It *was* the name given him at birth. He *was* Doris Paine's son, Chalker, the twin of Desdemona. The name's depressing origin filled his head as his visitor sent another insipid smile his way. He envisioned Doris laughing and saying she'd wanted to name him Iblis because it meant 'the devil' in Arabic. It would be a constant reminder that he was "the seed of the most evil father of all time," she said. Instead, taking the advice of a hospital orderly who was mopping her room right after his birth, she named him Chalker, claiming it had a nice, patrician sound to it. After his adoption, he hoped he would never hear the name again. He despised it.

"Well, Rankin, of course I am Chalker."

"You didn't get a new name when you were adopted?"

"I did, but what the heck? You know me as Chalker. Come on in.'"

Seconds later, his old friend took a seat on the settee in the parlor where the twins once sat during their mother's afternoon lessons. "I couldn't believe it when I saw you in line at the chicken place, Chalker. I'd just pulled in there myself—I'm hungry—haven't had anything to eat since some time yesterday—and I saw you up ahead. I blew my horn, but you didn't notice. You pulled away before I could get my food, and I watched you drive off, all the time wondering what in the world you were doing in Catalpa. After you left, I took out my phone and tried to call you. You may not believe it, but I still remember Doris' number—your old number. But when I called it, I got some woman who didn't know me from Adam's house cat."

"I had the landline disconnected last year. The line was still hooked up because Doris' will directed that her house and everything in it be maintained just as it was on the day she died. She required the trustee to keep paying the taxes, insurance, utilities, and the like until it was time to transfer it to me."

"I know she had lots of money. How much did you get?'

He shrugged. "I've already spent every bit of it." Although this was far from true, it seemed to satisfy his visitor.

"Anyway, after I finished my breakfast, I came on over to the house on the chance you might be here. And who should come to the door, but you! It's great that you're back in town, too!"

He nodded politely, but his thoughts were the opposite. *What in the hell can I do about this awful development? Annie's just a few doors down the hall, and Rankin shows up. For starters, he knows all about my boyhood and now, all about my return to Doris' house. He can ruin everything because I know he remembers what happened, just like I do. My plans, tonight, my one opportunity...*

"I'm not really what one might call, 'back,' Rankin. My mother left me the house in her will. Her instructions were that her entire estate be held in trust until I was fifty years old. It went on so long that the original trustee died and was replaced. I just got around to taking possession of everything last year, and I may end up selling the house. I haven't decided yet."

Turner leaned forward and spoke in a whisper as if Doris was still around, lurking behind one of the velvet drapes. "Knowing your mother like I did, and I knew her very well indeed if you know what I mean, I'm not surprised that her will was kind of strange. No offense, you understand."

"She was rather eccentric, wasn't she?"

An awkward silence followed while Iblis still wondered what to do about him.

Rankin stood and moved close to him, still speaking in a conspiratorial tone. "Chalker, this was the only room in Doris' house that I was not allowed to enter. She made me stand at the door because of 'too many nice things in the room.' I was allowed in her bedroom more than once but never in here."

"I'm sorry, but I don't recall any of that." In truth, he recalled every bit of it. Doris always looked down on the Turners, referring to them as 'trash of the Caucasian variety.' He remembered the bedroom incidents, too. His friend was older than the twins, and with Iblis' mother anything was possible. For all practical purposes, she was an oversexed prude.

Rankin smiled and stepped even closer. "So where have you been all this time?"

"Here and there."

"You have a successful look about you. What do you do for work?"

He caught a whiff of alcohol on Rankin's breath, and it sparked an idea. "I've had a career in which I've found great and lasting satisfaction."

His response seemed to puzzle his former buddy. "A career? So what are you? Some kind of big time lawyer? A doctor?"

He made a show of looking at his watch, pretending not to hear the question. "I'll tell you what—when I first returned to Catalpa, I brought two bottles of Blanton's bourbon with me. I envisioned sitting on the front porch in the evenings, having a drink or two, waving to my neighbors as they walked to and fro on the sidewalk."

This might have been true when he first returned to Catalpa. But his plans had changed altogether in June of the previous year when a photo of Reverend Will Rowan, the new pastor of the Catalpa Methodist Church, and his little daughter, Annie, appeared on the front page of the *Catalpa Times*. He'd seen it on a rack at a convenience store after buying gas. He'd just returned to Doris' house for the first time in over forty years, and the photo of Rowan and his daughter had shaken him, leaving him melancholic and consumed with a double dose of raw guilt for weeks.

"Twilight sitting and sipping sounds like a good idea," Turner said.

"Yes, it does. But I've been so busy since then with one thing and another that I haven't even opened the first bottle. You know what they say, Rankin—it's twilight somewhere. Why don't we go back to the kitchen right now and try some of that Blanton's? I don't want it to go to waste, do you?"

Rankin didn't hesitate. He accepted a seat at the kitchen table while his host found two glasses, opened a bottle of the bourbon, and poured a double portion for each of them. While they sipped the fine liquor, Iblis aka Chalker got him to talk about himself, hoping that something he revealed would help solve the serious problem he now represented. *How could he have just shown up, like a lump of dog feces on the sole of a Berluti loafer?*

"After they took me away from my dad and mom, Chalker, my foster parents helped me get a scholarship, and I got a degree in elementary education. I studied for a teaching certificate and took a job at a school up in Atlanta. After doing that for thirty years, I'd had enough. In Georgia, thirty lets you draw retirement, so I quit back in the summer. How about you?"

"About me? Oh, I was awarded an academic scholarship, the full load, room, board, books, everything. I probably wouldn't have been able to go otherwise. A part-time job at a clothing store at a mall helped out with spending money."

Rankin nodded. "I guess we were both lucky to get new parents back then, even if they didn't have a whole lot."

Bored beyond words, Iblis felt obliged to nudge his friend along with questions. "And what about your mom and dad, Rankin? What happened to them?"

"They never stopped drinking. Some years back, my mother lost our old house down on the corner to the bank. Before that, she asked me for money, but I refused. Daddy had taken off by then. He's dead, and she's got nothing but Social Security. I think she ended up moving in with her sister down in Valdosta.

"With my parents gone, I thought it might be a good idea to live in Catalpa again, but I wasn't sure, so I'm starting by renting a place over in one of those new developments. If I like it here, I may stick around. I haven't even sold my place in Atlanta yet. I never married. Did you?"

"No."

Rankin had been one of his few boyhood friends. He lived nearby in a red brick structure which still stood at the northwest corner of Methvin and Oglethorpe, but he was always hanging around the Paine house. Doris treated him like dirt. Now, he rattled on and on about his background, unaware that his one-person audience was stultified by such anecdotes as his torrid affair with a "good-looking, school secretary."

Iblis felt an urgent need to bring his chatty visitor back to the present. "So what are you up to now?"

"You may think it's crazy, but just a week or so ago, I took a position with the Catalpa First Methodist Church. I don't need the money. My school retirement is more than enough to keep me going. I just wanted some kind of mindless job to fill my days, and the church is a super place to work. The preacher, Reverend Rowan, is a nice guy. They tell me his wife passed on, and he has a little daughter named Annie. I have yet to meet her. I'm the director of maintenance there."

Iblis was so bowled over by this revelation that he almost fell out of his chair. *Is it possible? Is he really the janitor at Will Rowan's church?* What a stroke of luck! It was a gift, a gift from the gods or from *the* God, take your pick. It was a development that would tie up all the potential pitfalls that had pestered him over the last few months like floaters in an eyeball.

As Turner expounded on the intricacies of floor waxing machines and the problem of dust mites in old buildings, he formulated a plan. Satisfied, he filled his friend's glass twice more, smiling and nodding all the while at everything he said. Now he saw his old friend in a marvelous, new light, the proverbial one at the end of the tunnel.

He patted his visitor on the back. "I don't want you to enjoy my bourbon too much. Are you okay to go to work?"

"They'll never know the difference. Hell, when I taught school, I always had a buzz on. How else could I have stood it?" He reached into his pants pockets and took a packet of mints. "I never go anywhere without these."

"Good idea, Rankin." He turned around, opened a drawer under the counter behind him, and took out a blank pad and a pen.

"It just struck me that I don't know how to get in touch with you. You said that you live here in Catalpa, but I don't know where. If you don't mind, write down your name, your address, and your phone number on this pad. While you're at it, why don't you also include the name and address of the church and the church's phone number? I may want to contact you during work to go to lunch or to get together afterwards. Go ahead and jot down the names of the preacher and his daughter, too. I'm anxious to meet them."

His old friend took the pad and pen. "You could come by, and I could introduce you. I'll write down the door code for you, so you won't have to wait for the church secretary to buzz you in."

"Wonderful." Iblis watched him begin writing.

Turner paused and put down the pen. He reached into his back pocket and took out a worn, leather wallet. "I almost forgot. I've got something to show you. I've been carrying it around all these years."

He took a plastic sleeve from his wallet and placed it on the table. It appeared to protect a slender photo, possibly clipped from a larger picture. Iblis removed the photo from the sleeve and studied it. It was a picture of Desdemona in a two-piece bathing suit. He glanced at Rankin and said, "This was in a drawer in Doris' room with a stack of other pictures. I think I was in the picture with her. Where did you get it?"

"I removed it one afternoon when Doris was busy painting her toenails. I didn't want you in it, so I clipped you out. I sort of had a crush on Dessie back then, but you knew that. I could've tried something, and I probably would have, if everything hadn't happened like it did. She was young, but not all *that* young. Was she?"

The idea of Rankin touching Desdemona at all was appalling. It so irritated him that he felt like taking his head off right then and there. At the very least, as soon as the opportunity presented itself, he would rip the photo out of Rankin's wallet and tear it into little pieces. He had defiled it, and it needed to be destroyed. But that would have to wait. Right now, patience was required, and if nothing else, he was a patient man.

"Come to think of it, I have something I want to show you, too. While you're putting down that information for me, I'm going out to the barn to get it. I saw it there the other day, and I actually thought of you. I think it'll bring back old memories from the time we were boys."

"I'd like that, Chalker."

He went down the back steps, across the asphalt parking area, and into the old barn. He retrieved what he wanted, adjusted it for his purposes, and came back into the house. In the kitchen, he took up a position behind the janitor's chair.

His visitor was just finishing up his writing effort. When he spoke, his words were slurred. "What's that big coil of rope for? It looks like a hangman's noose."

He looked at his drunken friend and chuckled. "You don't remember what we did with this? Turn back around, and I'll show you. You'll get quite a laugh out of it."

"What are you talking about?" Rankin said, as he began to turn his head around. Those were his last words.

***

As Iblis sat in Desdemona's bedroom now, watching Annie sleep, thinking about his old friend's final hours, a word came to mind, one used over and over again by detectives and criminals alike in his favorite, old, films *noir* from the 1940s and 1950s. The word fit Rankin to a tee. He was the all-time, quintessential 'patsy.'

Chapter Thirty-Two

Thursday, Late Afternoon

Annie stirred on Desdemona's bed, sighed, and then sat up. Although the window blinds were partially closed, the fading, western light obscured Iblis' face. He watched her look around the room before her eyes fixed on him. "Daddy?"

"No. It's just me."

Seeming to accept that, she put her head back on the pillow, and soon she was breathing deeply again. While she slept, he left the room and went into the upstairs hall. An antique chair with a caned seat sat in a corner at the end of the hall. Doris had been very protective of it, claiming it once belonged to her great-great-grandfather. Time and again, she warned the twins to stay away from it or suffer a severe penalty. "It won't support you," they were told. He couldn't recall ever touching it, afraid that it would fall apart if he did. Now, he took great pleasure in sitting on it for the first time, plopping up and down for good measure. Nothing happened, not a snap, a crackle, or a pop.

From the forbidden chair, he leaned toward the window beside it and inched back the sheer curtains that hung there. He glanced up and down Methvin Avenue but saw no activity. He leaned closer to the window and pressed his face against it, looking down the street to his left. Nothing was going on at the intersection of Methvin and Oglethorpe either. No police cars, no FBI agents, no uniformed cops, nada. He smiled. They had no inkling of his identity. Nothing derived from the truck driver was revelatory to any significant extent. If it had been, the police would have returned. He chided himself for worrying about it in the first place.

The stars were aligned in his favor. His chance encounter with Rankin had changed things altogether, and now Annie was free from the confines of her prior life. Her 'kidnapper,' Rankin, was dead, a pitiable 'suicide,' and based on his note, she was 'dead,' too. From the people he'd heard conversing here and there earlier in the day, to the radio announcers he'd heard in his car, to the reporters he'd seen on the TV sets high up on the walls of the pizza parlor, everyone assumed it was the evil janitor who'd taken the poor, little girl. Yes, everything the media reported was taken as absolute truth, and he was in the clear. The irony of Rankin making all of this possible was not lost on him. Of course, killing him offered no pleasure; it was just a matter of necessity.

Looking back, it was astounding to think how everything had fallen into place. On Tuesday morning, his old friend was kind enough to provide excellent examples of his handwriting, and Iblis spent over two hours copying his modified-cursive, writing style. After he practiced to the point of near perfection, he wrote the suicide note. He used a ball point pen and a piece of paper from an old notepad, both of which he found in the glove compartment of the janitor's truck. Rankin's style was a scrivener's dream to copy, and even the most sophisticated of handwriting experts would deem the note his own.

Planting Rankin's Walmart receipt at the deserted fairgrounds in the early afternoon on Tuesday, and putting the hat, the locket and chain, the shoe, and the muddy shovel in his truck were all nice touches, too.

Hanging him from the church rafter was somewhat difficult. He'd thrown the rope over the high rafter by using a weight at the end of a piece of fishing line he'd found in the barn at Doris' house. The other end of the line was attached to the rope, and it was just a matter of pulling the rope over the arch and knotting it. He left the line and weight behind for the police to discover. But his poor friend, scrawny thing that he was in life, proved very heavy in death. By the time he finished, the hour was late. He was tired and his back ached from all the heavy lifting.

But notwithstanding his physical discomfort, he was pleased. He'd created a mountain of evidence against Rankin, what prosecutors would surely call a 'lock.' It was a given that the police would find that the evil janitor took Annie, killed her, and disposed of her body at some unknown location. Under the circumstances, the search for a living girl would cease, and no stressful law enforcement investigation into the identity of her kidnapper would take place. Soon enough, even her father would give up trying to find her remains.

In all of this though, one, nagging enigma lingered. *How could all of the coincidences related to his present endeavor be explained?* The list was disturbingly long, and just thinking of it over the last few days had brought a mild sense of uncertainty. He considered it now, asking how it could be:

That Annie, the only child of Will and Leah Rowan, should grow and develop to look just like his beloved Desdemona; that one year earlier, he himself should return to Catalpa for the first time in more than forty years because of Doris' bequest; that near the same time, Rowan should be assigned to fill the pastorate at the Catalpa Methodist Church; that near the same time, he should see a Catalpa newspaper photo of Rowan and Annie at a convenience store where he'd stopped for gas; that a week or so before he took Annie, his childhood friend, Rankin Turner, should become the janitor at Will's church; and that on the morning after he took Annie, both he and Turner should end up in the same drive-thru line at a Catalpa fast food restaurant, where Turner recognized him.

He wasn't usually one to question how or why, but so many coincidences begged pause for reflection. But just as he had before now, he let it go. If something else was at work here, something beyond his understanding, then so be it. Lady Luck had favored him thus far, and he had no reason to doubt that she would continue to do so.

When he'd told Desdemona's surrogate on Monday night that all he wanted to do was to save her, it was the absolute truth. After Doris died, the idea of a reenactment with a substitute became a lifelong obsession, the *raison d'être* for taking Annie in the first place. Although he'd never envisioned doing anything else with her, an opportunity for something more was on the table now— having her stay on. It was clearly feasible because no unruly complications or messy baggage would accompany his association with a young girl already dead to the world.

Her soft voice interrupted his thoughts. This time she was calling for him. He returned to the bedroom where she sat on the edge of the bed rubbing the sleep from her eyes. He sat beside her, doubting he'd ever seen anything more beautiful. "Annie, I have something to discuss with you. I told you to call me Iblis, but I never said it was my real name. The truth is that it was almost my name, but my adoptive parents gave me another one. So, you see, I didn't lie to you about it."

"You were adopted?"

"Yes, my mother died when I was a child just like your mother. Children are frequently brought up by men or women who are not their natural parents. You don't see anything wrong with that, do you?"

She studied him for a moment. "Not if there's no other way."

"In my case, it was a very good thing indeed. I turned out all right, didn't I?"

She nodded and lowered her head. "If Iblis isn't your real name, then what is it?"

"My mother gave me the name of Chalker when I was born, but I didn't like it, so, I was glad when my new parents changed it."

"So what did they call you?"

"It really doesn't matter, because as long as we're here in this house, I would prefer for you to continue calling me Iblis."

This last remark seemed to trouble her. "Where else would we be besides here in this house?"

He ignored her question. "It's time to go back," he said, taking her arm and leading her out of the bedroom.

"Please, I may die if you put me back in that little room. It's so lonely. Please don't."

Offering no response, he guided her down the stairs. When they reached the bottom, she balked, trying to pull away from him. "What am I supposed to do in there? I'm not sleepy. Do you really want me to sit for hours, doing nothing?"

He gave her a blank look. Her boredom was something he'd never even considered.

"I saw an old television in that parlor on the left," she said, pointing. "If it works, I could sit up there and watch it. I promise I won't do anything. Please."

"I'm sorry, but it doesn't work. I have another idea."

He took her to the closet, and strapped her down, surprised when she offered no resistance. Minutes later, he returned with a large, thick, leather book. He handed it to her. The title of the book, 'Pictures of Paine,' was stenciled in white letters on a yellow sheet set in a clear, plastic sleeve on the front cover. "Is it too heavy on your lap, Annie?"

Her eyes, questioning, went from the book to him. "I guess not, but what am I supposed to do with it?"

"It's a photo album. I've been enjoying it no end while waiting for you to join me. I want you to peruse it, too. It will help you to understand what comes next."

"Why don't you just go ahead and say what you plan to do with me?"

"That's something you should try to discover on your own. As you look at the photos, your future will open to you like two lovely blooms of a Camellia japonica, one pink and one white, both opening on the same bush."

She looked down at the book in her lap. A tear fell from her right eye, streamed down across her cheek, and onto the cover of the book.

Her tears upset him, but he didn't say so. "I'll be gone for a while, Annie, but I'll be back. Do you need anything else before I go?"

She shook her head and looked away.

He felt badly leaving her alone like this, but he'd been away from his own residence for several days, and such mundane tasks as opening his mail, paying his bills, and watering his house plants needed his attention. Life had to go on regardless of his little project on Methvin Avenue. Even so, things were going so well that he soon just might leave all of that banality behind and travel the world. Of course, obtaining a valid passport for his ward might be somewhat difficult, but money in the right place was bound to work wonders.

Chapter Thirty-Three

Thursday, Night

Except for its more modern annexes, Will's church was almost a hundred years old, and late at night after the building was deserted, it made odd, disconcerting sounds, including tapping, knocking, creaking, and even incredible, whispering sighs. The eeriness made him reluctant to return there alone after hours. He never discussed this phenomenon with anyone else because a structure which generated a feeling of unease didn't seem an appropriate venue for God.

On Thursday night though, he returned to the church out of necessity. He needed the private email address of Bishop Watson, and he couldn't find it at home. After he was served with Eileen's wholly frivolous lawsuit, he made a decision. Because of what had happened to Annie, he could no longer continue in the ministry; his faith was at too low an ebb.

As he entered the building, he wondered if Rankin's death would somehow increase the spectral sounds in the vacant church. He avoided even looking down the hall toward that older part of the facility and went straight to his office. Ignoring the blinking phone and all of the messages Callie had stacked on his desk, he went right to the drawer where he kept the notebook he wanted. Thumbing through it, he found the bishop's email address and put it into his cell phone's address book. At that moment, he heard a creaking sound much like someone walking on the old floors in the upper hall, so he cut off his office lights and hurried out. As he left the building, he decided that Rankin couldn't be the source of the noises. If hell existed, the janitor was already assigned to it.

On the way home, he reflected on his decision to resign. His plan was to go down to his mother's beach house on Tybee Island and think about his future, if, in fact, he had one. Things had developed in an odd way. What Eileen said in her suit had crystalized what he'd thought ever since Jack found Rankin's suicide note: Annie was gone, and he would never see her again. Even if she was still alive, she could be anywhere; and if she was not alive, her body might lie hidden forever. Jack was right about the futility of searching for her. Sitting around day after day, waiting to find out what had happened to her or her body would destroy him, just like dealing with Leah's fate almost had.

He didn't see a single Catalpa policeman as he drove across the courthouse square and headed to Atwater Street. He saw a lot of people out and about, but no police presence. It was obvious that they weren't looking for Annie, much like they weren't looking for her or Rankin the night before. They'd all treated the whole thing as a lost cause from the get-go.

As he was parking his vehicle at home, his cell phone chirped. He unlocked it and found a text message from Mae. *Will, I want to be with you tonight. Come stay with me.*

He paused before replying. *I'm not so sure that's a good idea.*

Yes, it is.

He hesitated again, looking for an out. *What am I supposed to do with Pete?*

Bring him with you. I love you.

He sighed. *Okay.*

Minutes later with Pete huffing and whining on the back seat, he arrived at Mae's condominium, wondering if he should tell her of his plan to leave town and doubting her willingness to accompany him if he did. She opened the door before he rang the bell, and the dog bolted inside, jerking the leash from his hand. A second later, she was in his arms, and they kissed.

Over his shoulder, she said, "Wow! You parked out front."

"I don't care what people think anymore."

"Neither do I. You round up Pete, and I'll finish up in the kitchen."

"What are you working on?"

"Supper."

The dog had already found his way to the kitchen, and he directed him to stay in a corner. Like him, Pete seemed enchanted with the odor of whatever she was cooking. Will had eaten very little since that morning, and he was famished.

She removed a large pan from the oven and set it on the stove top to cool. "This has to cool off. There's a bottle of red in the pantry. Why don't you pour us a glass?"

They sipped their wine for a few minutes, and then she served their plates.

"What is this, Mae? Some kind of pie?" He was looking at the large, pastry-covered thing she had put before him.

"It's called a pasty—sounds like nasty. They're English. My mother taught me how to make them. It's a lot of meat, potatoes, onions, and other things covered all the way around with pastry. It takes a man to eat a whole one."

They ate in a silence for the most part. After he was eating his second pasty and she had given Pete almost half of hers, he told her about his decision to leave the ministry and Catalpa. His eyes were on his plate.

He glanced at her, noticing that her fork was on her plate and her arms were crossed.

She seemed to be waiting for him to continue. His eyes went back to his own plate. "I was just getting ready to email the bishop when you called tonight. I'm leaving

Catalpa, too. Maybe I'll stay in Mother's house on Tybee for a while."

She said nothing. Her silence compelled Will to go forward. "Mae, you've got to understand. There's too much here to remind me of Annie. Everything does, every hour, every minute, every second."

She left the kitchen, and he could hear her going up the stairs. He followed her and stood at the foot, calling up to her. "Wait! I didn't mean I want to leave you behind. I want you to go with me!"

"I'd be happy to go anywhere with you, but not when you're leaving because you don't have the courage to stay." She disappeared from the top of the stairs.

He waited, but she did not reappear. He went up to her bedroom and found her standing at a window, looking out. He walked over and stood beside her. "You're all I have left, Mae. I don't want to lose you, too."

"Then stay here and face your demons. Be here when they find Annie, not on some beach somewhere."

"We both know she's dead."

"You're not dead, and neither am I."

"I might as well be."

"You have it in you, Will. You have it in you to climb this mountain. I want to climb it with you—God knows, I want to—but I'm not sure I can if you give up and leave. But that's beside the point. Don't stay here for me. Stay here for Annie. They'll find her. I know they will. And when they do, it's you who needs to be here to take her in your arms and hold her close, not Jack Carter or some stranger. Do you really think she'll ever rest if you're not the one to hold her?"

She was crying now. He took her in his arms, but she pushed him away. "I don't know what to do, Mae."

"Right now, just make love to me. Don't ask me why, but I need that."

An hour later, he left her in the bed and went downstairs. In her living room, he sat on the sofa in the dark with his elbows on his knees and his head in his hands. Pete, who'd been denied entry to the bedroom, met him at the top of the stairs and came down with him. Now he got comfortable at his feet, looking up at him.

He wasn't praying; he was trying to come to grips with all of the conflicting emotions that were raging inside him. He heard a sound and lifted his head, turning his eyes toward the staircase.

Mae had come down and was standing at the bottom of the stairs looking at him. "Don't you think you should put something on, Will?"

He looked down. He had left the bedroom in nothing but his boxer shorts. She started laughing, and so did he. He got up, and they embraced.

"Why don't you come back to bed? Tomorrow, things will look different to you," she said.

"There's something I need to do, Mae. It may some dumb, but I want to go over to Oglethorpe Street to the spot where the driver saw Annie. It's the only way I have of being close to her."

"Now?"

He nodded.

"Come on, Will. Really?"

Chapter Thirty-Four

Friday, Wee Hours

With Pete in the back seat and Mae beside him, Will headed across town to the intersection of Oglethorpe Street and Methvin Avenue. It was exactly one a.m. on Friday morning.

She remained skeptical. "I'm not sure why we're doing this. What do you hope to accomplish anyway?"

"I want to stand in the same spot in Oglethorpe Street where Annie was on Wednesday morning, right before Rankin picked her up and took her away. Then I want to go up Methvin Avenue just like he did with Annie in his arms. I want to experience the same place at the same time of night. It may seem strange—no, it *is* strange—but I think it will help me get through this somehow. It will make me feel closer to her."

He parked at the curb in front of the vacant, brick house at the northwest corner of the intersection. He put the leash on Pete, and all of them got out and stood on the sidewalk. It was very quiet. After a minute or so, he led the dog into the street, and she followed. They stood there for a moment, looking around. No cars, trucks, or other evidence of human activity disturbed the quiet streets.

"Well? Are you feeling anything out here? I can't say that I am."

At that moment, Pete began sniffing the ground and tugging at the leash. Will gave him rein, and the big dog pulled him down Oglethorpe to a location opposite a large dogwood tree next to the brick house. He nosed one spot in the street and circled around it, keening.

Will felt it, too. "This was where Annie lay when the truck driver first saw her, Mae. This is it!"

Still agitated, Pete stood on his hind legs, pawing Will's chest. He pushed him away and petted him in a useless effort to calm him down.

Mae was studying the shrubbery in front of the brick house. "Those bushes over there," she said, pointing. "Rankin came running out of them to get Annie. What was happening? I still don't get it."

"Let's walk up Methvin." He led Pete onto Methvin Avenue with Mae following. The closer they got to the second house on the right, the louder the dog whined. Will feared he might wake up someone.

"What's wrong with him? From the video, it didn't look like the man ever put Annie on the ground after he took her from the street, so what is Pete reacting to?" she asked.

"I don't know. It has to have something to do with that house." He pointed to the two-story, white house with the rounded front porch, the same one he'd investigated without success the day before. Like almost every other house on the street, it was dark.

As they came abreast of it, the dog yelped and bolted for the driveway, jerking the leash out of Will's hand. He barreled down the driveway and disappeared around the back corner of the house, barking all the way. They rushed after him, and turning the corner, they found him on steps leading to a back door. He was yelping, whining, and scratching at the door, trying to get inside.

Afraid that Pete would arouse whoever was in the house, Will ran up the steps, grabbed the leash and pulled the tugging dog back down to the asphalt parking area and over to the driveway. The dog resisted all the way to the street, still pulling on the leash as they rushed back down Methvin.

When they reached his SUV, Pete was still making noise.

"I can't believe we didn't wake up everybody within a mile of here," Mae said. "What was that all about?"

"He must have smelled something back there on the steps."

"Whatever it was, he almost tore that door down trying to get inside. You should call the owner tomorrow and offer to pay for the damage."

He nodded, but his thoughts were again on what Miss Janie Stewart had told him about the incident of forty years earlier. "Annie could be in that house for all we know. I need to call Jack right away."

"You'll have to wait a while. It's almost two o'clock in the morning."

When they arrived back at her condo, she reached for the door to get out, but he stayed where he was.

"Aren't you coming back in, Will? You need to get some sleep."

"I'm heading home. I've got to work out some things in my mind before I call Jack. It has nothing to do with you."

"Okay, but promise me two things. First, that you won't get in touch with the bishop until we've had a chance to talk again. And second, that you'll try to get some rest as soon as you can."

"I promise."

"We're finishing up with inventory at the store, but I can meet you for lunch."

He kissed her, and she got out. As he pulled away though, he saw her waving for him to come back. She had something white in her hand. He backed up until he was alongside her again.

"What is it?"

"I guess I must have sat on this when I got in your SUV tonight. Just now, when I got out, it came with me."

She handed the papers to him, and he unfolded them. It was what Jack had given him to study, the FBI list of all the registered guests on Tybee on the night the man had tried to grab Annie on the beach. He explained what it was, admitting that he hadn't looked at it yet. "The list doesn't make any difference at this point. Jack already told me that Rankin wasn't on it."

"Take a look at it, anyway," Mae insisted. "Okay? For all we know, somebody else may have helped Rankin."

"All right."

As they headed home, Pete was still agitated. On the rear seat, he moved back and forth from one window to another, keening and whining. Will was agitated, too. *What if Mae is right? What if someone else was involved, someone who knows where Annie is resting 'in the arms of the Good Lord?'* "Someone who knows where Annie is buried," he whispered.

Chapter Thirty-Five

Thursday, Night

After Chalker left the closet, Annie opened the book he'd left with her. Pictures filled it, each protected by its own little sleeve. She didn't mind spending her time this way because she wanted to know if the book *would* reveal what was to come next. *Besides, what else do I have to do?*

The pictures nearest the front seemed very old. Her father would call them 'snapshots,' square, little, black and white pictures with white borders. One showed a two-story white house with snow on the ground. *It might be this house.* In another, a pretty girl posed in an old-fashioned, one-piece bathing suit. In others, the same girl was shown with two adults who must have been her parents. The man always had his arm around her waist or shoulder, while the woman stood to the side, not touching the girl or the man. Once or twice, the girl was in the man's lap, even when she looked like a teenager. *Could she be Doris?*

As she turned the pages, the pictures were in color and more modern-looking. The pretty girl from the older pictures appeared in some of the newer ones but all grown up. She had red hair, and it was shorter, framing her face.

Most of the newer pictures featured a boy and girl growing up together from the time they were babies until they were about seven or eight—second graders maybe. The girl had blonde hair, and she was the same girl shown in every picture on the wall in the little closet. The boy had dark hair, and he was in many of the wall pictures, too. *Were they brother and sister?* A second boy who looked older was in some of the photos. Annie remembered him from some of the wall pictures, too. No one else was in the pictures.

For the most part, the younger girl and boy were side by side, touching, holding hands, or arm in arm. In one picture, they bathed together in a tub. *The tub upstairs?* In another picture, they were standing in front of a giant, valentine heart, leaning forward and kissing each other on the mouth.

She saw no pets, nor the usual school plays, soccer matches, volleyball games, or vacation shots. For these children, Disney World didn't exist. Blank passages filled the back of the book, and it looked like photos had been removed. *The photos on the walls now.*

After a time, Annie tired of looking at pictures, and she closed the book. She was at a loss to understand what the pictures were supposed to tell her. Soon she fell asleep with the book in her lap.

Several hours later, she woke up with a start. She didn't know what time it was or what day it was, only where she was. Something had woken her up, a vibration, a scratching, a shaking. She could feel it in the floor.

What is it? What's happening?

Then she heard something. *What did I hear? Was it a barking dog?* She couldn't be sure.

She stomped her feet and screamed. She screamed over and over again, but nothing happened. The vibrations stopped. Her chin fell against her chest, and the tears came. She was so alone. It wasn't fair.

Every time Chalker left, she wondered if he would come back. *If he doesn't, will I rot and die in this closet without food or water or a bathroom? Will I be mummified in this little coffin of a room?* She had seen movies like that with people in walls and basement rooms, dried up and hollow-eyed. They were always found years after they had died. If you so much as touched them, they turned to dust.

"Iblis! Chalker! Iblis! I hate you! I don't want to die here!" she screamed at the top of her voice, but no one came.

All at once, she knew. She knew what was going on right here and now. It was what Iblis had said and how he'd said it. It was the sum of everything that had happened to her since he'd taken her away.

Iblis is the younger boy in all of the pictures in the book and on the wall. He once lived in this house, and Doris is his mother. He's not just some neighborhood boy who'd watched Doris and her children in the bathtub together. Iblis is Doris' son, all grown up. And her other child is a girl, and she's the girl in the pictures in the book and on the walls. And this little room under the stairs is all about his sister not just some other girl that he liked. Iblis has a crush on his own sister!

Was that why Iblis had given her the stupid book? And where was his sister now? If he liked her that much, why didn't he go find her and put her *in a closet? It's because he can't find her! She's gone! That's the only reason I'm here. It's because I look just like his sister, just like the girl on the wall. He wants* me *to become* her*!*

Angry and frustrated, Annie took the photo album in both hands and threw it as hard as she could. It hit the closet door and sat there leaning against it, opened at an odd angle, looking somewhat damaged. The tears came then, and she wished that she hadn't thrown the book. She stretched as far as she could, but she couldn't even touch it.

Maybe it was better that I can't reach the sorry book. If Iblis likes those pictures, then I don't like them. I don't like him. He's weird.

She began to imagine all kinds of things about Iblis as a boy, putting him in situations that she and her girlfriends would've giggled about. He would've been the boy who liked to read but was too shy to kiss a girl on the cheek or hold a girl's hand. Then she imagined him kissing her.

"Ugh," she said out loud. "I have to leave here. Oh, Jesus, I have to leave. I have to leave right now!"

Chapter Thirty-Six

Friday, Early Morning

Will woke up early on Friday morning, having gotten no more than two or three hours of fitful sleep. He was tired, but last night's visit to the house on Methvin Avenue was still fresh on his mind. He wasn't sure what it proved, but he did know that it offered hope where things were hopeless before.

After he showered and dressed, he let the dog out and made coffee. While it was brewing, he walked to the end of the driveway and picked up the morning paper. He knew without looking at it that it would feature a story about Rankin.

At the kitchen table with his coffee, he turned to the *Catalpa Times* and found an oversized headline across the entire top of the front page, 'Custodian Found Hanging in Church.' A sub-headline announced, 'Police Stonewall Details.' The police might have 'stonewalled details,' but the article which followed left no doubt that Rankin had abducted Annie from the fairgrounds, taken his own life, and left a suicide note confessing to the kidnapping. The paper referred to 'an anonymous, credible source,' and he wondered just who that might be.

Inside the paper, he found another story. This one was headlined, 'Where is Little Annie Rowan?' Anyone reading the article would think she was dead. The reporter speculated that she could be 'resting' anywhere in Tanotchee County and that people walking in the woods might want to be on the lookout for freshly turned earth.

When he finished reading the articles, he located the number for the *Times*, and called it. Newspaper people kept schedules almost as ridiculous as his own, so he wasn't worried about the hour. As the phone rang, he opened the newspaper to the article about Rankin. Will had never met Warren White, the reporter who wrote it.

After White answered, Will introduced himself and got right to the point. "Mr. White, throughout this ordeal, I've been repeatedly cautioned by the police not to share information about their investigation with the public. I just read your article about my daughter's kidnapping, and it includes a great many details that I was led to believe would be kept confidential. I know that reporters are reluctant to reveal the name of a source when privacy has been requested, but in view of my obvious interest in this, I was wondering if you might tell me where you got this information. I'm especially concerned that it might've come from someone on the church staff."

"I can understand your concern, Reverend Rowan, and your interest is clear. Even so, I can't tell you who talked with me. If I do, my source may not be willing to help me out in the future."

He sighed. "I can't believe this. My daughter was taken, you've written a story about it, and you won't even tell me where you got the information you shared with the public. Did your source ask for protection?"

"Not directly, no."

"Well, then…"

White was quiet.

"Mr. White, think of what I've been through these last few days. The person that talked with you—in so many words—said that my child is dead. Can't you just tell me who it was?"

"Okay, I guess it's only fair. His name is Lieutenant Carter. He's right under the chief at the police department."

"You're kidding! Jack Carter gave you all that?"

"Yes, but please don't tell him I told you. And, Reverend, so sorry for your loss."

He called Jack. A voice, unnaturally hoarse and deep, said, "Carter." Will let him have it, a one-minute tirade of frustration and disappointment.

His response surprised him. "Slow down, Will. I've never talked to Warren White in my life."

"Then who did?"

"I don't know, but I intend to find out. I read the article, too, and whoever called White, posing as me, knew as much about the death of Rankin as I do. Maybe more."

"Then I guess I should apologize, Jack. I should have known you would never make a disclosure like that."

"Don't let it worry you. I'm glad you called anyway. I have a question for you. This morning, I woke up with one thing on my mind. It was keys."

"Keys?"

"I hate things that don't make sense. Turner's wallet, his truck key, and his cell phone were all in his pockets when you found him. He had no problem keeping up with those items, but where were his church keys and his house key? Tell me—did you ever happen to see him with a key ring? What did it look like?"

"When we hired him, I gave him two keys. The large key opened several outer doors at the church, and the smaller one was for some cabinets that stay locked. I saw him put both of them on a key ring. I noticed only one other key on the ring at the time, probably his house key."

"So his truck key wasn't on it?"

"Not that I saw."

"Anything unusual about the ring? Was some kind of tab attached to it?"

"Not really. It was a silver ring with a silver, oval fob. It had engraving on it, but I didn't pay attention to what it might have said."

"I'm sure we haven't come across that," he said, sighing deeply. "Thanks. I'll be in touch."

"Wait one minute, Jack. I need to talk with you about something else."

He described his visit the night before to the intersection where the truck driver saw Annie, including Pete's strange, aggressive reaction at the house on Methvin. "Jack, we've already talked about what Janie Stewart said about the incident of forty years ago right there at the same spot."

"So, you think they're connected?"

"They have to be."

Nothing followed but silence. "Jack? Are you still there?"

"Yeah, I'm here. My reaction is 'so what.' If they all lived around there forty years ago, chances are they're long gone. What did you think you were doing out there in the middle of the night anyway, Will? You and your dog could have gotten yourselves shot messing around somebody's house at that time of night. You had no business involving Mae either."

"But, Jack…"

"I don't think what your dog did at that house means a damn thing. Dogs go after all kinds of animals at night—cats, possums, raccoons, you name it. Furthermore, we've already been to that Methvin house once, and the man who came to the door seemed as innocent as you or me. He seemed completely harmless to the detectives; he was in pajamas as I recall."

Their conversation went downhill from there, turning into an argument back and forth about whether or not the dog's reaction was important.

Jack brought it to an end. "Hold it. That's enough. Let's don't do this. You're giving me a headache, and I've got a heck of a lot to do."

Will was too upset to respond, so he didn't.

"Look, Will, I haven't forgotten about what Miss Janie said. As a matter of fact, when you called yesterday morning to tell me about Rankin, I was at the newspaper office looking into that incident she told you about. I didn't wait around to see if they had something, and I haven't been back since *because* of Rankin. I'll go to the paper again this morning and see what they can find. Fair enough?"

Will remained quiet.

"I seriously doubt that anybody beside Rankin was involved, but I'll check into the history of the house on Methvin anyway, just to see if there's anything funny about who owns it now. In the meantime, you stay away from it."

Jack was still talking, something about the necessity of a warrant, when Will brought the call to an abrupt end. He was sure Jack was wrong. Pete was on to something, and it would take more than checking into the history of that house to find out what it was.

Chapter Thirty-Seven

Friday, Early Morning

On Friday morning, Iblis opened the door to the closet under the stairs and stumbled over the album he'd left with Annie. He picked it up. "You didn't like the pictures?"

"I was looking at them, and the book fell out of my hands. When I tried to catch it with my legs, it went flying across the floor. I couldn't reach it after that." Never a good liar, she avoided eye contact with him as she offered this explanation.

"I see. I'll put it near your chair, and you can continue looking through it if you wish." He leaned the album against her chair and smiled. "I can't stay very long this morning because I have to attend to my duties. To make up for leaving you alone again, I want to give you more freedom for a little while. Would you like that?"

She nodded and smiled even though she didn't know what he meant by 'a little more freedom.'

He leaned down and unstrapped her. "No chain today. Let's get some breakfast."

He let her use the bathroom and then escorted her to the kitchen. The table was already set. He motioned for her to sit down and served their plates with sausage biscuits, yogurt, and fruit, adding glasses of milk and juice for her. He never stopped smiling.

While they ate, he entertained her with an anecdote about Doris. "She took us to the drive-in theater."

"What's that?"

"It's an outdoor movie theater with a giant screen. A couple in a red convertible was parked next to us. They were engaged in what mother called, 'vehicular acrobatics.'"

"Was your sister with you?"

He studied her for a moment as if he wondered how she knew. "Yes, she was."

"What was her name?"

"Desdemona."

"And I look just like her, don't I?"

"Yes."

They were both quiet for almost a full minute, and then he spoke again. "My mother's eyes were glued to what was going on with the acrobats, but she ordered us to watch the movie. Guess what was playing that night?"

"Was it 'The Wizard of Oz?'" It was the first old movie that came to mind.

"No. That night, and probably many other nights for years, a certain featurette was being shown. I know that because she took us back there many times. It always came on before the main feature. It was called 'The Birth of Twins,' and it showed twins being born in a hospital setting. It was in full color, quite graphic, somewhat sickening, and supposedly educational. The twins were a boy and a girl."

She noticed that his eyes glazed over as he spoke. He went on to explain exactly how it felt to watch the twins being born. He seemed to remember every tiny detail of the process, but she wasn't paying close attention.

She was preoccupied with something on the floor under her left foot. When he removed the plates and took them to the sink, she leaned down and picked up the object. She glanced at it and then pushed it between her legs out of sight. It was a key ring holding three keys. A silver, oval thing was attached to it. "Something strange happened here last night, Mr. Iblis."

He was at the sink washing the dishes. When she spoke, he looked in her direction, smiled, and then turned back to the sink. "Let me guess. You heard some odd noises, didn't you? Old houses are like that."

"Yes, odd noises. I could barely make them out, but they sounded like a dog barking. It was real faint. My dog's a big, black lab, and his name is Pete. It could have been him, I guess. I yelled as loud as I could, but I didn't hear the sounds again."

He turned and looked at her. He wasn't smiling any longer. "You heard a dog? You must have been dreaming, Annie."

"That's what I thought at first, but then I felt vibrations from somewhere in the house, like somebody rattling a door."

"Back or front?"

"Maybe the back."

He looked first at her and then toward the back porch. He left the kitchen and walked onto the back porch. At the same time, Annie reached for the keys, got up, and headed for the front door. She took great care not to alert him.

***

Iblis wondered if the closet was as soundproofed as he'd thought. He opened the back door and was amazed at what he saw. He'd been in a hurry when he came in, and he hadn't noticed the lower part of the door. Now, he leaned down and ran his fingers over what seemed to be…scratches. *A dog*, he thought. *A big dog!*

He turned toward the kitchen, considering what the scratches meant. In his mind's eye, he saw Will Rowan and a big, black dog at the back door in the dark of night, shaking it, scratching it, and trying to get inside. He quaked at the thought.

He returned to the kitchen only to find that Annie wasn't there. He called for her, but she didn't answer. He felt a bolt of panic and strode past her chair, through the dining room, and into the hall. There he saw her. She was at the front door. She had keys in her right hand, and she was trying to open the door with them.

Keys? he thought, walking quickly down the hall in her direction. "Wait, Annie. Please stop that at once."

What she was attempting to do didn't concern him because she would not be successful. He reached her and took her right hand in his. He took the keys from her, and she sunk down on her knees and let out a wail. He put the keys in his pocket and helped her up.

"Come with me, Annie."

His tone was soft but direct. He led her into the parlor on the right and told her to sit on the settee once shared by him and Desdemona. He sat beside her. She lowered her head and began crying softly. She asked if he planned to hurt her, but he ignored her question.

He reached into his pants pocket and removed the ring of keys he'd taken from her. The fob was a heavy, silver oval. The initials, 'RT,' were engraved on it. No doubt, the keys were those which opened the First Methodist Church and Rankin's house. They must have fallen out of his pocket when he was being throttled on Tuesday afternoon. They weren't required when he'd taken him to the church because his friend had given him the entry code. Law enforcement would already have noticed the absence of the keys on Rankin's person or in his truck or anywhere on the church premises. That was a certainty, and it was a problem. "Stupid on my part," he said out loud.

"What are you going to do to me?"

He looked in her direction. "These keys don't open a single door in this house, Annie."

Then he questioned her for ten minutes or so about her dog, its size, its breed, its bark, the last time the vet had cut its nails, and its fenced-in status at her house.

Throughout, she was emphatic about one thing. It was *her* dog, not her father's.

When he'd finished, he was convinced that her dog paid a visit to Doris' house the night before, and because it was usually confined to the backyard at home, it hadn't come alone.

Up until this moment, everything had gone so well. As far as the police were concerned, Rankin had taken Annie, killed her, and then himself. His call to the newspaper reporter impersonating the black lieutenant, even to the extent of adding dialectal touches, sent the word throughout the community. Annie was coming around, too, accepting him and looking forward to their time together. "It was so easy to imagine that I was in the clear and that this could go on forever," he said, speaking out loud again, forgetting that she sat nearby.

"I'm so sorry about the keys, Mr. Iblis."

"And there's the scroll, too."

"I don't know what you mean."

He looked at her but said nothing. *Did I ever touch the scroll without the benefit of rubber gloves?* He despised rubber gloves; he liked to touch things, to feel them in his hands. He'd never envisioned losing the scroll, so maybe he'd been lax in handling it. He didn't think he'd been remiss, but it was possible. The video, the missing scroll, the keys, the dog at the door, and Annie's attempt to escape were all causes for concern. *Is it all falling apart now?*

He stood, and she cringed, seemingly expecting the worst. He put his right hand on her shoulder and bent down so that his face was close to hers. "Don't worry, Annie. I forgive you for trying to leave, and I'm sure that you're sorry that you did."

"I won't do it again," she whispered.

"I've got a wonderful idea. Why don't we go on a picnic this evening? I'll pick up what we need and come back for you. I know just the spot. It's out on Rickety Back

Road. Beyond the woods, there's a meadow filled with wild flowers, leading down to the moss-covered bank of a beautiful, rippling stream. It will be an evening you'll remember as long as you live. Trust me on that."

Chapter Thirty-Eight

Friday, Morning

After his conversation with Jack, Will left his house and drove over to the church, still irritated by Jack's attitude. Annie's dog wouldn't have attacked the back door of the Methvin Avenue house unless he sensed something or someone important inside. *So what if no cause for a warrant existed?* They should just go on in with weapons drawn and look around. But, no, they had to have a little piece of paper signed by a judge, and they couldn't get it based on the 'testimony' of a dog. A quote from Charles Dickens came to mind, something about the law being 'an ass.' It was so true.

In his office, he wished for a punching bag but settled for a small trash can which he kicked over his desk and against the far wall. Its spewed contents, mostly crumpled paper, littered the floor in the process. Ignoring the mess, he picked up his keys and left the church. It was getting to the point that he couldn't face people anymore, even his staff.

With nowhere else to go, he headed to Mae's bookstore. She'd mentioned something about inventory, and even though it was early, he supposed she might already be at work. He had no real purpose in going there other than a need to vent about Jack's lack of interest in Pete's behavior.

At her shop, the lights were on, but the 'closed' sign was still posted. He parked out front and knocked on the door. Inside, Brad Dixon was moving through the stacks. He opened the door and invited him in, explaining that Mae had gone over to the newspaper office.

"She didn't mention what she planned to do at the paper, but I'm guessing she wants to place an ad for a little sale we're planning. She should be back any minute now."

"I'll just wait, colonel."

Will went over to the shelves and began idly eyeing the books. He came across a book entitled, *The Philosophy Book: Big Ideas Simply Explained.* It brought back the worst of memories—those of Leah's wasted career, her last, terrible day, her death, and her funeral. *Has Annie already joined her?* he wondered.

He left the stacks and walked over to the checkout counter. Her assistant joined him there, holding up a set of spreadsheets. Although Will neither asked nor cared, he explained what the sheets represented.

"These are lists of all the books in the shop. They are separated into three categories, then separated again by genre, and then listed by author. We have some that Mae bought outright for resale; others are in the category of print-on-demand; and a few others are on the shelves under some sort of consignment arrangement with an author."

When he didn't comment on this, the colonel continued. "We have newspapers, too, but they are not part of the inventory."

He nodded. He was not in a mood to chat right now.

"I don't know whether you're aware of it, but Annie's case made the *New York Times.* I know because we take it here. It was just a short article, published before that janitor hanged himself. I guess everything is different now. At least that's what the Catalpa paper says."

He gazed at the man but remained quiet.

"I'm so sorry it all happened, Will. At least they know who did it now, don't they? I mean they don't think anyone else was involved, do they?"

"I don't know what they know or what they think, colonel. I hope you don't mind, but I'd rather not talk about it."

"What are they doing to find Annie? They haven't given up completely have they?"

He wondered how a retired Army colonel could be such a dolt. He was about to respond when Mae unlocked the front door and came inside. She waved some papers she was holding in her right hand.

"Will, I'm glad you're here. I've been at the newspaper office. They have all of the old papers on microfilm. We couldn't find a write-up about the incident Miss Janie mentioned, but that doesn't mean it didn't happen. One of the older employees said they never printed anything like that back then. To make the paper, it had to be what she called, 'happy news.' Obituaries though were an exception, and I copied a couple of them I think you should see."

Dixon seemed puzzled by this. "Mae, what incident was this 'Miss Janie' talking about? Who is she anyway? I don't believe I've met her."

Ignoring him, she passed one of the obituaries across the counter to Will. He put his elbows on the counter and began to read it, Col. Dixon read over his shoulder.

Doris Delaney Paine

Doris Delaney Paine, age 36, of Catalpa, died suddenly at her home on April 7, 1980. Doris was born on April 1, 1944, in Catalpa, the only child of Drs. Lance and Lurette Paine, both of whom predeceased her. She graduated both Catalpa High School and Auburn University where she earned a BA degree in Ancient Studies. She taught Georgia history briefly at Gunne Middle School before giving up her career to devote all of her time to raising her children. Doris was a voracious reader, a loving and devoted mother to her children, and an active member of the Nehemiah Baptist Church where she served for many years as a candle snuffer attendant for the Wednesday night services.

She was predeceased by her daughter, Desdemona Paine. Her survivors include her son, Chalker Paine. It was her wish that no memorial service be held, but contributions in her memory to any local charity will be deeply appreciated. Obituary courtesy of Peeler Funeral Home, Oglethorpe Street, Catalpa.

No picture accompanied the obituary. Will put it down and backed away from the counter, bumping into Dixon who almost toppled over.

"Excuse me, Will," the colonel said. "Wasn't there another one, Mae?"

"Yes, Brad, but I need for you to get back on the inventory. I want it wound up before we reopen the store."

Dixon nodded and headed to the other side of the store where he recommenced his inventory.

Mae touched Will's arm. "Let's go back to my office."

He followed her into her small office in the rear of the store, and they sat down, she behind her desk and he in a chair across from it. "Is there something you don't want your assistant to know about?" he asked.

She sighed and looked down. "No, not really. I just thought you would want privacy when you saw the other obit. Let me read it to you, and then I want you to take a look at it. It's not very long. It's the obituary of Desdemona Paine, and it includes a picture. Here's all it says:

"Desdemona Paine, age 10, of Catalpa, died on September 19, 1979 in Catalpa. Miss Paine was born on February 13, 1969, in Catalpa, the child of Ms. Doris Paine. Survivors include her mother and her twin brother, Chalker Paine. Her maternal grandparents, Drs. Lance and Lurette Paine, predeceased her. A private memorial service is planned. Peeler Funeral Home in charge of the arrangements."

"That's it for Desdemona Paine, Will. There's no mention of her father or her paternal grandparents. Her obituary omits any reference to why she died. It doesn't even say that she died 'suddenly.' It's all very strange."

Will was perplexed. "So what? What does it have to do with Annie? Miss Janie recalled that Doris Paine's daughter got hurt on Oglethorpe Street one night forty years ago, but she didn't seem to remember anything else. How can we find out what happened to her? Would there be a death certificate somewhere?"

"I don't know, but I want you to see this." She bit her lower lip and handed the obituary to him.

He took one look at it, and his hand began shaking. His mouth fell open before he glanced up and said, "It might as well be a picture of Annie."

"It *is* Annie! Jack needs to see it right away."

Chapter Thirty-Nine

Friday, Morning

Will left the police department disappointed. Jack wasn't there, and although his vehicle was in the parking lot, he was 'out and about,' according to the officer at the front desk. As he left the building, he tried to reach Jack on his cell phone but was sent to voicemail.

He put away his phone, walked up to the courthouse square, and entered the nineteenth century building housing Sam Franklin's law firm. Following a short wait, an assistant ushered him up to his office on the second floor. Sam, a courtly man of medium height with light brown hair, directed him to a chair in front of his desk. The lawyer expressed concern for Annie's plight before he steered their conversation to the lawsuit filed by the Cuttinos.

"I know they're your daughter's grandparents, Will, but I have to say this—their complaint is a mountain of manure. I'll file a timely answer and prepare an affidavit for your signature. After discovery, we'll use the affidavit to move for a summary judgment in your favor."

He noted that the attorney never once suggested that he might defend the claim on the theory that Annie was, after all, still alive. *Was Sam just being kind, or had he and everybody else already written her off?* There was no way to know.

As talk of the suit began to wind down, the attorney's assistant tapped on the door. He motioned her inside, and at his desk, she leaned over and whispered something to him. He nodded and said, "Have him come on up."

"Jack Carter is downstairs, Will, and he's here to talk about your case. He's on the way up."

A few seconds later, Jack appeared, and Sam directed him to the other chair across from his desk. The policeman seemed surprised to see Will but didn't inquire about why he was there, too.

Sam leaned forward. "Jack, I'm not sure why you're here, but my assistant said your visit was urgent. As you can see, Will is here, and we aren't quite finished with his business. Would you like for him to step out for a moment while you and I talk?"

"No. It concerns his daughter's case, so it's fine if he stays." He removed a document from his coat pocket, unfolded it, and passed it over to Sam. "I have some questions for you about this deed."

Sam studied the deed while Jack continued. "A little while ago, I was in the office of Tanotchee County Tax Collector. I wanted to know what their records showed about the house at 15 Methvin Avenue, the second house on the right coming up from Oglethorpe."

Sam looked up. "And what did you find out?"

"The owner of the property is Chalker Paine. Oddly enough though, the tax bill isn't being sent to the house on Methvin. At the request of Mr. Paine, they send the bills to a post office box in Atlanta.

"From there, the tax clerk directed me to the record room in the Superior Court Clerk's office at the courthouse. There, I ran into a helpful deputy clerk who located the most current deed to the Methvin property and made a copy for me. The deed I just gave you and the same post office box in Atlanta were the only tidbits of information they had on Mr. Paine."

Will interrupted. "So the Paine family does still own the house. I've seen Doris Paine's obituary, and she had a son by the name of Chalker."

"I don't have a clue about why this might pertain to your daughter, Will, but maybe I can answer some of your questions about Chalker Paine," Sam said, holding up the deed. "This is what's known as a 'Trustee's Deed,' and I was the one who signed it eighteen months ago in my capacity as trustee of the Doris Paine Testamentary Trust. Doris owned the house at 15 Methvin Avenue when she died forty some odd years ago. She left a will which directed that the house be held in trust until her son, Chalker, attained the age of fifty years. After that time, she wanted it deeded to him.

"Does he live in the house?" Will asked.

"I guess he may have at one time, but now, I don't know."

Jack frowned. "Isn't he your client?"

"Technically, no. We represented the estate of his mother, Doris. I'm told she died when Chalker, her only surviving child, was just a boy. Of course, that was before my time. After her death, he was adopted through the Tanotchee County Department of Family and Children Services. At least, that's what happened according to an old memo in our file."

"Was his name changed in connection with the adoption?" Jack said.

"That usually happens."

Jack gave every indication of becoming frustrated with the attorney and his vague answers. "Is there *anything* you can tell me about Chalker Paine or this deed?"

"Let me see." Sam leaned back in his chair. "In her will, Doris Paine directed that everything she owned, including her house, be held intact and delivered to her son on his fiftieth birthday. I suppose the poor boy would just have to get by as best he could until then. When the estate was distributed though, it certainly proved worth waiting for. He got the house and a heck of a lot more in investments and cash. Aside from the house, his mother's estate was worth over three million when she died, and the corpus produced considerable, compounded income over the ensuing four decades. I don't mind talking about it because as trustee I was required to file annual reports with the Probate Court. It's all public knowledge."

Will still wanted to know who was in the house. "Has Paine ever lived in the house?"

Sam shrugged. "I know it seems like I don't know much about him, but I got involved with the estate long after the fact. My senior partner prepared the will, and Doris appointed him to serve as sole trustee. He retired from the firm about ten years ago. However, under an agreement with me, he kept one lucrative client—the Estate of Doris Paine. But just three years after he left the firm, he died, God rest his soul, and I was appointed by the court to serve as successor trustee of the Paine Testamentary Trust."

Jack had a question. "Does he still go by Chalker Paine, or does he use the name he got in the adoption?"

The lawyer joined his hands and put his elbows on the desk. "Our file doesn't reflect who adopted him. In Georgia, all adoption records are confidential with certain limited exceptions. If he was given a new name after the adoption, and I assume that he was, I don't know what it is."

"So you're telling me that you don't know the name your client uses now?" Will said.

"No."

Then Jack chimed in. "Sam, how could you have deeded property to a man that you can't identify by his current name? You don't know who he is!"

"I admit that it sounds odd. But my late partner was a poor record keeper. He did put a memo in the file though, dated and signed by him, stating that he had located Chalker Paine and that he had confirmed his identity after meeting with him in Atlanta. He also stated that his correct mailing address was an Atlanta P.O. box. My partner apparently did not consider it essential to include Chalker's current name and address in his memo."

"So how did you ever get in touch with him about transferring the house and the balance of the estate to him?" Jack asked.

"I sent a letter to his P.O. box. He replied and requested that the entire transaction be handled by mail. He said it was not convenient for him to come to Catalpa, and he declined my offer to come up there to meet with him."

Will sighed. Sam's explanation was getting them nowhere. When the police knocked on the door at the Methvin house on the night Annie was last seen, a man answered it. He had to be living there. "Jack, when the officers went to the house, did the man give a name? Was it Chalker Paine?"

"He did give a name, but I don't think it was Paine. I'd have to look at the file again."

Frustrated now, Will said, "Sam, I don't think you understand how important it is for us to find out the identity of the man who's in that house now."

"Keep in mind that it was my solemn duty to distribute the estate in accordance with the will of Doris Paine, and in the Trustee's Deed, I had no choice but to show 'Chalker Paine' as Grantee. That was the name which appeared in the will, and the only one I had at the time. In my correspondence to Paine, I enclosed what's known as a name affidavit for him to complete and sign, inserting his current name and confirming that he was one and the same person as 'Chalker Paine.' It should have been recorded on the real estate records along with the Trustee's deed, but he never returned it to me."

Will stood up. "So if there's a man living in the house on Methvin, it may or may not be Chalker Paine."

"I wouldn't know. I've never met Mr. Paine. I suppose the person living in the house could be a tenant."

Jack stood to leave, too. "If we ever find out who he is, I'll be sure to let you know," he said sarcastically.

"Why don't you just go over there and knock on the door if you want to know who lives there, Jack?" Sam offered.

"I've already tried that," Will said, turning to leave.

As they headed out the door, he heard Sam say, "Wait a minute. You haven't told me why you want to know about Chalker Paine in the first place."

Ignoring his question, they left his office.

241 • The Closet

Chapter Forty

Friday, Late Morning

Mr. Iblis hadn't returned, and Annie spent her time looking through the photo album again. She was bored with the pictures of the Paine family, but she was concerned that he might question her about various aspects of it. He'd said that he wouldn't punish her for trying to escape, but she wasn't so sure about that. The thing with the keys was a dumb move. She couldn't even get them to go into the lock.

She was tired. She looked at a few pages of the book, and then she dozed; she read and dozed, read and dozed. If it would keep her from being punished, she would keep looking at it.

By now, she'd lost track of how many days she'd been in the closet. She wondered if it was the same way for Pete when they left him in the backyard for the day or closed him up in the kitchen all night. Every time, he probably thought they might never come back like she thought the same thing about Mr. Iblis. It made her realize that they couldn't have done anything worse to her poor dog. "I'm so sorry, Pete. If I ever get away from here, I'm never going to leave you alone again," she said out loud, as if he were sitting at her feet.

Of course, her words meant nothing because no one outside the closet could even hear her.

The night before, she had come to a decision. She would look at the album or do anything else Mr. Iblis wanted her to do to get out of the chair and out of the closet, but she wouldn't hug or kiss him. She was neither his daughter nor his sister, and she never would be, no matter what happened.

This morning, or yesterday, or three days ago, she was not sure when, he told her that her father had given up on trying to find her. *How does he know that? Has he seen my father on TV? Has he talked to him?*

"My father won't come get me, and I will be with Chalker forever," Annie whispered. Saying it helped her to face what she was beginning to think might surely happen. *If I'm not in the closet, it won't be so bad. He could have punished me this morning, but he didn't. He forgave me because he understood. He'll let me out of the closet soon enough. Maybe Daddy will marry Mae. He likes her. Maybe they'll have babies. If the children they have love each other, would that be wrong? Was anything ever wrong if love was involved? Love is the most important thing in the Bible. God is love. Love one another. Love thy neighbor.*

She was so confused, and she had so many questions but no answers.

When was Mr. Iblis coming back? Were they still going on a picnic? What day is it? Has the night already come and gone? If I stay with him, where will I go to school? Will I ever see my friends again? What will my clothes be like?

She closed the album and let it slide to the floor. She lowered her head to her chest. She didn't know what to think anymore. She would truly rather die than be the sister of Mr. Iblis.

Chapter Forty-One

Friday, Late Morning

After they left Sam Franklin's office, Jack and Will returned to his office at the police department. Jack motioned for him to sit in front of his desk and then closed the door.

"Jack, I want to show you two obituaries that Mae found in the *Times*. The first one is for Doris Paine. She died in 1980. She had twins. One of them, her daughter Desdemona, predeceased her. The other twin was her son Chalker. Both of the twins and Rankin Turner were involved in the incident recalled by Miss Janie. It happened at the intersection of Oglethorpe Street and Methvin Avenue, right in front of Rankin Turner's house. Ms. Paine and her children lived on Methvin in the second house on the right coming up from Oglethorpe. That's the house that Annie's dog tried to get into last night, whining and barking up a storm." He pushed the obituary of Doris Paine across the desk and watched Jack read it.

When he finished, he glanced at Will. "I know all of this already. I wish I could say it proved something, but it doesn't. A lady passed away. She had twins and one of them died before she did. That's all."

"The Paine family still owns the house on Methvin, and odds are that Chalker Paine is the man your people saw there the other night. Maybe Rankin had help. Chalker and Rankin were both involved in something that happened at the same intersection forty years ago. We've got to get inside the Paine house because Annie may be there right now."

"Wait a minute." Jack pushed aside some papers on his desk and picked up a file. He opened it and pulled out several sheets of paper stapled together. After studying them for a second, he nodded and said, "That's what I thought. This is a report from the officers who canvassed Methvin Avenue on the night Annie was seen. At the Paine house, the man who came to the door said his name was Iblis, not Paine."

"What was his first name?"

"It's not given here. I guess they felt they didn't need to get it."

Will glared at him.

Jack sighed. "Look, I'll share some things with you, but only on the condition that you won't get involved on your own again. I want to give you hope, so you'll forget the urge to take matters into your own hands, so you'll let me do my job."

Will nodded. As far as he was concerned, just nodding didn't amount to an agreement.

"You promise, Will?"

He nodded again, and Jack seemed satisfied.

Their conversation was interrupted by a uniformed officer. He barged through the door, and the lieutenant waved him over to his desk. The officer whispered something to him, and looking troubled by what he heard, he issued instructions of some kind, and the officer left. All Will could hear was the name, Agent Baxter. Jack shook his head, glanced at Will, and said, "Let's get out of here for a minute. If we don't, it'll be one thing after another. Okay?"

He agreed, and they headed out through a back door. A block later they found a table and two chairs inside a combination bakery and deli on a side street. Jack ordered coffee for both of them. Will was anxious to hear whatever Jack thought might give him 'hope,' and he said so.

"All right, Will. I've been troubled since I woke up this morning about the extent of Turner's involvement in Annie's taking, or at least, his solo status. It was his keys. I can't think of any reasonable explanation for our failure to find them. Then, later this morning, I got a call from the crime lab in Atlanta. I'd asked that the autopsy be expedited, and they've finished, but they found anomalies."

"Anomalies? What kind?"

"Turner's pants were stained, but we didn't find any urine or bowel contents on the floor under his body. That was of some concern to the crime lab technician, too, but he said it only occurs in about fifty percent of the hanging cases. He said that the amount of discharge is also affected by when and what the deceased had eaten prior to death. Depending on how long Rankin had been dead, it could have been hours since he last ate."

A cell phone pinged, announcing a text message, but both of them ignored it. When it pinged twice more, Jack looked down at his phone, frowned, and said something under his breath that Will couldn't quite catch. Then he continued. "We detected a fecal odor on the body and another odor, too, one hard to pin down. We thought some kind of substance he'd been using on his job might have tainted his clothes."

"What did it smell like?"

"His body had a chemical smell about it. One of our guys thought it was the odor of Freon when it leaks a little bit—what you get when you open an old refrigerator."

"So what did that tell you?"

"I talked to the lab folks at length about the odor. They detected it, too, and apparently there was also a great deal of discussion about time of death. If you saw Rankin drive across the courthouse square right after midnight on Thursday morning and then found his body more than seven hours later, then he should have died within that time frame. And the pathologist thought that Turner had been dead for no more than six or seven hours, which seemed to fit within the known facts. But get this. His assistant was ready to swear that he died at least twelve hours or more before you found him, and more than five hours before his truck crossed the square."

"If the assistant was right, who drove his truck across the square that night?"

Jack shrugged. "Because of the Freon odor, they ran a series of tests on the body tissue, but all they were able to determine was that it hadn't been frozen. However, they couldn't rule out the possibility that the odor came from some kind of refrigeration short of freezing. If his body was preserved that way and then brought to the church, then the pathologist may be wrong about the time of death, and his assistant may be right."

Will leaned across the table. "And in that case, somebody besides Rankin may have been involved in taking Annie."

Jack nodded. "There was something else. The lab folks found a print on Turner's belt buckle. It wasn't his, and there's no way that it belonged to one of us. On his belt buckle, Will! How could it have gotten there?"

Will's expression advertised his dismay. "Could it be Annie's print?"

"It wasn't that small."

Just then, the owner of the shop brought their coffee. "Jack, you usually have a cupcake, too," he said. "Can I bring you one?"

Jack eyed the glass case filled with cupcakes over to his right but shook his head. "Thanks, but not today."

After the owner withdrew, Will said, "I didn't know about this place. Annie would really like…" he started, but he couldn't finish.

"You still have hope, don't you, Will."

"I want to," he said very softly.

Jack reached across the table and patted his hand. "I'm not quitting until we get all of this straightened out."

Will looked at him and nodded slowly. "Thank you. Neither am I."

They were both quiet until Jack spoke again. "Another thing jumped out at me with all this talk of Chalker Paine. This morning, we got a report on Rankin's cell phone. No red flags showed up until Tuesday. Early that morning, two calls were made from his phone to the same landline number on the north side of Atlanta. The number is in the name of a woman who just moved down here from Ohio to be near her daughter. She's only had the number for seven or eight months. The caller asked for 'Chalker.' She told him she didn't know anybody by that name and hung up. The same man called back and asked for the same person again, so she hung up a second time. The lady has no connection with Turner. His phone was never used again."

The more Will heard, the more his anguish flared up. He leaned forward. "Can't you see it, Jack? It's all too much. You may still think she's dead, and maybe she is. But I'm telling you that somebody besides Rankin is involved, and we've got to get inside the Paine house."

"*We* are not going anywhere, and *you* need to stay out of it regardless. You've got to let me handle this."

Will pulled a folded piece of paper from his pocket. His voice was shaking now. "I told you that Mae found two obituaries. One was for Doris Paine, and the other one was for her daughter, Desdemona. She was Chalker's twin, and she died at age ten—the same age as Annie—in September, 1979. I've looked at a calendar for that year. She died on a Friday during the third week in September. She must have died from her injuries in the incident described by Miss Janie, the one at the same intersection where Annie was seen two days ago." He pushed the paper toward Jack. "This is Desdemona's obituary. You take a look at it, and then tell me one more time that we need to wait before going into that house."

Jack unfolded the paper. "My God in heaven," he whispered. "It's Annie's double. My head is spinning. What does all of this mean?"

"There's one more thing to think about, Jack—Annie not only looks like her, but this is the third week in September, and today is Friday!"

Chapter Forty-Two

Friday, Noon

Iblis' confidence was ebbing away in the wake of the missing scroll, the unexpected video, the discovery of Rankin's keys, and the barking, scratching dog. Will Rowan or the authorities or both were somehow making connections which would bring them inexorably back to a man named Chalker Paine and the house on Methvin Avenue. Doubtless, his freedom and perhaps his life, too, were now in jeopardy. No later than that evening, he would have to leave Catalpa and the state of Georgia behind forever, but Annie could not come with him.

He found it necessary to make a final appearance at his place of employment. Although some slight risk was involved, his absence might arouse suspicion at what was a crucial time in his dealings with Annie.

While at work, he went through the motions, trying to appear normal and composed while churning inside. At half past eleven, he gave up and left his job, departing on the premise of going to lunch. It would be a long lunch hour, indeed, one from which he would never return. He'd been foolish to think that he wouldn't need to spend these last, few hours with her. But after years and years, that would be the end of it all and Desdemona, too.

Throughout his life, he'd accomplished what was necessary regardless of the consequences. On occasion, such necessity included doing physical harm just as it had this week and another time, long ago. Those situations had been fundamentally different from the one he faced now. As for what he did to them, it was like slicing warm bread, a prelude to essential sustenance, but as to what he would do today, not so. This time, it was like the tossing away of good, fresh bread and that was what made the present circumstance so terribly difficult.

Behind the wheel of his vehicle, sadness engulfed him, and he stifled a moan. Arriving at the grocery store, he wiped his face with a tissue and steeled himself. He rushed through the store, sparing no expense in buying provisions for Annie's picnic. He wanted her to have the best time of her life, eating the most sweet and tasty foods available in a small town.

At the house, after unloading the groceries, he let her out of the closet and led her to the kitchen. No chain restrained her, and none would ever do so again. At the table, she ate a hot dog, French fries, and a soft drink he'd bought at the grocery store deli. He'd never seen her so calm and collected.

While she ate, he placed some eggs in a pan to boil and leaned against a counter, watching her. When she finished her lunch, she talked about the photo album he'd left with her. He could tell that she was trying to impress him with her understanding of his relationship with Desdemona. It was pitiful really because it didn't matter anymore whether she understood or not. The whole scenario made him feel painfully dishonest.

She was enjoying an ice cream bar when she asked a question he'd avoided answering in the past. "Where is Desdemona, Mr. Iblis? What really happened to her?"

He brushed her question aside again. "I'm busy deviling eggs for the picnic. Do you want to help?"

She finished her ice cream and came around to stand with him at the counter. She began taking the shell off one of the eggs, something she told him she'd done many times before at home. "Mr. Iblis, you have all those pictures of Desdemona, so she must be very important to you. Will she be mad if you give me her room?"

His reticence no longer made any sense. After this evening, his beloved sister would be nothing but a memory. "Desdemona is dead," he said quietly.

She dropped the egg she was working on and said, "Oh!"

He reached down, picked up the egg, and threw it away. "Do you want another egg?"

She nodded, picked one up, and began shelling it. "I'm sorry. I didn't know. Would you tell me what happened to her?"

Why not? Her knowledge is no longer a concern.

Noting that the shells had been removed from all of the eggs now, he put them in a bowl and placed them in the refrigerator. "The deviling can wait," he said.

He had her sit at the table, and he sat across from her.

In telling the story of that night, he was transported. As he talked, he was there, and it was happening all over again. Ever since, he'd remembered every action and every word said.

***

"It was a late Tuesday afternoon in September, a school day. Desdemona and I were sitting on the front porch here at the house with our only neighborhood friend, Rankin Turner. Doris, our mother, was in the backyard, cutting shrubbery.

"Rankin had a pup tent, and over the weekend just past, Dessie and I helped him put it up under a big dogwood tree beside his brick house. He lived just down the street from us. The house is still there but empty now.

"He bragged about how he'd spent the night in his tent, but neither of us believed him. We knew he was afraid to stay out there by himself, and I suppose Dessie wanted to call his bluff. She suggested that we all sleep out in the tent together.

"She said, 'We'll come down to your house around midnight, Rankin, and then we'll sneak back home before daybreak. Mama will never know we were gone.' He pointed out that his parents wouldn't care. Doris often referred to them as 'lushes,' 'alkies,' or 'juiceheads,' among other appellations.

"That night, we got out of the house without waking Doris and joined Rankin inside the tent. Dessie sat between him and me, holding our hands while we swapped ghost stories. I liked just sitting there holding her hand, but she got bored. She wanted to play a game. I hoped it was a kissing game, but she had something entirely different in mind. She'd heard boys talk about it at school. It was called, 'trick-a-truck.'

"Back then, transfer trucks still ran up and down Oglethorpe Street all night long. 'Here's what we'll do,' she said. 'One at a time, we'll lie in the middle of Oglethorpe Street like we're dead. When a truck comes along, and the driver sees us out there and starts to brake, we'll run over and hide in the bushes. It will make the driver so mad!' We both expressed doubts about the idea, but when Dessie called us 'pansies,' that was all it took.

"She talked me into going first. I went into the street and lay down on my back near the centerline. I waved to her and Rankin. They were hiding in the tall, dark bushes surrounding his house. The game played out just as she said it would. A transfer truck came up the street from their left toward me, and the driver applied his brakes as soon as he saw me. As the truck began to come to a screeching stop, I jumped up and ran into the bushes. To our great pleasure, the frustrated driver made an obscene gesture in our direction and drove off.

"Rankin went next, and the same thing happened. However, this time, the driver got out of his truck and bellowed something profane before driving off.

"Now it was her turn. She added a twist though, one she probably had in mind all along. After we hid in the bushes, she started taking off her clothes. When she was naked, she ran out into the street and lay on her back with her hair under her shoulders, her legs slightly spread, and her arms crossed over her chest.

"Rankin turned to me. 'Chalker? I can't believe her.' I shrugged, not knowing what to say.

"No trucks came right away, and for the longest time she was in full view, her white skin and blonde hair glowing in the soft, street lights. I couldn't take my eyes off my beautiful sister. It was the most exciting thing I'd ever seen.

"But then a truck came. It kept coming and coming, but she didn't move. At first I froze, but soon I yelled and rushed out of the bushes toward the street, just as the driver was applying his brakes. I wanted to pull her to safety, but I was too late. The truck was on top of her. The underside of it caught her chin and dragged her up the street.

"Then, I did the only thing I knew to do. I tore up Methvin Avenue yelling for Doris. When I burst through the front door of our house, she was already waiting at the bottom of the stairs with crossed arms. She jerked me up, planted her face right against mine, and said, 'What *has* that little bitch done this time?' With every word, saliva flew across her lips and landed on my face.

"A few minutes later, Doris and I were in her car, following the ambulance to the hospital. We could've ridden with Dessie, but Doris refused. I wailed all the way to the hospital. While I cried, she ranted. 'Here's your sister, buck-naked and lying in the street, same as a common whore rolling in the gutter, and you, hiding in the bushes like some kind of pervert. I'll never live it down.'

"My sister didn't wake up, not that night, not ever again. She was placed in a room, with tubes running in and out from machines making humming, beeping sounds. The noises annoyed my mother, so we sat in the waiting room most of the time, and at night, we went home. This went on for two days.

"Early on Friday morning, she told me that we needed to visit her room for the sake of 'appearances.' There, we stood together beside her bed, looking at her. She was whiter than any person I'd ever seen. They had put something over her mouth, too, to help her breathe. I noticed a dark liquid seeping through the bandage above her left eye. Doris dabbed some of it with her index finger and raised it to her nose, sniffing it. She called it 'filthy.' Once she reached under the covers and began shaking Dessie's left foot back and forth, demanding that she wake up, but she didn't.

"She shook her head and left the room, and I climbed onto the bed and put my face close to Dessie's. I took her hand and told her that I loved her. I think she squeezed my hand then, but I'll never be sure. I was still on the bed when she returned with the doctor. She jerked me off the bed and onto the floor. I stayed there, afraid to say or do anything.

"The doctor said that her brain was 'functioning minimally, at best.' Doris wanted him to confirm she was 'brain dead for all practical purposes,' but he wouldn't commit one way or the other. He talked about rare cases of people waking up from comas after years of 'hibernation' and then leading perfectly normal lives. He theorized that this could happen to Dessie.

"According to the doctor, it was 'financially impractical' to keep her in the hospital. Hearing that, my mother told me to wait for her in the hall.

"Outside the room, I cracked the door and heard some of her conversation with the doctor. She didn't want to pay 'that kind of money.' For what, I wasn't sure. She said that we would just go on and take Dessie home. This seemed to upset the doctor. I'll never forget what he said,

'But Ms. Paine, if we disconnect the life support apparatus, she may not survive.'

"That didn't faze Doris at all. I can hear her now, almost yelling, 'Unplug my baby! I want her home with me.' She could be quite intimidating at times. By then I was really getting worried about my sister.

"The doctor left to get some papers for mother to sign. She told me to return to the room and speak to Dessie 'one more time,' before they got her ready to come home. I couldn't hold back any longer. I begged her not to unplug my sister. 'We need her! I don't want her to die!' Doris ignored me, and when the doctor returned, she signed the papers. With that done, she told the doctor that we would be in the cafeteria eating breakfast while they finished 'de-tubing my darling Desdemona.'

"While we were downstairs eating, a nurse came up and whispered into Doris' ear. The nurse left, and she kept eating, humming some kind of church hymn. I was desperate to know what the nurse had said, so I asked. She swallowed a mouthful of sausage and grits and said, 'The little trollop croaked.'

"I was speechless. I didn't even know what 'croaked' or 'trollop' meant.

"She kept on eating and eating, and I asked her again what had happened to Dessie. She said, 'Your slutty sister got her due. It's just the two of us now.' Hearing that, I vomited all over the table and fainted dead away."

**

Iblis looked at Annie. Her color was somewhere between green and ashen. His own face was wet with tears. Although he'd never told the story of that night to anyone else, revealing it was cathartic. He walked around the table and put his hand on Annie's shoulder. He could tell from her expression that she was beginning to understand at last.

"How awful, Mr. Iblis."

After that, she was quiet. When the eggs were deviled, he made little tomato sandwiches with rounds of white bread, and prepared a seafood salad with the finest of crab meat, jumbo boiled shrimp, iceberg lettuce, celery, green peppers, and condiments. Then he sliced some Alpine style cheese and put it together with slices of the sweetest apples available at the store. With the addition of the other items he'd purchased at the grocery store, they now had the makings of an unparalleled feast. He'd already brought down a light, plaid blanket from a linen closet upstairs, and he put it on the kitchen table along with a picnic basket from the pantry.

It was almost time to go. However, one other detail remained. He turned to Annie and put his right hand under her chin, drawing her face up close to his.

"I've got to go out to the barn for something we'll need for the picnic. Can I trust you to stay right here in the kitchen until I get back?"

"Yes."

"Is something wrong, Annie?"

She lowered her eyes to the table. "I'm still upset about what happened to Desdemona. Doris is the meanest mother I could ever imagine."

He looked toward the door leading into the dining room. "Don't say that *too* loud, Annie."

"Why?"

He pretended not to hear her. He stepped onto the back porch and out the back door. He went into the old, white-washed barn at the end of the driveway. In one of the stalls, he found a round point shovel and put it in the trunk of his vehicle.

She was still sitting at the table when he returned. He lied, saying that while outside he'd received a call on his cell phone, and something had come up that would require his absence for a few minutes.

"It's a little problem at work. I'm afraid that you'll have to go back into the closet for a while. It won't be more than twenty minutes or so. I promise."

She stood and grabbed his shirt sleeve.

"Please don't. Please. Just take me with you. I swear I'll be good."

"Annie, I promise you that this will be the very last time that I will ever make you stay locked up in the closet."

"Really and truly, Mr. Iblis?"

"Cross my heart." And he did, with his right forefinger.

"Okay then, but how am I supposed to know how long twenty minutes is?"

"You'll just have to trust me on this, Annie. I'll be right back."

He took her to the closet, strapped her in the chair, and locked the door. He could hear her saying something inside, but it was so faint, he couldn't make it out.

In truth, his agenda included an errand which might take longer than twenty minutes. It was a good thing that she couldn't tell how long that he was gone. He didn't want the picnic spoiled because she was upset with his tardiness.

Chapter Forty-Three

Friday, Afternoon

After Will returned to his house, he paced, sat, and moped, going from room to room, out in the yard, and back again. He wanted to do something—anything—to help with the search for Annie. He had been ordered to hold tight and wait for Jack's call, but no call had come yet.

He'd picked up a chicken sandwich on the way home, thinking he might eat it for lunch. Now, with the day more than half gone, he took it out of the refrigerator, unwrapped it, and ate some of it. Staring at what was left of the sandwich, he thought, *Annie loved these things*. Pete did, too. He pulled the rest of the chicken out of the bun and handed it to the dog. It was gone within seconds.

Watching Pete gulp down the chicken, he made a decision. If he hadn't heard from Jack by late afternoon, he would leash the dog and head to Methvin Avenue.

As the afternoon dragged on, his cell phone rang. The display indicated that the call was coming from the church. It was Callie. "Will, I'm so upset. The FBI men have been here. The FBI! They're looking for Wycke...Dr. Randolph. It's crazy, but they think he had something to do with what's happened to Annie."

He had to think for a moment before the name rang a bell. "Do you mean Dr. Taliaferro's associate? That Dr. Randolph?"

"Yes."

"That makes no sense. Why were they looking for him at the church?"

"They came here to talk with me because Wycke's nurse told them about us. I don't know why they want to talk with him."

"Why do you say 'us,' Callie?"

A few seconds of silence followed before she sighed and continued. "I've been seeing him for a while. He begged me not to mention it to anybody because he's in the middle of a nasty divorce up in Atlanta. He and his wife have been separated since last year, but now she's trying to take everything he has. He was afraid that if she found out we were dating she could use it against him. I don't know how since we haven't done anything but talk."

"This is shocking news, Callie. How long has it been going on?"

"It all began in July. He came by the church one day when you were out. He said you were in his office earlier, and he wanted to speak with you about joining the church."

"I have been to his office with Annie, but we didn't see him. We were waiting for Dr. Taliaferro. Have you been with Dr. Randolph today?"

"We were supposed to have lunch. It would have been the first time in two weeks or so. I picked up something, and he planned to come to my house. He didn't want us seen out together."

"Where is he now?"

"I don't know. He never got to my house, and my calls to his phone went to voicemail. So, I came on back to work."

"Has he ever mentioned Annie to you?"

"Yes, and he seemed curious about you, too. I guess some of the things I told him may have been of a personal nature. I can't tell you how upset I am about all of this, Will. You don't think he was using me to find out things about Annie, do you?"

He could tell she was crying. "You've done nothing wrong, Callie. If you hear from Dr. Randolph, call Jack Carter right away."

"I despise keeping secrets from people. It always turns out badly."

By the time the call ended, Callie was so distraught that he was worried about her. He called the church's youth minister, explained the situation, and asked her to check on Callie for him.

At least the FBI was doing something, but he wondered what Jack was up to. He tried to reach him again without success, hoping to find out if Dr. Randolph was a suspect, and if so, why. A call to the police station was just as fruitless. "The FBI guys are back there, but Jack isn't. I'll let him know you called."

He thumbed through his contacts and found Maggie Carter's number. She had no idea where he might be. "You know how police work is—we haven't heard from Jack since he left for his office early this morning. We're so hoping they find her, Will."

He put Pete in the backyard and drove to the police station. After he told the officer at the front desk that he had some information to share about Annie's case, he was escorted back to an office where Todd Baxter and another FBI Agent were sitting. Baxter was on his cell phone, and the other agent was reviewing some kind of paperwork. He nodded and sat, waiting for Baxter to finish his call. From what he overheard, it had something to do with Brad Dixon. *And what's that all about?* he wondered.

Baxter put his phone on the table and looked across at Will. "Reverend Rowan, you're here for what reason?"

"My assistant mentioned that one of your associates has been at the church asking about Dr. Randolph. I just wondered why."

Baxter listened to his question but said nothing

"Where's Jack?" Will asked.

He answered without looking up. "I'm sure he'll be back soon."

"But where is he?"

The agent gave him a tired look and shook his head. "He'll be back, and I'll have him call you. Okay? Before you go, let me ask you something. Your secretary is Callie Rainwater, right?"

Will nodded.

"Has she mentioned Dr. Randolph to you today?"

"Yes. She was seeing him, but they kept it a secret from me. It was something about a pending divorce. Why?"

"Do you know him?"

Will explained Randolph's offer to treat Annie when they visited his office last January. "I just talked to his nurse that day. We never saw him, and I wouldn't know him if he walked through that door right now. Is he a suspect?"

"Let's just say that a blip came up on his background check, something that happened a long time ago when he was a juvenile, a statutory rape that was never prosecuted. We just want to talk to him, and that's all I can tell you. Now you head on home and wait for Jack to call you. Okay?"

"Agent Baxter, you were talking on your phone when I came in. I heard you say something about Brad Dixon. What's that all about?"

Baxter hesitated. When he spoke again, his words were measured. "I can't talk to you about that right now, but I will tell you this. Some questions have come up about the extent of Rankin Turner's involvement in this whole thing, and because of that, our investigation remains ongoing. Please understand that we're doing everything in the world that we can do to find your daughter. We'll be in touch, Reverend Rowan. Why don't you go on home?"

He left the police station and headed over to Mae's shop, where he found her alone. She came from behind the counter and hugged him. While they were still embracing, she said, "I'm so glad you're here. I was just getting ready to call you. A customer was browsing the shelves, and I was waiting for her to leave."

The concern in her eyes was obvious. "I wish I knew what was going on, Mae. I haven't reached Jack yet."

She turned away, saying, "I haven't seen him either, but one of his detectives, Ted Bridger, has been here. You met him out at the fairgrounds the other day." She went behind the counter again as if she needed a momentary buffer. "I went to school with Ted, and I always thought he had a crush on me. It seemed like he was trying to impress me."

He waited, having no idea where this was going.

"Ted was looking for Brad. He's been ordered to bring him in. The police think he had something do with what happened to Annie."

Will was flummoxed by this. "Why?"

"When they checked, they found out he's been lying to me all along. He's not a retired colonel, and he's never even been in the Army. He certainly never knew my husband or served with him in Afghanistan. He may have taken a job at the shop just to get close to you…and to Annie. They're planning to come back and check my phone lines just in case he's been listening in on my conversations with you."

His voice shot up an octave. "Have they found him yet?"

"When Ted came by, Brad was still at lunch. I told him where he usually goes, and maybe they found him there. He hasn't come back, so I'm thinking they got him, but I haven't heard from the police again."

For all Will knew, Dixon was being held at the police station when he was there. He might have already told them where Annie was. "Mae, I need to go. I have to go back to Jack's office."

"Will, I feel like such a fool. I hired Brad without even checking him out. All I know about him is what he told me. I'm so very sorry."

"It's not your fault, Mae. We'll talk later, but right now I've got to go." The possibilities were becoming endless. *Was it Turner? Randolph? Dixon? Was it two together? Was it all three at once?*

Five minutes later, he was back at the receiving desk in the foyer of the police station, addressing the desk sergeant. "I need to talk with Agent Baxter again. Would you tell him I'm out here? I want to know if anybody has been to the house on Methvin yet." The officer got Baxter on the phone, listened to his response, and then sent Will on his way. "About the house on Methvin, he doesn't know what you're talking about. He said for you to go on home."

Will considered arguing with the officer but turned and walked out instead. He couldn't find Jack and the FBI wouldn't give him the time of day. Only one option remained.

Chapter Forty-Four

Friday, Afternoon

After Iblis lost his beloved Desdemona, a desperate need to control his life had colored all of his activities, and that need continued until this day. Now, as he returned to Doris' house after winding up his minimal, pending affairs, control remained at the forefront of his warped psyche, and he wasn't about to lose it. A great sadness was there, too, but that couldn't be helped. Now, more than ever, he had to do what was required.

Entering the house, he noted that all was quiet. In the kitchen, he placed a bucket of fried chicken in the refrigerator. Then, he went to the downstairs bedroom and put on a casual outfit suitable for a picnic. While he was changing, he heard footsteps on the front porch. Buttoning his shirt, he left the bedroom and stepped into the hall. A black man stood on the other side of the front door. As Iblis stood very still and watched, the visitor pasted his face against the door's glass panel and tried to peer inside.

After knocking on the door several times for over half a minute, he turned and left the porch. Iblis assumed that he'd given up. He went to the door, parted the window curtains, and looked out. Neither the man, nor any vehicle was in the front of the house. Relieved, he headed toward the closet to free Annie, but a noise sent him to the kitchen and the door leading into the back porch. He cracked the door and peered across the porch, confirming that the stranger was now at the back door.

Soon, the knocking resumed, and this time, he would have to answer it because the door wasn't locked. But first, he pocketed a six-inch knife from a rack on the kitchen counter. When he stepped onto the back porch, his visitor had already pushed open the door without an invitation. His appearance and demeanor gave him away. Iblis recalled seeing him just two days earlier when he and another cop were rummaging through the bushes in front of the brick house at the corner of Oglethorpe and Methvin.

The man held up a badge and ID. "I'm Lieutenant Jack Carter of the Catalpa Police Department." Craning his neck, he looked around the back porch, and then his gaze settled on Iblis, staying there for several seconds before he spoke again. "This used to be Doris Paine's house. Are you Chalker?"

He was taken aback but recovered quickly, nodding and smiling broadly. "I'm surprised you know my family, lieutenant."

"I've lived here all my life, and I try to keep up with folks."

"You must have been the one knocking at the front door. I was busy in the kitchen and didn't hear it at first. Then, when I did hear it and went to the door, I didn't see anybody or any vehicle out front. I'm glad you came around back."

"It's a pretty day. I left my car at the station and walked over. May I go ahead and come inside?"

"Sure. What can I help you with?"

As the lieutenant stepped across the threshold, Iblis noticed the large pistol holstered on his belt behind his back. He stood facing Iblis. "You do live here, don't you, Mr. Paine?"

"Actually, my residence is elsewhere. This was my mother's house, and I stay here every now and then to salve my nostalgia."

"And where do you reside?"

"I have my own home. I acquired this house a little over a year ago from my mother's estate. I'll probably end up selling it." *Here's hoping the lieutenant didn't notice that I dodged his question about the location of my home. The less he knows about me, the better.*

The lieutenant paused, seemingly considering that, but then moved on. "Mr. Paine. I'm sure you've heard about the disappearance of little Annie Rowan. Because she was last seen nearby, we're canvasing the neighborhood for any clues as to her whereabouts."

"Oh, yes. The police have already been here once, the night the girl was seen, I guess, but you're coming back now for some reason?"

The policeman's eyes went to the floor and then back up to meet his. "As a precaution, we're taking a look at every house on the street. No one was at home next door, so I'm starting with your house."

Iblis decided to play along. *But, if an opportunity presents itself, I'll stop playing.* "Isn't a search warrant usually required for something like this?"

The lieutenant seemed nervous. He kept looking down, avoiding his eyes. "It takes a great deal of time to get a warrant, and time is something that we don't have. A little girl's life is at stake."

"But still, lieutenant…"

He sighed. "Let's just say my visit is unofficial. Will you agree to let me take a look around? That way, no warrant will be required."

"Of course, you can look around. I have nothing to hide, lieutenant. Why don't you start on the second floor?"

He did, even looking in the small attic opening off Doris' bedroom. Of course, it was all fruitless. Annie wasn't making a sound at the moment, and Iblis guessed that she must have dozed off. He took the policeman through the downstairs rooms, too, ending in the bath and bedroom off the short hall that housed Annie's closet. It was dark in the hall under the stairs, and Iblis made a point of not turning on the light. The officer walked by the closet door twice without even noticing it.

"Well, lieutenant, that's the tour. I certainly do hope you find the little girl." Iblis guided the officer toward the front door. Throughout, the policeman had never turned his back on him, and he was still facing him now.

"Before I leave, I want to ask you about something that happened a long time ago right down there at the intersection of Methvin and Oglethorpe. It involved you and your sister and a boy named Rankin Turner. You may have seen Turner's name mentioned in the paper today or heard it on TV."

Iblis stiffened. "Yes, I'm very much aware of the incident you're talking about, but what do you want to know about it?"

"What were the three of you doing together down there that…" Suddenly the lieutenant stopped and cocked his head.

"Did you hear that thumping noise, Mr. Paine? I could just make it out. It sounds like somebody stomping their feet."

"I don't think so. What are you referring to?"

"It's coming from the direction of the stairs."

The policeman began walking that way at a brisk pace with Iblis following close behind. He stopped next to the stairs, listening. The thumping commenced again.

"These old houses have all kinds of funny noises, lieutenant. I'm sure it's nothing at all."

"Somebody's doing it." He followed the sound over to the short, dark hall under the stairs.

"Is there some kind of light in here, Mr. Paine? If so, please cut it on."

Iblis found the switch and flipped it on.

"Is that a closet?" the lieutenant said. He moved to the door and tried the knob, finding it locked.

While the policeman's hand was still on the knob, Iblis placed the point of the knife on his neck, piercing the skin. He froze as a trickle of blood found its way down between his shoulder blades. A second later, Iblis spoke into his right ear with the calmest of whispering voices.

"Lieutenant, raise your hands and rest them on the door frame. Otherwise, don't move at all, or I will slice your spinal cord into two separate and quite distinct portions. At that point, you will sink to the floor, having lost all control of every nerve in your body and every accompanying function below your neck."

Chapter Forty-Five

Friday, Afternoon

Driving home from the police station, Will gave Mae a call. He wanted to know if she'd heard from Brad. She hadn't. As they talked, he couldn't hide his frustration with law enforcement. "Nobody knows where Jack is, and the FBI agent won't give me any details about what they're planning to do. You saw Pete's reaction to that house last night, and if somebody doesn't get in there right now, it may be too late."

She sighed. "You're not thinking of going back there, are you?"

"If I do, I'll have Pete with me."

"Please don't do that, Will. Wait till you hear from Jack. Maybe he's already been over there. You couldn't have gotten much sleep last night, and you must be exhausted. Just lie down for a while, at least until he calls."

He was silent.

"Will?"

"Just think of who's on my side, Mae."

"Do you mean Pete?"

"You know I don't."

At home, he let Pete in the house and checked one more time for missed calls or messages on his cell phone or his landline recorder and found none. Then, with Pete on his heels, he went to his bedroom and took down the wooden, presentation case which contained the revolver his mother had given him after Leah was killed. He carried it to the kitchen and sat at the table.

He opened the case and took out the gun. He'd never fired it before, but his father showed it to him when he was a boy. At the time, they were on the bank of a small lake, getting ready to put a john boat in the water to fish for bass. His father planned to take it along to kill any snakes that might come their way. He let him hold the gun before he loaded it. At the time, the gun seemed big, heavy, and dangerous, and he still remembered what his father called it. "Smith and Wesson, Model 10."

He showed him how to load it and engage and release the safety. After that, his father had fired a round into a stump nearby. He declined to let him shoot the revolver that day, although Will would later shoot others with him.

He placed the gun on the table. When his mother gave it to him, she'd told him it was loaded, and he released the cylinder now and found that it was. He thought the safety was on, but he could not be sure. He unloaded the gun and checked. The safety *was* on.

As he placed the gun back in the case, old Mr. Tolley's question at the fairgrounds on Monday night popped into his head again. *Would a preacher ever kill a man?*

He stared at the gun. It was still big, heavy, and dangerous, a purveyor of death, a terrible, ungodly thing in the hand of whoever pulled the trigger. *Could I ever kill a man?*

It was a question that would have to remain unanswered for the time being. He looked at his watch and came to a conclusion. If Jack didn't call within the next thirty minutes, he and Pete would go to the house on Methvin Avenue. He pushed the gun aside and put his head down on his folded arms. Soon he was asleep with his head on the table. At his feet, Pete drifted off, too.

271 • The Closet

Chapter Forty-Six

Friday, Afternoon

Iblis dealt with Lieutenant Carter in short order. He began by telling Catalpa's second highest ranking law enforcement officer that Annie was indeed still very much alive and located in the closet under the stairs. He also threatened to cut off Annie's right index finger for starters, unless the policeman provided some very important information. Under the circumstances, he was more than willing to cooperate.

First, the lieutenant admitted that no one else engaged in law enforcement had connected Iblis with the Methvin Avenue house or a man named Chalker Paine. Among policeman, he, and he alone, had put it all together. "Even the lawyer, Sam Franklin, didn't know anything but the name your mother gave you when he transferred this house to you."

This comment brought a chuckle from Iblis. "He was too concerned about money to worry about who I really was."

Second, the lieutenant explained why he'd come to the house in the first place. It was a combination of things. It involved the recollection of an old woman named Janie Stewart, the contents of an old obituary, records from the tax office and Sam Franklin's office, a report from the State crime lab, and Will Rowan's dog. And to his knowledge, he was the only one who had made these connections.

Third, he confessed that his visit to the Paine house this afternoon was "secret by necessity." No one else knew that he was here. "I didn't even try for a warrant, and I was afraid I might lose my badge if someone found out that I broke into your house."

Lastly, he confirmed that his police vehicle was still parked at the police station.

When the lieutenant finished, Iblis said, "So, it's just you. You don't know of any reason why any law enforcement types might show up here looking for you or me or Annie?"

"None whatsoever. By the way, scumbag, if you have laid one hand on her, I'll hunt you down and kill you."

This brought a smile to Iblis' face. "I assure you that I haven't touched her, lieutenant."

***

Now, with the police officer taken care of, Iblis was ready for the picnic. He removed the pieces of fried chicken from the bucket and put them into a more appropriate plastic container. His visit to the chicken place had taken some time because they were out of dark meat, which he preferred. They fried it while he waited.

"It wouldn't be a picnic without fried chicken," he commented to himself as he removed the other picnic items from the refrigerator and packed everything into the picnic basket. He poured sweet tea into the thermos and added ice. He took the basket and the thermos out to his car and placed them on the passenger seat. At the same time, he removed the policeman's handgun from his pocket, wrapped it in a linen napkin he'd brought out with him, and put it in the trunk next to the blanket and shovel.

Now everything was ready, and it was time to go get Annie. Although happy to see him, she was more than a little put out. She scolded him for being gone for more than the twenty minutes he'd promised.

"How do you know how long I was gone?"

"I counted the seconds in my head. You didn't come back for almost two hours. And even when you came back, you didn't let me out. I could hear someone talking outside the closet door. Was it you? Why didn't you let me out?"

He smiled. She'd heard both him and the police officer, but he wasn't about to let her know that. He knelt down in front of her and put his hand on her shoulder.

"I would ask you to forgive me, Annie, but it wasn't my fault. I was delayed by one thing after another. When I returned, I got tied up on my cell phone. It was me talking on my cell phone that you heard. A call came through right when I was at the door to let you out. It doesn't matter now anyway. I promise you I will never lock you up in this closet ever again."

"I hope you're telling the truth this time."

She was so overjoyed with leaving the house that she didn't complain at all when he asked her to lie down on the back seat of his car. He told her she could sit up as soon as they reached the turn off to the spot where they would picnic.

It was a beautiful, September afternoon. A cool breeze and low humidity blessed the day, and the sky's rare shade of blue beckoned one to come outdoors and stay there until sunset.

After following Rickety Back Road for a while, he turned onto an old, dirt, logging road which ran through a large, wooded tract owned by the power company. He'd investigated the area a month earlier just in case it might be needed, finding it unoccupied. A farmer living nearby volunteered that hunting was not permitted on the property, so it was rarely visited by anyone.

The logging road snaked far back into the woods, and as soon as they were on it, she sat up, looking around and smiling. Through the rearview mirror, her visage brought a smile to his face, too.

When the dirt road came to an end, he stopped and turned his vehicle around so that it was facing in the direction of Rickety Back, now quite a distance away. She exited the car still filled with joy at just being outdoors. He took the basket, and she carried the thermos and blanket, and they walked a short distance through the woods and across a grassy meadow until they reached a wide, deep creek. He spread the blanket on the mossy bank, and they sat together, for the moment doing nothing more than enjoying the lovely setting.

Her happiness was infectious, and it inspired him to entertain her with humorous stories of childhood antics, both his and Desdemona's, but mostly hers. At least half of the tales involved avoiding the wrath of Doris, however and whenever they could. Now and then, Rankin was mentioned, too.

At one point, Annie touched his arm. "You loved Dessie, didn't you?"

"Yes."

"I mean like boyfriend and girlfriend."

He was silent, but his eyes were smiling.

As the sun got lower, but well before it dropped behind the horizon, they had their picnic feast. Annie's appetite was hearty, but she didn't seem to notice that he wasn't eating much. During the meal, he kept up a steady banter about the many quirks of Doris.

"Your childhood wasn't happy, was it?" Her mouth was full of chicken.

"No."

"You've never told me what happened to your mother. Is she dead like mine?"

"Yes, she's dead."

"My mother died in a hospital. My Grannie Eileen told me that a man hit her over the head. How did your mother die?"

Her questions about his childhood and the death of his mother caught him off guard. His mind left the pleasant meadow by the creek and roared back to the house on Methvin Avenue. In a flash, his last, bad days there came back, and for a moment, he lost control. While Annie stared at him, he sat in a trance-like state, remembering every detail of his mother's death and what led up to it, not by telling Annie, but rather in his head as if he was sharing it with another person for the first time.

***

My mother let Desdemona die. That might have been all it took, but she didn't quit there. Callous on a good day, she cancelled out my dead sister in every way imaginable, including throwing out her belongings. But somehow, I secreted away some of Dessie's things and saved them from Mother's wrath.

One thing was a pair of her pink panties. I hid them in my dresser stuffed inside a plastic, Easter egg. From time to time, I brought them out and fondled them, and once or twice, I even wore them to bed. Was that so wrong of me?

I rescued another thing, too—the note Ravenel gave her. I had it laminated at an office supply store, and then I rolled it back up into its original form as a little scroll and tied it with a ribbon. But now I've lost it forever.

My fear that Doris would throw out all of our pictures of Dessie made me hide them, too. One day while she was taking a nap, I collected the family photo album and all of the pictures of Dessie I could find in the house and put them inside a folded blanket on a shelf in my closet. She never looked at pictures of us anyway, so she didn't notice they were missing.

Those effects became my most prized possessions. Mother never discovered the note or the photos, but she did find the panties and played havoc with them later on in the worst possible way.

With Dessie gone, Mother smothered me with cloying, unwanted attention, making my life miserable. When I wasn't in school, she dragged me along everywhere she went, even to her hairdresser and gynecologist. I was a pre-teen for goodness sakes!

But the putrid icing on the sour cake of my young life began to spread in earnest a month or so after Dessie died. Out of the blue, Doris allowed me to select a new school outfit, something she'd always done herself in the past, her taste leaning toward 'sensible' clothes. At a department store on the courthouse square, I chose a light blue, button-down shirt, straight-legged jeans, penny loafers, navy blue socks, and a tan, water-proof cotton jacket. I'd never been so proud. If only Dessie could have seen me! Even now, I treasure the reaction of the girls at school. They looked me up and down, not giggling and pointing at me as they usually did, but with a new curiosity arising from my grand ensemble. I liked my new clothes so much that I wanted to wear them every day. Of course, she wouldn't let me.

One late, October day several weeks later, Mother and I were sitting on the back porch steps after supper, enjoying pecan pie and vanilla ice cream scrunched together in jelly glasses. It was one of her favorite things. Both of us were already dressed for bed. It was a mild evening, and the pleasant weather had me feeling pensive, even melancholy. My thoughts turned to Dessie and then to the father I'd never met. Without giving sufficient thought to the consequences, I touched Mother's arm, gazed up at her, and asked if I would ever get to meet my father.

Her over-loaded spoonful of ice cream stopped halfway to her open mouth, and her face hardened into a grimace. Sporting the wisdom of a doofus, I persevered, mentioning that other boys had fathers and wondering out loud when I might get to meet mine. All at once, her ire gushed forth like the putrid contents of a volcanic, squeezed pimple. She grabbed my arm and shook me violently, dislodging my glass of pie and ice cream. It bounced off the steps, shattering on the asphalt driveway below. I feared the worst, and my fear was altogether justified.

She dragged me into the house and shoved me into the closet under the stairs. The door was closed and locked behind me. It was dark in there, and the only light switch was in the hall. I sat on the floor with my arms wrapped around my knees and began to cry. I'm almost certain that she was on the other side of the door, listening. My mother was a witch, just like Dessie said she was.

After an interminable time, I fell asleep with my head on my knees. I woke up much later, cold and needing to urinate. I pounded on the door, yelling to get out. But she didn't return, and after waiting as long as I could, I wet my pajama bottoms. The odor of urine mixed with that of the cedar walls was vile and nauseating. Within minutes, I vomited my supper into a corner of the little room.

When at last the door was opened the next morning, I stumbled into the hall, disoriented and blinded by the morning light. She was standing there, still wearing a long, white, silk nightgown. Smiling, she patted me on the head. 'I'll fix you a nice breakfast, Chalker, but first I want to show you something. Close your eyes real tight and follow me.'

Even with my eyes closed, I could tell that she was leading me to the back door, down the steps, and onto the asphalt below. I stood there at the bottom of the steps, shaking, with my eyes closed.

'Now open your eyes and look up here, young man.'

I opened my eyes, squinting in the morning sun. Doris was at the top of the steps, looking down at me and smiling. She was gesturing with her left hand toward a point above her head. As my eyes adjusted to the light, something stretching high across the backyard came into focus.

I gasped in disbelief. My new school clothes had been cut into thin strips and woven together to form a long blue and tan rope. The colorful rope stretched from a bolt above the back door, right over Doris' smiling face, all the way to another bolt on the barn.

'And now look over here,' Doris said, pointing down to her right.

Again, a loud gasp left my throat. My brand-new shoes had been nailed to the house and filled with syrup. The syrup was dripping down the white wood siding to the shrubbery below. My navy-blue socks had been nailed up, too, likewise filled with syrup.

But the worst was yet to come.

'Now look back up here, Honey Bun.'

As I watched in horror, she pulled her nightgown high above her waist, revealing Desdemona's pink panties. They were drawn tightly across her crotch, cutting into her white thighs. 'I've known you had these all along, you prissy, little dirtbag. Don't you ever mention your father again. Do you understand?'

She popped the elastic on the waistband of the panties. 'And if you ever want to see these again, you'll have to take them off me.'

She concluded her performance with a curtsy and let her gown fall back down to her ankles. I dropped to my knees, my head on my chest, unable to look at this revolting spectacle for one second longer. A moan rose deep in my throat and left my open mouth in a rushing wail, as if my soul had been gathered up and expelled with it. In truth, I think it had.

It was on that day, right there at the bottom of the steps that I resolved to kill my mother. My own life was in the balance. I had no choice but to do it and no clue as to how to go about it. After all, I was just a boy. But at last, an opportunity came, and I made the most of it.

It arose several months later because of her penchant for trimming shrubbery. Any yard man that ever worked for her was allowed to cut the grass but not the shrubbery. She got too much pleasure from doing it herself—cutting, chopping, slicing, chunking, paring, and shaving bushes right down to their photosynthetic bones.

On her last day on earth, she felt the need to trim a large holly. More than once, she asserted that a holly should never be allowed to grow into tree form. It was 'bad luck,' she said, although I never understood why and still don't.

The holly she wanted to trim that day was very high, indeed, and the ground under it was quite uneven. So, she enlisted me to steady her tall, folding ladder while she did the cutting. She gave me specific instructions about how to hold the ladder, where to stand under it, and how to shift my position while she moved back and forth, cutting away. Ever the dutiful child, I took an extra-firm hold on the swaying ladder as cut branches and leaves pummeled down on my head.

So as to reach the tallest part of the bush, Mother needed to step onto the very top of the ladder and spread her legs wide for balance. Gazing up from the ground, I had a clear view of the boggy area under her short, wrap-around skirt. I blinked, disgusted by what I saw. Under her skirt, between her bare legs, small, red hairs protruded from Desdemona's pink panties. Knowing that I would see them, she had to have worn them again only to get my goat.

The lurid sight proved too much for me, and my troubled psyche snapped. I let go of the ladder and walked away, first mumbling about needing to use the bathroom and nudging the ladder with my shoulder as if by accident.

She teetered and tottered as the ladder began to sway wildly back and forth. 'Come back here, Chalker!' she yelled.

But I didn't go back, and she lost her footing. She soared off the ladder in a modified swan dive and hit the hard ground below face down, first her knees and then her elbows, all to the sound of cracking bones.

To my horror, the fall didn't kill her. Broken and breathless, she was still very much alive. I stood motionless, ready to run, afraid that she might somehow leap up and seek retribution. Then her breath returned. 'What have you done to me, you little, wop bastard? I can't turn over. I can't move. Get me up right now!'

Instead of helping my mother though, I ran around the yard with my eyes to the ground. At last, I found what I needed and picked it up.

'What are you doing, Chalker? I can't see you!' she whined.

I returned and stood behind her. I will never forget the weight and rough texture of the red brick I was now holding in my right hand. 'I'll help you turn over now, Mother.'

With my left hand, I took her left shoulder and turned her toward me. When the left side of her face came up, I brought the brick down on her forehead as hard as I could, just above her left eye. The edge of the brick dented her skull, making a sickening, crunching sound. Her whole body jerked once, and then she went quiet, never to move again. I turned her head back around and put the brick under it, so that its edge matched the dent in her skull.

That done, I ran into the house, found what I needed, and returned to my mother's side. Manipulating her limp body just enough to remove the pink panties, I replaced them with a white pair taken from her chest of drawers. Finished, I sat on the grass next to her.

Then I said to her, 'No one knows whether death may not be the greatest of all blessings.' It was a quote that she had made me memorize during one of my many supplemental lessons on the antiquities.

Everyone assumed that my dear mother had met a terrible, accidental fate, leaving me a pitiful, homeless orphan. Those days were so wretched that I can't bring myself to share them with Annie or anyone else. But

Desdemona knows, and she understands. Yes, Doris is dead, and she always will be.

***

Iblis felt Annie nudging his shoulder, and as his eyes focused, his mind returned to the present.

"Are you okay, Mr. Iblis? You seemed to go away for a little while, and you never answered my question. What happened to your mother?"

He pretended not to hear her and instead pointed to a hawk sailing above the trees, around and around in graceful circles. "I like to think of Desdemona as sailing across the sky like that hawk, altogether free of this earth, smiling and looking down on me, waiting to lift me up there, too. I hope better places than this exist, don't you, Annie?"

"If you mean heaven, that's what my father says." Just as soon as those words came out of her mouth, her eyes dropped to her plate. When she raised her head again, tears wet her face.

He put his arm around her and pulled her close. *Poor, poor girl. You have no idea what lies ahead for you.* They sat like that for a little while, and then he clapped his hands. "It's time for some pie!"

He gave her a piece of pie but didn't put any on his plate. After she was eating again, he stood suddenly. "I almost forgot. I have some things we need, Annie, but I left them in the car. I'll just run up to the car and get them. It's parked just on the other side of that rise."

"Promise me you're coming back, Mr. Iblis."

"Don't be silly. I always have."

As he walked through the woods to his car, his heart was heavy. When he reached the edge of the woods, he stopped, turned, and saw her sitting with her knees drawn up and her arms wrapped around them. She was gazing at the beautiful green pasture on the other side of the creek.

All at once, a song that Doris used to sing to him and Dessie came to mind, one he always associated with death. He couldn't remember all of the words, but it was about the Promised Land, about crossing the River Jordan to the sweet, green fields on the other side.

And then as he continued into the woods, something else came to mind. It was what his mother used to say to him and Dessie almost every day. *I wouldn't be doing this to you, children, if I didn't love you.*

Chapter Forty-Seven

Friday, Evening

At the kitchen table, Will was awakened by the ringing of his cell phone. The digital read out on its face indicated that he'd been asleep for over an hour. Still groggy, he studied the number of the caller. It was coming from the church. He didn't want to talk with anyone from the church right now, even Callie, and he let it go to voicemail. His current mood was antithetical to what the church stood for.

The gun was still on the table in front of him, and Pete was still at his feet. He put some food in Pete's bowl, and while the dog was eating, he called Jack's office and then his home. Jack hadn't been in touch with either one, and Maggie sounded worried.

"Please let me know if you hear anything, Will. This isn't like Jack."

In his bedroom closet, he found a light, nylon jacket and put it on. Back in the kitchen, he tightened his belt, and put the gun behind his back in the waist of his trousers. He draped the jacket over it, just like he'd seen done in the movies. He practiced pulling it out several times to make sure that he could access it with ease.

At that moment, he heard Mr. Tolley again, as surely as if the old soldier was sitting right there in the kitchen. *Would a preacher ever kill a man?*

"God help me, Mr. Tolley, I don't know," he muttered.

He sighed and looked around the kitchen wondering if he'd forgotten anything. For just a second, he considered leaving the gun behind but nixed the idea. Displaying the gun might be the only way to get whoever lived there to tell him where Annie was. *Surely* that *won't require shooting anybody, will it?*

He put his cell phone in the vibrate mode and pocketed it. As soon as he took down a leash, Pete began wagging and huffing in anticipation of an outing. Bending over to attach the leash, he felt the gun pressing hard against the small of his back. He prayed then, asking God to protect him and Pete and to allow them to bring Annie home, regardless of whether she was dead or alive.

On the way to the front door, the dog started barking for no apparent reason. Will unlocked the door and put his hand on the knob. As he did, it began to turn. He removed his hand, placed it on the gun, and stepped back. By that time, Pete's barking had reached a fever pitch.

The door was opened from the outside, and his mother was standing there dressed in tan jeans, a blue sweat shirt, and sneakers. A small duffel, sprinkled with appliqued flowers, sat at her feet. "Don't look so shocked, Will. I told you I would come on up if you didn't call. You didn't, so here I am."

He was speechless. She opened her arms to hug him, and he reciprocated. He was sure she could the feel the gun in his waistband, but she didn't mention it right away. After she knelt down and greeted the dog, he picked up her duffel and followed her inside.

"I was afraid you might be at the church."

"I haven't been back there since this morning."

Amelia Rowan studied him for a second and then said, "So what's going on? What's with the gun?"

He ignored her question, offering instead to take her bag to Annie's room. "I've got it," she said, picking up her bag and following him to her granddaughter's room. She placed the bag on the bed, next to the big, pink rabbit.

Picking up the rabbit and hugging it, she said, "Oh, Henry, it's so good to see you again." She put it back on the bed and avoided Will's eyes, but he could see the tears.

"You must be worn out from the drive," he said. "Would you like some coffee or a Coke?"

While he made coffee, she told him she'd browsed through all the media reports on Rankin's death, and cited them as one reason why she'd come on up. "I know you've got Mae, but I thought you might need even more support right now."

He told her that the investigation had been moving in several other directions today and that Rankin might not have been the only one involved. He gave few particulars and left out his middle-of-the-night visit to the Methvin Avenue house.

"You mean there's a chance she's...is it possible?" She looked away and put her hand over her mouth, unable to finish her question.

"Maybe."

She poured two cups of coffee. "You still like sugar?"

He nodded, took his cup, and they sat in silence for a minute or so, sipping the coffee.

"Why exactly are you carrying a gun?"

"You never know when you might need one."

"Will, I'm not sure what that means, but if you want my advice, stick with what you do best—praying—and let the police do their jobs. Ministers don't go around shooting people, and from what you've told me about that police lieutenant friend of yours, he seems very competent. If Annie can be found, I'm sure he can do it. There's a big difference between having a gun for protection and carrying one on a mission to shoot somebody, don't you agree?"

Her question went unanswered. "Look, before you got here, I'd promised Pete that I would take him for a long walk."

"I'll put my stuff away and come with you."

"No. I want some time to think. But I'd really appreciate your fixing something for my supper. Do you remember that grocery store on the other side of the courthouse square?"

"I do, and I'd love to cook for you. It'll be in the works before you get back." As she spoke, she eyed some folded papers he'd left on a kitchen counter and then picked them up. "Is this important, Will?"

Months before, he'd told her about the incident on Tybee Island, and now he explained that she was holding the FBI's list of all the people staying on the island at the time. "I haven't had a chance to look at it today. If you run out of things to do, why don't you see if you recognize any of the names on it?"

"I'll do it as soon as I get back from the grocery store and get dinner started. Give me a hug before you go."

She hugged him again, this time avoiding the gun.

Before their embrace ended, he said, "Mother, I love you," and when they separated, her eyes searched his, but he turned away.

"Will, what…"

He cut her off. "I need to go now." Picking up Pete's leash, he left the house. As soon as he was outside, he put his phone in the silent/vibrate mode. All the way to Methvin Avenue, the gun rubbed against his back, causing him to debate the wisdom of what he was doing.

Chapter Forty-Eight

Friday, Evening

Iblis was no longer in the woods off Rickety Back Road. He was sitting on the concrete steps at the back door of Doris' house. Behind him, the sun was low in the sky, shadowing the back yard. It was a most fitting place to reflect on his relief at last from the racking guilt and dispiriting baggage which had haunted him for half a lifetime. Unfortunately for some, his absolution had come at an exorbitant price, especially for the cost paid today.

The star-crossed surrogate, Annie Rowan, was deep in the woods, soon to be 'resting' if you will, far off the nearest public road, not be disturbed any time soon. The power company was most likely holding the land for investment, and numerous signs on the property attested to the prohibition of hunters. By the time she was found, if she ever was, he would be living a different life far from Catalpa and the troubling remnants of his past.

He'd guaranteed his own obscurity. Almost forty years earlier in a Georgia town north of Atlanta and far removed from Tanotchee County he'd been adopted and given a new name. Ever since, he'd been someone else. Even if the county where he was adopted ever came to light, which was doubtful, the records of the proceeding were forever sealed by law. Nor could his adoptive parents provide any information, revelatory or otherwise. When they adopted him, they were already late-middle aged, and they'd both died natural deaths years before, virtually penniless. Perhaps some smart detective would one day connect a man named Chalker Paine with Doris and what happened to Annie, but no one could ever connect Iblis with that man. *Chalker Paine did it, but who is he now?*

Where is he? Those were questions which might someday echo through the halls of law enforcement offices from Tanotchee County to Atlanta and beyond, questions without answers.

Thanks to his despised mother, he was now a rich man. In fact, one could almost say that she'd made all of this possible. He wouldn't be returning to his current position because he had no need to do so. The world was his, and he could live anywhere in it. Neither his own residence nor this house was of further use to him, and he would gladly leave them behind, never to return. Let the tax collectors have it.

He was satisfied that over time, in a different place and life, his still vivid memories of Doris would fade. He would forget Rankin and Annie, too. Of course, he would always be mindful of Desdemona, but she would cease to be the focus of his life.

He was so filled to overflowing with the joy of leaving the past behind that he whispered, "Excelsior!" He'd not experienced this kind of exultation since the death of his mother. *Death brings life,* she would have pointed out.

As he sat in this blissful state, reveling in his newly found freedom, he glanced at Doris' Ligustrum hedge, tall, green, and still surrounding the back yard. *It needs cutting,* he thought.

Then, something else caught his eye. It was a large, metal eye bolt protruding from the corner of the house, above the steps, just below the lower roof. From the metal bolt, his eyes followed an imaginary line to a companion bolt still high up on the corner of the old barn. The bolts were no longer joined by a line as they once had been.

Just thinking of those bolts and his mother still brought forth apprehension, and in defiance of the cool, evening air, one droplet after another of sweat rolled off his forehead onto his shirt. That the drops weren't blood red surprised him.

Here, in the setting sun on the back steps of Doris' house, he vowed never to sully his mind with her memory again. For all he knew, she might still be in the house right now, up there in her room waiting for him, but he didn't care. In a few minutes, he would leave her far, far behind forever.

At peace now, he stood to go inside. But at that very moment, a large, black dog stuck its head around the corner of the house and let out a roaring bark.

Chapter Forty-Nine

Friday, Evening

Will and Pete reached the corner of Oglethorpe Street and Methvin Avenue as the sun was announcing the coming darkness with a final, brilliant burst of gold. By then, the dog was already jerking him onto the Methvin sidewalk as if he knew exactly where they were headed.

Soon they stood before the second house on the right, the one with the rounded front porch, now dead white in the gloaming. From the sidewalk, he saw no lights coming from the house or any other signs of life. At that moment, his cell phone vibrated, unnerving him. It was nothing but a text from his mother, *Just wanted to let you know...Mae's coming for dinner*. He shook his head; eating was the last thing on his mind right now.

Returning his attention to the house, he got a firm grip on the leash with his right hand and thumbed in Jack's number on his phone. This time, a recording said, "The number you are trying to reach is not in service at this time." That was it; he'd tried over and over again to get Jack but couldn't. He would wait no longer.

He'd already decided on a course of action, even if someone *was* at home. Should Pete's agitation apex again as it had the night before, he was going inside, hang the consequences. He leaned down to the huffing dog and whispered two words, "Find Annie." Right away, the big canine yanked the leash out of his hand and took off down the driveway. He dashed after him, yelling, "Pete, no!"

The dog rushed around the corner of the house and commenced barking before he could catch him. When he rounded the house seconds later, he was shocked to find a parked car back there. The sight brought him to a sudden stop. Recovering, he bounded up the steps, grabbed the leash, and pulled Pete off the door.

He stood fast for a moment, restraining the dog and entertaining the possibility that whoever lived in this house had nothing to do with Annie's kidnapping. Pete's extreme activity seemed to disprove that, but even so, he couldn't just barge in making accusations and brandishing a gun with no idea of what he might find inside. He *was* going in, but unless he remained calm, wary, and collected, a disastrous result might follow.

The dog was a powder keg. When somebody answered the door, he might explode helter-skelter into the house, taking Will with him. He opted to hold him in reserve for the time being even though it meant giving up any protection he might afford.

An iron railing ran along the steps, and he knotted the leash around its bottom post. Pete reacted with jerks and pulls so violent that they threatened to bring the railing down, but it held fast. Having restrained the raging animal, he climbed the steps and knocked on the back door. To his surprise, the force of his blows pushed the door open, inviting him to come inside.

First, he took off his jacket and hung it over the railing. Then, he eased across the threshold into an enclosed back porch. He stood still and listened, but the house was as quiet as a mortuary. Beyond the porch, a dark hall waited, offering no semblance of life. He called out in that direction, voicing the classic, "Hello? Is anybody at home?"

After a stressful pause, a strong, articulate, male voice responded. "Reverend Rowan? Is that you? I saw you and your dog heading down the driveway, and I'm at a loss to understand why you chose to use the back door instead of the front. Be that as it may, please just come on in. You are certainly welcome in this house."

***

Never looking back, Iblis had gotten inside the house just as he saw the big, black dog begin to round the corner. He closed the back door but had no time to lock it. Doubtless, the snarling hound had come for him, poised to rip him to shreds. He longed for the policeman's gun, but it lay in the trunk of his car to be thrown away miles from here along with the muddy shovel, the picnic basket, Annie's clothes and anything else from Doris' house that might implicate him. In its absence, he grabbed a long-bladed knife from the rack on the kitchen counter, the same one he'd used on Jack, now cleaned of blood.

He knew the black lab on sight, having seen it in Rowan's backyard on one of his drive-by forays several weeks earlier. Now though, it was pulling at a leash, so the preacher was surely right behind it. The knife would protect him from the animal if it got too close, and he could use it on Rowan, too, if need be, but he was far more concerned about the animal. By their very natures, preachers were kind and gentle, but dogs could be killers.

As these thoughts ran through his head, a question popped up. *Am I sure it's Rowan and not some cop come to find Lieutenant Carter? Better to confirm it.*

He jogged through the downstairs bedroom into the same bathroom once used by Annie. Hidden at the window, he watched Rowan tie up the dog and head up the steps. *Good! Preacher but no dog! I can certainly deal with that.*

He hurried back through the bedroom to the short hall in front of the closet under the stairs. From there, he heard Rowan call out, and he replied. Then he stepped into the dark closet, leaving the door cracked so the intruder could hear him. He sat in Annie's chair with the knife in his right hand, hidden beside his right thigh. If the pastor was brave enough to leave the back porch, Iblis was sure he could lure him to the closet. Without the dog, he was more

293 • The Closet

or less at his mercy because the odds of his having a weapon of any kind were almost nil.

When the preacher opened the closet door, the photos on the walls would shock him at first. Then, a second later, he would see Iblis. The further jolt of that revelation would have him so off balance that the knife could find its mark with ease. The poor man of God, confused, off-guard, and vulnerable, would have no means with which to fight back.

In the dark, he sat very still and listened. He heard Rowan call out again and then go from room to room on the first floor. When he heard the Bible booster coming into the short hall leading into the downstairs bedroom, he smiled. Now he would surely investigate that room and finding nothing, return to the hall. When he did, Iblis would bring him into the closet like a fish on a line. He regretted the ensuing mess he would make and considered whether he would even bother to clean it up. Most probably, not.

Chapter Fifty

Friday, Twilight

The voice inviting Will to come into the house had sounded so pleasant that he wondered if his visit was a big mistake, if Jack was right, and if Pete *had* smelled something other than Annie. The washer and dryer on the back porch suggested that this might be some innocent person's home after all. He hesitated, but as he listened to Pete barking and whining outside, something told him to trust the dog.

Of the three doors off the porch, one opened onto a long, dark hall, another looked like it might lead into a small closet, and a third led into a kitchen. He walked toward the hall because he thought the man's voice came from that direction. Then he called out to the owner again. "I'm inside the house now. Where are you?"

He got no answer, so he proceeded up the hall. Ahead, a small foyer greeted guests at the front door with sitting rooms on either side of it, both deserted, and a stairway to the second floor on his left. He went through a door across from the stairs into a dining room and the kitchen, but he couldn't locate the man.

So far, the decor made him feel like he was stepping back into the era of his grandmother. At her house, it was altogether pleasant, but here, it was sinister. If any lights were burning, he couldn't see them, and as he wandered through the first floor, the daylight coming in from the outside began to dim. In the hall, he stopped, reluctant to go up the stairs yet. "I'm having trouble finding you," he said loudly but got no reply.

Unease over the décor, the silence, and the growing darkness led him to reach back and put his fingers around the butt of the gun, but he left it in his waistband. In his pocket, his cell phone vibrated, startling him. Thinking that it might be Jack, he pulled it out and found another text message from his mother. *Will, there's a familiar name on the Tybee list. Call me as soon as you can.*

He put the phone back in his pocket and looked up the stairs toward the second floor. He was about to go up when he realized he'd missed an opening under the stairs. He walked over and investigated. Finding a short hall leading to a bedroom, he went back there. But the man was not in the bedroom or its adjoining bath. This silly game annoyed him. The only time the man spoke, his voice seemed to come from somewhere on the first floor. He must have since gone upstairs.

Back in the main hall, he called up the stairs. "I can't find you, sir. Are you upstairs?"

"I'm in here, Will."

The man's voice, although softer this time, alarmed him. He could have sworn that it came from the bedroom he just left. "Where?"

"I'm right here in the closet under the stairs. There's a light switch by the door. Turn it on."

He walked back into the short hallway. It was so dark he hadn't even noticed the closet door before. He found the light switch and flipped it. A slither of light shone through the door of the closet, and he began to sweat. "I've come to take Annie home. Is she in there with you?"

A long, anxiety-producing pause followed before the man spoke again. "Of course not. Why would you even think that? Just open the door and come on in. There's something I want to show you."

Will was bewildered by this strange arrangement. *Who or what is behind that door?*

He thought of getting Pete but hesitated, considering all the commotion the dog might cause. If Annie *was* in the closet, she might get hurt in the resulting fray. He was conflicted. *What if the man had done nothing wrong and was in the closet performing some kind of perfectly legitimate task? Not possible! He'd been sitting in the dark.*

Either the man was very eccentric, or something very unpleasant awaited him as soon as he opened the door. He reached for his cell phone thinking he might call the police, but he stopped. They would laugh for sure at his story about an agitated dog and a man who wouldn't come out of a closet.

"I'm waiting, Will."

Something in the tone of the man's voice caused him to reach for the gun. He pulled it from his waistband and held it down by his side. He stood behind the door and with his left hand, took the knob and inched it open. Light poured into the hall from the closet, but nothing else happened. He opened it further, pushing the gun forward so the man could see *it* but not him.

The man guffawed. "Good heavens, a preacher with a gun! What in the world do think you're going to do with that thing, Will?"

The truth was, he *didn't* know. He moved slowly forward, trying to keep the gun from shaking, and peered around the opened door. He'd been holding his breath, but as the little room came into view, he let his breath out in a rush and spoke one word, "Annie." She was not in the closet, but the walls were covered with pictures of her.

He then turned his head toward the man surrounded by the pictures. He sat on a wooden chair in the middle of the little room with his legs crossed, seemingly relaxed

He was stunned. "Henry! It's you...Henry Pylant! Leah's..." He couldn't finish his thought. He couldn't have been any more dumbfounded if a reincarnated John Wesley had been sitting there.

"Yes, Will, it's me."

"What are you doing *here*? Where did you get all of these pictures of Annie?"

The Emory professor uncrossed his legs. His body seemed to tense as if he was getting ready to stand.

He was still in the doorway. All at once, his senses kicked in, and he gestured with the gun. "Don't get up, Henry. You need to stay right where you are until you tell me what in God's name is going on."

"Fine, but we're friends aren't we? Please stop pointing that gun my way. It makes me nervous."

Will ignored his request. "What are you doing here?"

"Okay, I don't care. Leave your gun like that, but please don't pull the trigger. It's simple, really. I'm here because this is my home. It's where I grew up. It once belonged to my late mother, Doris Paine, God rest her soul."

"Doris Paine? Wait a minute! You're her son. *You're* Chalker Paine!"

"I went by that name at one time. But when I was a little older than your daughter, Robert and Mildred Pylant adopted me and changed my name. I haven't been a Paine since then and good riddance to that deplorable name of Chalker. This house is mine now. I admit that the pictures on the wall seem to depict your daughter, but I assure you that they really don't. They're pictures of my twin sister, Desdemona, who died long ago. This room is my tribute to her memory. I'm only hiding in here because I'm deathly afraid of dogs. I saw you bring one up the drive."

Will lowered the gun to his side but still kept his distance from the smiling man. He glanced at the walls again. "I don't care about your twin sister or your adoption or even your name. Is Annie somewhere in this house?"

Henry's response was soft and inviting. "Annie? Goodness gracious, no. By the way, how's she doing? I'll bet she's a young lady by now." He gestured for Will to move closer. "I have to tell you that I don't like to talk to someone standing in the shadows. Please come on in here, so I can see you."

Will took a step forward. His eyes now focused on what the man in the chair was wearing—a dark sweater, dark brown jeans, and old-style, black sneakers. His mouth formed the word, "oh." At the same time, he pointed the gun toward Henry again. "It was *you!* You were the man at Tybee Island! You put Annie in the street on Tuesday night!"

He nodded and grinned. "I give up, preacher— guilty as charged."

Will's knees were threatening to buckle. He was afraid they might give way. "Tell me what you've done with her, Henry."

His eyebrows shot up. "Or you'll do what? Do you really expect me to believe that you'll actually use that thing? You don't want to end up killing me. Just think of the mess."

This gave him pause. *Can I shoot him? What if I kill him? If I do, I'll never find her.*

The gun was shaking now, so he put another hand on it. He leveled it with the taunting man's head, yet unsure if he could or should use it.

"You're already aware of everything that I know, Reverend. You must be aware of Rankin Turner's suicide note with its unequivocal statement that your daughter is 'resting in the arms of the Good Lord.' I suppose Rankin is the only one who could tell us where she's resting, but unfortunately he's no longer with us."

All of Will's Christian principles were in the balance—his beliefs, his hundreds of sermons, everything he'd ever taught Annie—but the scales were tilting heavily to the dark side. This man was mocking him like Satan himself.

"You must want to die," he whispered.

"What did you say?" The professor tucked his left hand behind his ear, as if straining to hear. "Come closer, Will. You're speaking so softly that I can hardly hear you."

He didn't move. "Can you hear this? Tell me where I can find Annie, or I'll kill you!"

The professor chuckled. "Do you really think I believe that? I may die someday, but you aren't the man who'll bring it about. Such an act would contravene everything you've been espousing for years. *Thou shall not kill!* Who knows where your little Annie is anyway? Maybe she's joined your darling Leah in the great beyond."

Hearing Leah's name caught him off guard. The gun began to shake in his hands. "Shut up about Leah. For the last time, what's happened to my daughter?"

Henry leaned forward, lowered his head, and put his left hand to his forehead. He looked like he was praying. In that pose, he spoke again. "Or you'll do what, preacher? You have that gun, and before you leave this room, I suppose there's a very slim possibility that you may shoot me. Please understand that I'm sorry for everything that's happened to you. You're a good man. On the other hand, Rankin Turner was a fool. I don't know what he might have done to Annie or where she might be, but I do need to confess something else to you. You're a minister of the Gospel, and if I'm about to die, I want to make my confession. If you allow me nothing else, I want your understanding and forgiveness. I can't bear to keep it inside for one minute longer. Please come closer, so that I may seek absolution."

Will didn't move. All of the resolve he'd ever known was fast leaving him. "So what is it you want to confess? That it *was* you that took Annie? Okay, fine. But where in the name of God is she?"

Henry shook his head and looked up. His face took on an imploring expression. He appeared ready to cry. "It's not about your daughter. I'm not even referring to her. I want you to know what happened to Leah, your wife."

Just the mention of Leah's name jolted him, and he almost dropped the gun. "What's that supposed to mean, Henry? Do you really know something about what happened to her? Did one of your students kill her?"

"Just be patient, Will, and listen to me for a minute. When I first met your wife, I was just an assistant professor at Emory. I'd been trying to get tenure for years without any real prospect of success. As the years went by, it was made clear to me that I would need to publish again before I would even be considered for that sainted status. Several proposed projects of my own doing were nixed by the higher-ups. Then your lovely wife came along."

Why does he keep talking about Leah? "That has nothing to do with what happened to her. You don't know anything. It's a stall! If you don't tell me where Annie is, I'm going to blow a hole in you, and while you're bleeding to death, I'll go get her dog and let him rip you to shreds."

"Come on, preacher, just hear me out."

Will said nothing and moved closer, agonizing over his surging, volcanic hate of this man. *Can I shoot him? Can I?*

Henry sat back and smiled. "Over time, as Leah and I worked together, I came to realize just how brilliant she was. Her idea about the formation of the philosophy of Socrates was flat-out revolutionary. She theorized that his early training as a sculptor or stone mason greatly influenced the structural patterns of his thinking. Whether his father worked with stone is somewhat controversial, but most believe that he did. I knew from the get-go that her concept was an absolute winner, one that begged for widespread publication."

"Leah! Leah! Leah! If you know something, say it, Henry! Say it! And say it *now*!"

"That day—oh, that terrible day—I'll never forget it. You may not recall that I couldn't join the two of you for dinner that evening because I had a faculty meeting. And what a meeting it was! Before it was over, I was given an ultimatum. My career at Emory would cease twelve months hence unless during that time I offered concrete proof that a paper authored by me had been accepted for publication in a reputable, academic journal."

In a flash, Will lurched forward and landed a kicking blow on the professor's right shin. He withdrew just as quickly. "Forget Leah, Pylant! Where is Annie?"

Henry flinched but remained upright. He held up his left hand, warding him off. "That hurt like hell, Will. Please just listen. That same night, while you were at your meeting, I paid Leah a visit. Of course, she let me in. Why shouldn't she? We were very good friends."

"You were *there* that night? You were in *our* house?"

"Yes, right there in your kitchen, I pled my case. When I told Leah what had gone on at the faculty meeting, her concern made me feel that I had a chance. You see, I begged her to let me have her idea, her research, everything in her prospectus so that I could offer it for publication as my work and mine alone. I vowed to help her develop another theme, even one more notable than her own. I said I'd even write the new dissertation for her. I confided that if my career tanked, I was going to take my own life. Oh, in typical Leah fashion, she was very sympathetic to my plight, but her sympathy fell short of letting me have her work."

Pylant's calm attitude was ripping Will apart. The gun, in both hands now, was in danger of shaking loose. "Was somebody else in the house, too? A drug addict? The one who did it? For God's sake, Henry, what happened?"

"I'd already confirmed that she and I were the only ones aware of the substance of her prospectus, and that it could be found on her laptop. She hadn't even shared the details with you. It rather made me feel like her secret lover. Even so, I knew that she might refuse my request. You must understand that I was desperate; it was my life or hers. I had no choice, none whatsoever. When she wasn't looking, I removed a small hammer from my pocket and hit her as hard as I could on the side of the head. I felt certain the blow was fatal, and ultimately, it was. Right afterwards, I hurried to create a convincing, burglary scenario. I rushed to remove her rings, and I placed them on the counter next to her laptop and purse. Then I went straight to the back door, opened it, and knocked out a glass pane. I was heading into the house to grab more stuff when I heard your car in the driveway. I have to admit that I panicked at that point. I ran back to the kitchen, grabbed the laptop and the other items from the counter and went out the back door. It was that simple, and it all worked."

Every tenet of Will's faith had left him by then, and he was consumed by a monumental, uncontrollable rage. He pointed the gun directly at Henry's head, with his finger ready on the trigger. "Jesus Christ! You *murdered* her! It was *you*!"

Henry wiped a fake tear from his left eye. "Sorry about that, but, yes, I did. I had to do it, all for the sake of my career—my life, really. My visit to your house months later was just a ruse to find out if you had found another copy somewhere in the house. You hadn't, so I was good to go. And by the way, it ended up making a nice little book for me, sold over two thousand copies in academic circles. Not to mention that I'm tenured now and a full professor at Emory, although as it turns out, I couldn't care less. Poor Annie though…that's a different story."

"You're going straight to Hell, Henry!"

"Maybe someday I'll go there, but today? I don't believe so. Look at your weapon. You might want to take the safety off."

It was an effective bluff. When he glanced down at his gun, Henry's hidden right hand came up. As the knife flashed in the light, ripping through the air toward Will's chest, he pulled the trigger.

Chapter Fifty-One

Friday, Night

"God help me. I've killed him!" Will whispered.

He backed away from the horror on the floor, still holding the gun in front of him. Blood splattered the pictures on the walls, dripping to the floor. It was on him, too—his face, his right arm, his chest, and his pants. He was standing in it. The sweet smell made him sick.

He could feel a trickle under his shirt, but if it brought pain, it went unnoticed. When he fired the shot, he was leaning toward the mad man. The knife sliced through his shirt on the pocket side, cutting a thin line from his gut to the top of his chest. Blood seeped through.

The rest of the blood was all Pylant's. The gunshot had blown across the left side of his head, knocking him off the chair, leaving him crumpled and motionless on the floor in a bloody pool. He looked dead.

He stumbled out of the closet into the short hallway. There, he leaned against the wall, breathing rapidly. He let the gun slip to the floor and took out his cell phone, punching in 911. His call was answered right away.

Before he could speak, the responder said, "You're calling from a cell phone. Please tell me your name." Will gave his name and began to explain why he'd called, but the responder interrupted him.

"Please wait. What's the address you're calling from?"

"Address? It's 15 Methvin. I have to go. I've got to find her."

"Who? Is she hurt?"

"Annie…my daughter…I don't know where she is. I'm calling about the man I shot."

"Tell me exactly what happened."

"I shot the man…blood everywhere."

"How old is the man you shot?"

"I don't know."

"Is he conscious?"

"Not moving."

"Is he breathing?"

"He took Annie. He's on the floor…dead."

"Do you want to check to see if he's breathing?"

"Got to find my daughter."

"Wait, Mr. Rowan. Are you hurt?"

Will ended the call. His phone vibrated almost immediately from a call back, but he ignored it. He stepped to the closet door and glanced at Pylant. He hadn't moved. Closing the door, he bolted into the long hall, through the back porch, and out the back door, leaving it wide open. Seeing him, Pete began barking and jumping up and down.

Will ran down the concrete steps and took off Pete's leash. Pete could not get enough of sniffing Will, seemingly fascinated by the blood. Will pushed him away and pointed toward the steps.

"Annie! Go find Annie!"

The big dog looked up at him and then rushed up the steps and through the door. He followed, trying to keep up with him, flipping light switches on along the way. Pete went straight to the closet under the stairs and scratched at the door.

"No, Pete! Annie!"

Pete turned away from the closet and began sniffing his way methodically and rapidly through the house. Will had a hard time keeping up with him. After he'd covered the downstairs without success, the dog rocketed up the stairs to the second floor. Before he could get to the top of the stairs, he heard Pete furiously barking at something. He found him scratching at a small door inside a dark bedroom at the end of the hall, one filled with pillows and furnishings covered in floral lace and yards of cloying fabrics.

Amid all the barking, he detected a muffled, guttural sound coming from behind the door. He pushed the dog aside, flipped a light switch beside the door, and threw it open. Halfway down the long, narrow, attic-like room, Jack Carter stood on a frail-looking, wooden, bar stool with a rope around his neck. The other end of the rope was affixed to an exposed cross-beam. It wasn't taut now, but if Jack left the stool, he would be hanged before his feet hit the floor. He was naked except for a pair of white boxer shorts. His hands were cuffed behind his back, and his mouth was covered with duct tape. His eyes were wild.

"Jack!" Will cried.

At that moment, Pete barged through the door and headed for Jack. Will went after him, but he was too late. The dog lunged forward, crashing into the stool, causing it to wobble back and forth. A second later, Jack made a loud, unintelligible sound, as he and the stool began to topple over.

Chapter Fifty-Two

Friday, Night

Will took four leaping steps and caught Jack just as the stool crashed to the floor. He was heavy, and it took all of his strength to keep him up. No way he could do that and reach the noose on his neck, too.

"Sit on my shoulders, Jack!"

He cupped his hands and caught one of Jack's feet, and somehow Jack got one leg and then the other around his neck. *What do I do now?* Will thought.

With Jack on his shoulders, the noose remained out of reach. Although the stool lay at his feet, it was out of reach, too, and if he leaned down to bring it upright, the rope would choke the lieutenant. The agitated dog was adding to the chaos.

"Listen, Jack. I have to reach down for the stool. When I do, you may start choking. Hold on tight with your legs, but don't break my neck in the process. Try to stay still up there. It won't take but a second. Do you understand me?"

Jack grunted and nodded. As Will bent down, he glanced up and saw that the rope was going taut and heard a gurgling sound deep in Jack's throat. He grabbed the stool and came back up with it, while Jack tightened his legs around his neck.

He put Jack's feet back on the stool and pulled away from him, letting out a whoosh of air. He'd been holding his breath the whole time, a subconscious expression of empathy for the dilemma of his friend. "That was too close. Are you okay?"

Wet with sweat, he nodded.

Will rummaged around the attic and found a sturdy table. He dragged it over to his noosed friend and got up on it. He pulled the nose over Jack's head and the duct tape off his mouth.

"Thank you, Lord God!" Jack shouted.

After Will helped him down off the bar stool, he collapsed on the floor almost on top of Pete, shaking and breathing hard. "I've been up there for hours, thinking that I couldn't stay on my feet one second longer. I would've gone down for sure, Will, but you saved my life, you and this dog of yours. My clothes are over in the corner by the door. There's an extra cuff key hidden in the little pocket on the inside of my shirt near the bottom button."

Will retrieved the key and unlocked the cuffs, taking a look around in the process. The attic was filled with some kind of strange equipment reminiscent of his one-time visit to a chiropractor.

While Jack was dressing, he explained why Pylant had left him like that. "He was thinking out loud the whole time. He considered shooting me but didn't want to upset Annie or alert a neighbor with a gunshot. He rejected every other method of bumping me off as being too messy. He didn't want to get covered with blood, didn't have time for a bath. He made me take off all my clothes because he was worried that I might have something hidden on me like a knife or a cuff key. He wanted to keep me from going anywhere until he settled on the best way to dispose of me, but I could've choked to death while he thought about it. I think he has a sadistic bent. He did mention that he wanted to give Doris some company. Apparently, that's her bedroom you just came through to get to this little attic."

"What did he say about Annie?"

"She's in the closet under the stairs. He admitted that much."

"No. She's not, but Pylant is."

"All that blood on you, Will. Are you okay?

"I got cut, but most of it is Pylant's. I shot him in the head right before Pete found you. I think he's dead."

"You? You shot him?"

He was quiet, looking at the floor, so Jack continued. "He asked me a lot of questions. He said he would kill Annie if I didn't cooperate, so I told him things. Some of it, I made up. Most of it was true."

"Where is she, Jack?"

"When I got here, she was right there in the closet under the stairs and still alive. I heard her stomping her feet. If she's not there now, my guess is we'll find her somewhere in the house."

"So she's still alive?"

He looked at Will but said nothing. When he was dressed, they headed out of the attic. The distant sound of sirens indicated that the first responders would soon arrive. In the upstairs hall, he told Will that he needed to sit down for a minute, and they did, on the top step of the stairs.

Will thought about Pylant. What he'd said about Leah was true, but the rest was all lies. He took Annie, and Rankin had nothing to do with it. By then, his chin was on his chest and his adrenaline was gone along with any remaining scintilla of hope. He would never find her now because he'd killed the only man who knew where she was.

Jack stood and put his hand on his shoulder. "Okay, let's take a look at the closet before the EMS folks arrive. Be sure to hold the dog."

He nodded but remained where he was; he didn't want to visit the closet again. When Pete followed Jack, Will grabbed his collar and held him back. Less than a minute later, Jack called up to him. "If you have a phone, bring it down. Pylant crushed mine, and I need a picture of this."

He headed down the stairs with the dog in tow and handed Jack his phone. Then he took the dog outside and tied him to the railing again.

Jack came outside just as law enforcement and EMS personnel arrived. He suggested that Will wait for him in the kitchen while he ushered the responders to the closet. Twenty minutes later, he joined him there. "Pylant's not dead, but your bullet pretty much made a mess of everything on the left side of his head. The main focus right now is to stop the bleeding, treat him for shock, and get him stabilized enough to move."

"Is he awake?'

"No. And he may never wake up again."

"He'll die, right?"

Jack shrugged. "Somebody will be coming to look at your wound. It's still bleeding."

He looked down at his chest and pulled at his shirt. It was sticking to his chest, wet with blood.

"I saw a kitchen knife on the floor near Pylant, and I'm sure it has your blood on it. Todd Baxter and his people are in there now, and I told him to make sure that the techs preserve the knife properly. I found what must be your gun on the floor in the hallway. They'll be taking that with them, too."

"What about Annie?"

"As far as we can tell, she's not here."

While they waited for the EMS tech, he related that the FBI had cleared both Wycke Randolph and Brad Dixon. "Dr. Randolph was at the hospital when Annie disappeared, and the old, statutory rape charge was never prosecuted. When they checked into it, they found that the girl who'd brought it did so because she was mad at Randolph for dumping her."

"Callie will be overjoyed to hear that."

"Dixon admitted lying to Mae to get her to give him a job, but he had a good reason. About the time his wife was diagnosed with cancer, he was laid off from an executive position. He was overqualified for most jobs and desperate for work of any kind when he approached Mae. My bet is that she'll keep him on.

"The man you shot was once known as Chalker Paine, but his wallet says his name is Henry Pylant."

"Pylant is the name I know him by. He was—and maybe still is—a professor at Emory University. You know that Leah was a student there when she was murdered. Before I shot him, he told me he killed her because he wanted to steal her dissertation prospectus."

"You're telling me that the same man who took your daughter killed your wife? That's hard to believe, Will."

He stared through Jack, not listening now. All he could think about was the pending death of the only man who knew where Annie was and his responsibility for it. He was still in that mode a few seconds later when he realized that an EMS tech was leaning over him, unbuttoning his shirt. "You need to go to the hospital and get this stitched up. In the meantime, let me clean your wound and apply some butterfly tabs to hold it temporarily."

He nodded. It was the least of his concerns. When the tech finished with him, Jack reached into his pocket, took out his car keys, and spoke to the tech. "Give these keys to one of the officers outside and ask him to go get my vehicle. It's at the station. Tell the officer to take the preacher's dog with him and leave him with the desk sergeant. When he gets back, I'll run the preacher to the hospital. We'll pick up the dog later."

He turned to Will. "I forgot to mention that when I was using your phone, a text came in for you." Jack pushed his phone across the table, and he found a message from his mother.

You and Pete really are taking a very long walk indeed. When can we expect y'all to return? Mae's already here. She's concerned because you told her of a plan to visit some house. Where are you? Thank goodness it's a cold supper! By the way, the name I recognized on the list was that Emory professor of Leah's, Dr. Henry Pylant.

Will's spirits sank even further. He thumbed a short reply, *I'm fine. I'm with Jack. Be home soon.* Then, he closed his message app. If he had bothered to look at the list, he would have seen Pylant's name, just another sorry omission on his part. He looked up at Jack. His eyes sent a message that Will didn't want to receive. "You feel sorry for me, don't you, Jack?"

"I feel sorry for you and for me and for everybody involved in this mess."

Chapter Fifty-Three

Friday, Night

The Catalpa General Hospital emergency room was busy on most Friday nights, and tonight was no exception. Will's wound was closed, and he was given antibiotics, a tetanus shot, and pain killers. The ER doctor put his bloody shirt in a plastic bag and gave him a scrub top to wear home. The nurse was helping him get dressed when Jack came and said, "Pylant's conscious now."

Will slid off the ER bed. "Tell me what he said."

Jack put his arm on his shoulder. "The blow to Paine's skull may have caused bleeding on the brain. He's suffered a stroke and can't talk. He's got some paralysis on the right side of his body, too, so he can't use his right arm. I'm going up to his room now. They've agreed to let me try to figure out a way to communicate with him."

"Let me go with you."

***

Chalker was whiter than the sheets he was lying on. His eyes were closed; his head was heavily bandaged; he was connected to more tubes and monitors than Will had ever seen inside a hospital room. He stood in a corner with the attending nurse while Jack and Agent Baxter approached the bed.

"Henry?" Jack said.

Chalker didn't open his eyes or otherwise acknowledge him.

He tried again. "Chalker?"

Chalker's eyes flew open, and he looked at Jack and Baxter. His eyes then moved around the room and settled on Will and the nurse. A tear rolled down his left cheek.

Jack leaned closer to him and spoke again in a strong voice. "Where is Annie?"

He seemed confused. His eyelids fluttered, and the left side of his face formed a half-frown.

Jack held up a pad and pen. "If you can write, tell us where she is. Do it now."

Chalker closed his eyes.

***

In darkness, he tried to get his muddled mind to focus. *Whatever this life has been, whatever I've done, it just doesn't matter anymore. Death may be the greatest of blessings after all.* With great effort, he raised his left hand off the bed.

***

Jack placed the pad under Pylant's hand and his fingers around the pen. "Wherever she is, write it on the pad."

They all watched as he moved the pen across the page. His hand fell back down, and his eyes closed again.

Baxter picked up the pad and looked at it and then at Chalker. "Is this the best you can do?"

A monitor began beeping rapidly, and a nurse stepped forward. "You'll have to leave now, lieutenant."

He moved toward the door, and the others followed. Anxious, Will tried to look at the pad over his shoulder. "What did he write on the pad?"

"This." He gave the pad to Will, and he looked down at the words scrawled across the paper.

off ric b by creek

"What does this mean? We need to go back in and find out what he was trying to tell us."

"No. You wait right here."

Jack and Baxter went back into the room, leaving Will in the hall. Seconds later, they returned and headed rapidly down the hall with him on their heels. Jack spoke without turning around. "The man is down for the count.

We need to get in touch with my office. Let me use your cell phone again."

He took the phone and punched in his office number. When they came to the hospital chapel, he motioned for them to go inside. They sat down on a pew, and he activated the speaker on Will's phone. The others listened as he asked the desk sergeant to give him the name of every road or street in the county that began with the letters, 'ric.'

Minutes later, the sergeant came back on the line. He had the county map in front of him and read off road names. "There's Ricebank, Richardson, Richmond, Rickety Back, Rickett, Rickle, and Rico. That's all of them."

This information did not connect the dots for Will, but when he glanced at Jack, he noticed that he was smiling. "Okay. The only roads that include both a 'ric' and a 'b' are Ricebank and Rickety Back. Take a look at those two roads on the map. Tell me if you see a creek running close to either one of them."

The sergeant paused before speaking again.

"There's no water near Ricebank. There's a pretty good size creek running sort of parallel to Rickety Back though. It's way off the road, on the west side. I'd say it's close to five miles from the paved road."

"That's it," Jack said.

They sped away from the hospital in Jack's vehicle with Baxter in the passenger seat and Will in the back. As they left, the lieutenant called one of his men and gave him instructions for organizing a search party. Then, with siren blasting and lights flashing, he ramped up the speed.

Ten minutes out, he got a call on his radio. It was Detective Bridger. "We searched Pylant's car. I wanted to let you know what we found in the trunk—a Sig Sauer P226 that looks like yours, girls' clothing, drug paraphernalia, a picnic basket with half-eaten food, a blanket, and a muddy shovel."

"He buried her," Will whispered.

"Okay, Ted," the lieutenant said. "Had my gun been fired recently?"

"Let me go find Tompkins. He was taking the gun to the office."

The three of them waited in silence, and then Bridger was back on the radio. "Sorry, Jack. I don't know about the gun, and it looks like Tompkins has already left. I'll run him down and let you know."

None of them spoke again until they reached Rickety Back Road. As Jack turned onto it, he explained what he knew of the area. "Rickety Back runs north-south. We'll start here at the north end and go up. The other searchers will come up from the south to the point where we started. This area is truly rural, and there hasn't been much development on either side of the road. I think Southeast Power has owned most of the land on the west side of the road for years, running all the way back to the creek. I don't remember any access roads off Rickety Back into the power company property, but I could be wrong."

This confused Will. "If no roads go into the property and the creek is five miles back, why did Chalker even mention the creek? Surely, he didn't walk that far to..."

The G-man interrupted Will. "Look out, Jack!"

A deer leapt out of the woods and across the road right in front of them. Jack braked and swerved, just missing it. "I'm going to have to slow down. This area is crawling with deer this time of year."

When he reduced his speed, they began to have a better view of the thick, dark woods on the west side of the road. A half-mile later, Jack suddenly slowed his vehicle, made a U-turn, and headed back the other way.

"What the hell, Jack?" Baxter said.

"I saw an opening back there on the west side of the road. I would have missed it if I'd been going any faster."

The opening was a dirt road, and he turned onto it. "It's a logging road, and it may go all the way back to the creek."

As Jack careened through the woods on the rutted road, Baxter telephoned the man heading the other searchers. "We're going in now. Go ahead and move through the woods off the west side of Rickety Back until you come to a creek. Then head north along the creek covering a fifty-yard span. We may end up going north, too, and if we do, we'll leave some kind of marker showing where we started."

The dirt road seemed to go on forever, but at last it came to an abrupt end at a shallow ravine bordered by woods. They got out, and Jack produced three flashlights. With the lights in hand, they hurried into the ravine and up a hill on the other side. Jack led the way. "The creek shouldn't be too far beyond this rise. If we don't find her here, we'll start moving north."

Will was doubtful about their prospects. "She could be anywhere out here. If she's been…we may not find her until the sun comes up."

The agent patted him on the shoulder. "I think it's time you said a prayer or two, preacher."

Chapter Fifty-Four

Friday, Night

At the hospital, Chalker opened his eyes. He'd been awake for some time, but he had no desire to answer any more questions from nurses, doctors, or law enforcement. He wondered if they would find Annie. Behind closed eyes, he'd been thinking about his last minutes with her. He shut his eyes again, and thoughts of what he'd done to her returned.

***

H*e left her alone and returned to the car for the policeman's gun and the shovel. He was careful to hide the gun in his waistband, but he couldn't keep her from seeing the shovel. When he came back, she seemed overjoyed to see him. Oh, how very difficult she was making it.*

She sounded a little worried, but she wasn't concerned about anything that really mattered. "I'm glad to see you. I was afraid you would leave me out here, Mr. Iblis."

He put his hand on her shoulder. "You know I wouldn't do that. Have you had enough to eat?"

She smiled and patted her stomach. "I'm full."

She was eyeing the shovel, so he felt compelled to offer an explanation. "There are some marshmallows in the basket. Not to mention that it's getting cool. I thought I'd dig a fire pit right over there," he said, pointing to soft ground nearby. "Then we can warm up and roast the marshmallows."

"What fun! It's been forever since I've done anything like that."

"Annie, why don't you look around for some big sticks and start piling them up?"

She did that, but by the time she'd gathered a good bit of wood, he was only halfway done with his digging project.

"Why are you making the fire pit so deep, Mr. Iblis?"

***

Chalker sensed someone else in the room. He opened his eyes and saw a uniformed policeman standing at the foot of his bed, looking at him.

"I thought you were awake, Paine. I just got here on a shift change. I wanted to come in and see what a true pervert looks like. I hope they fry your ass like a piece of Black Label bacon and serve it to a pack of howling dogs."

Chalker closed his eyes again. He wondered if he'd have to put up with this kind of abuse for the rest of his life, if he'd ever again enjoy the peace of solitude.

Soon, his thoughts returned to Annie. Something about being close to death brought clarity. It made him think not only of what had happened but also of why. All of the many coincidences which had led him to Annie and to this moment had only one purpose, and that purpose was to punish him for what he'd done to Annie's mother, Leah.

Just then, a familiar quote came to mind. It was from Albert Einstein via Doris: "Coincidence is God's way of remaining anonymous." *Could all of this be His doing? Could it be?*

Chapter Fifty-Five

Friday, Night

When the three men came over the rise, the woods thinned out and about fifty yards down an open, grassy slope, their lights brushed the creek. As they headed down the slope, something else came into view. It was a mound of fresh earth not far from the creek bank.

"Jesus," Will said, breaking into a run.

Jack caught him and grabbed his arm, holding him back as Baxter reached the mound and looked down. "It's an empty hole," he said.

The pastor slumped. "Thank God," he said. "Is she not out here?" He kept trying to convince himself that they weren't looking for a body, but he noticed that both Jack and Baxter were focusing their lights on the ground. They moved up and down the creek bed, twenty yards both ways but found no sign of her. Jack suggested that they mark the spot and head north along the creek.

Will started in that direction but hesitated, shining his light back towards the wooded area. He stepped in that direction, and when he did, he thought he heard a soft voice.

"There's somebody in there!" he shouted, as he began running up the slope to the woods.

"Wait," he heard from Jack behind him, but he didn't stop.

As he reached the edge of the woods, he heard the voice again, this time speaking words he would never forget.

"Mr. Iblis, it's dark, and I'm frightened. And who are all those men with you?"

"Annie!" Will shouted.

"Daddy?"

"I'm coming!" he said as he bolted through the woods to the source of that wonderful voice.

***

When the nurse returned, Chalker kept his eyes closed, feigning sleep. He was mulling over the last of his time with Annie, and he didn't want to be interrupted.

In the end, he just couldn't do it. He couldn't shoot her, much less bury her in the ground. It took getting to a point just short of killing her for him to realize that it was no more possible for him to do that than it would've been for him to dispatch his beloved Desdemona. In his heart, the two were one and the same.

Now, in his mind, he played out what he had done to Annie one more time.

It started with a lie. He complained that she hadn't gathered enough firewood. "We need to go deeper into the woods to get more, Annie, and I'll need your help. Otherwise, our marshmallow fire won't be sufficient."

He led her up the grassy slope and into the woods. After puttering around for a moment, pretending not to find the right type of wood, he said, "This isn't working out. I need to go through that bramble thicket over there to get more wood. I'm dressed for that sort of thing, but you aren't. You will have to stay here until I come back. I trust you, Annie, but it'll soon be dark, and I don't want you wandering off and getting lost. I have a little cord in my pocket, and I'm going to use it to tie you to that tree over there. Please understand that I just want to be sure that you'll be right here when I get back. Otherwise, I may not be able to find you."

The sun was getting low, so she didn't question his motive or put up a fight. She trusted him. It was ever so sad leaving her there, but he convinced himself that she'd be safe from harm in the woods for a little while, if somewhat lonely and afraid. After he was far, far away, starting his new life, he would call Will Rowan and let him know where she was. At least that's what he told himself at the time. Of course, if that wasn't convenient, or if something happened to her in the meantime, it just couldn't be helped.

All in all, he was somewhat pleased with the way things had turned out, assuming one could be at peace after having half of his head blown off. He'd mitigated his circumstances by providing Annie's location, and in view of that, he was sure that only a jail term would befall him for that offense. Aside from his 'confession' to Will Rowan, there was no evidence whatsoever to suggest that he had killed Leah. His admission could be explained away as an untruthful effort to provoke Will into doing something stupid enough to allow him to escape the preacher's ire over Annie's plight. If otherwise, then his admission would amount to nothing more than his word against Will's—a case of 'he said versus he said.' And Chalker knew that such proof rarely let to a conviction. On top of that, he had tons of money to pay lawyers.

To the extent that he could, he smiled.

***

It didn't take long for the doctors at the hospital to determine that Annie had not been physically harmed in any way. Strange as it might seem, her kidnapper had taken good care of her. Will hadn't told her about shooting Chalker yet because she'd already expressed concern for him more than once, asking in each instance if he was okay.

She would need counseling, and so would he because he'd done something he would never have thought possible. He'd tried to kill a man, and he'd done it with pure malice. Others might not blame him, but he was going to have a hard time forgiving himself for it, if he ever could.

Now, the three of them stood together on the small porch of Will's house on Atwater Street—a worn out minister wearing a doctor's scrub top and blood-stained pants, a young girl dressed in funky clothes typical of the seventies, and one very happy, whining dog.

Will put his arm around Annie. "How would you like to surprise Mae and your grandmother by just ringing the bell?"

She grabbed her father's arm and giggled. "What fun! Let's do it!"

Then she pressed the doorbell, letting it ring and ring.

The End

About Joseph MacNabb

Joseph MacNabb was born in Newnan, Georgia, where his ancestral roots date from 1827. His forebears include a Scottish sea captain, gentlemen farmers, a circuit-riding minister, a newspaper editor, and a lot of strong women. Early on, most of his writing consisted of legal briefs and judicial orders, but in recent years, he took up fiction. He and his wife, Patty, live in Newnan where he likes to read thrillers and mysteries, take long walks, and fly fish. He's a born story-teller, and he loves to write. *The Closet* is his first book. His second book is currently in rewrite, and he soon hopes to complete a third. All of his narratives are set in mythical Catalpa, Georgia, a decent-sized town, growing in a good way but still hanging on to a small-town flavor. It's a fine place to live, but, like most southern towns, it's stained by a sinister underbelly.

Social Media

Website: www.josephmacnabb.com

Twitter: https://twitter.com/JosephMacNabb
@josephmacnabb

Facebook: https://www.facebook.com/joseph.macnabb/

Acknowledgements

Heartfelt gratitude to my wonderful agent, Pam Ahearn of The Ahearn Agency for her wise counsel and tireless efforts on my behalf; to my wife, Patty, for reading and editing my manuscript and all of its many rewrites and for much more.

Made in the USA
Columbia, SC
01 June 2021